WIZARD OF
THE MARCH

WIZARD OF THE MARCH

by
S. Van Haitsma

To my family and friends
whose support made this book possible

1

May 1413, Welsh March (the borderlands west of England)

"Sometimes we must help our friends in their time of need," Clum assured himself as he passed through the crowded market towards the stable. "Even when it seems like utter foolishness, simply because that is what friends are supposed to do."

"Eni?" he said softly as he poked his head into the shadows. The smell of hay and horse filled his senses. His eyes, etched with the bright sunlight, tried to make out the contours of the barn's dark interior but could see nothing past the first horse who turned and stared at him carelessly, content with a mouthful of hay. A bay mare, tied to a hitching post just outside the stable, snorted at the injustice of being outside the shade and food of the barn.

It was typical on market days for the stable to be crowded with all the merchants and visitors in town, but the threat of rain earlier had filled the stalls to a breaking point since sunrise. Once the weather cleared and the crowds arrived, horses and carts began lining up around the field outside the city gate.

Clum could never figure out why it always seemed darker in the stable on sunny days than when it was overcast, he had thought the opposite should be true. He tried to make his way between the stalls, not knowing if the next shadow would be wooden timber or the hind quarters of the horses, which shuddered at his touch and stirred the litter beneath them as they shifted in their stalls hoping for more than just a pat on the rump as he passed by.

Clum had to blink several times before his eyes would take in all the features of the stable: the timber posts riddled with iron spikes on which harnesses and bridles hung like tinsel, pitch forks and shovels

1

lined up against the last stall, ready for the call to duty.

A few strands of last year's hay twisted and turned from the open portal above, ensnared in cobwebs that clung to the underside of the loft, fluttering like fish on a line as they rode the currents of the air.

It wasn't until he passed the last horse that he could make out the figure huddled in the corner of the hay pile. A sliver of light caught the boy's head from a split in the barn wood that had fallen to the elements.

"Eni," Clum whispered, as the boy looked up from the bundle on his lap that held his attention. "He's here!"

"Good," the other boy answered, looking up reluctantly.

"But…" Clum started to say but stopped. He knew from experience that Eni wouldn't listen; he never did. Not that he could be blamed for that. Eni was English- at least, half of him was- and the son of the lord's Steward, while Clum was only a Welsh peasant. The Welsh were told time and again they were there for their brawn; not their brains.

"You better come then," he said, turning to walk back through the gauntlet of horses and disappearing into the shadows, leaving only a swirl of dust shimmering in the light that poured through the crack.

Eni sighed, his stomach ached as he thought about what his father would say, but looking down at the bundle of hay and fur what choice did he have? He slid up the timber post as he struggled to his feet but had to adjust mid-way up to free his tunic from a sliver of wood. Bits of hay clung precariously to his garments as he passed the horses and made his way out the open stable door.

The grayness that had held the county for more than a fortnight had finally lifted and the sun bathed the countryside. Mud splattered and oozed out of the wagon wheel and cart tracks, drying in the sun like loaves of deformed bread, only to be flattened by herds of sheep making their way baa-ing into the market. The change in weather had raised the spirits of both villagers and travelers alike, but to Eni, emerging from the shadows of the barn, such brightness was unwelcomed.

Glancing up, Eni figured it must be well past noon since the spring sun was positioned so high in the sky. He had been in the barn ever

2

since it happened, soon after breaking his fast that morning.

"Come on," Clum's head sprang up over the back corner of a cart. His attempted whisper was loud enough to cause several of the women who were strolling the market to look his way. Seeing it was only the red-headed Clum, who quickly ducked back down again, they merely shook their heads and went back to their bartering.

"Typical Clum," thought Eni upon seeing the episode from the stable door, though for once he was thankful for Clum's reputation.

Eni stepped from the barn's shadows, hunched over slightly so as to hide the bundle wrapped in his arms from the sun's discovery, or that of anyone else. He quickly wobbled over, stiff from sitting so long, and joined Clum behind the hay cart.

"There," Clum said, pointing though the crowd. Eni had no trouble following the direction. The meandering market crowd was usually as chaotic as a battle, with the combination of sheep, dogs, and people, but when the old man was at the market, the crowd would break as if he were the king himself, giving him a wide berth as he made a port of call to all the merchants. Eni turned and sat down with his back against the spokes of the cart's wooden wheel.

"You wanted to wait, though…" Clum said, more to calm himself than to ask Eni what they were doing. His head bobbed up and down as he looked into the crowd for the old man. "You don't want to do it with so many folk around…" he said, looking down at Eni before nodding again that he understood the plan. Eni didn't answer but continued to keep both arms wrapped around his bundle.

Market days came but once a week and even those who couldn't afford to buy would come just to see and hear the latest news from all around the March, and even that of England. Occasionally, the old man would disappear from Clum's view, swallowed up by the crowds that moved en masse until the man moved again, the crowd dividing in front of him like minnows before a bass.

"There's your Mum…" Clum said on his bob up and was about to point at the woman in the blue dress. Eni pulled his arm down and almost caused Clum to tumble down on top of him. "What is she doing here?" he questioned, poking his head over the cart for a look of his own.

Lady Mali, though Welsh by birth, was by her rank as the Steward's wife not expected to shop the market like a commoner. She had servants for that, but she liked to escape to it when she had the chance and find out the happenings with her kin.

"We do not want to see her?" Clum asked.

"No," Eni said, returning his arm to its place snuggled around the bundle as he settled back behind the wheel. "We do not want my mum, your mum, or anyone else's mum to know where we are... at least not right now."

"Right," Clum nodded, "no mums."

The crowds had thinned before the old man again parted the sea of people and made his way out of the market. Clum, who had continued to pop up and follow the man's progress through the merchants' stalls, started to report it to Eni in his typically hurried voice. Eni pulled the red-headed boy back down behind the cart. "Shh," he motioned silently as the man passed by.

Clum hunkered down next to Eni, his brown eyes wide with a mix of excitement and fear as he waited for Eni's approval to look back over the railing of the cart at the passerby.

The man's footsteps were drowned out by the clanking of copper pots that trailed behind him in gathering intensity, but everything stopped just past their hiding spot. Before Eni could stop him, Clum stole a look.

The man had one end of the rope tied around his waist and was busy tying the other end of the rope to the top of his walking stick. Once done, he picked up his parcels and the clanging copper pots continued their chorus out of the village green.

Eni soon joined Clum, watching the man until his velvet green cloak passed a tree and disappeared from sight into the surrounding forest.

"Are you sure?" Clum finally asked in a voice that was much quieter than was typical.

4

Eni didn't answer right away and Clum hoped he was reconsidering and had seen the danger in this plan. "There's no other way," the older boy said at last, looking at the bundle in his arms, "he's my only hope…"

September 2018, London (605 years later)

Wendy imagined the building would be older, a couple of hundred years at least, given the story. But with its tan brick and teal trim, it was more Elton John than Elizabethan.

She checked the address again- 'Suite 75', the scrap of paper undeniably said. The building wasn't that large and it only had one entrance. *Maybe they rebuilt after the war*, she thought, folding the paper and stuffing it in her jeans. *Or, more likely, this is a complete waste of time*. She actually hoped it was, given the circumstance; she knew she was late - which was becoming all too common for her, today she was just a bit later than usual.

The day was cool and damp, causing her to shiver as she closed the car door and crossed the car park, puddles still spotted the asphalt from the night's rain. She paid her parking fee and headed toward the building.

She stopped to check her hair in the glass door and shifted the loose curls behind her ears. The reflection of her diamond stud flashed like a giant wart on her nose; she had planned to pull it out that morning, but the thought faded once she left the bathroom mirror. Standing here in the front window, it was too late, so she shrugged and went in. What did she care what they thought? Just another stiff old professor, as if she hadn't had enough of those over the last four years.

Like a cicada in a tree, the door buzzed when she entered, the sound hanging in the air until the door brushed closed again with a magnetic click. She stood there for a moment looking around. The entry was walled-in by cardboard boxes stacked four or five high, leaving only a gap for the two doors and front window.

A middle-aged lady popped up from behind the boxes. Her long, thin neck looked for a moment like a lamp post planted in the cardboard. Her silver hairdo and round face radiated with her smile. "Here for a pick-up, love?"

Stepping forward, Wendy could see the boxes filled most of the office but for a small passage-way that meandered past the first few rows of desks. Their tops, bare of all but a layer of dust, left no indication of their former tenant's occupations.

"Ah- no, to drop off…" Wendy answered, patting the book bag slung over her shoulder.

"Sorry," the lady answered, as her smile dropped. "We aren't accepting anymore deliveries here; they have to go to the university address," she said, her hand reaching over the stack with a ready address card.

"Oh…" Wendy said taking the card with a sense of relief. She started backing away to the door, but stopped and looked at the card. "Would Dr. Brown be there?" she asked cringing, fearing it a far-fetched question. "You see, my Grand asked me to drop it off to him, but she was…"

"…Oh no, Dr. Brown is still here," the lady cut her off after dropping back down behind her cardboard wall. "You can find him in there," she said with only her hand making the effort to get back up again as it pointed to a frosted glass door down the box-lined hall.

Wendy reached for her bag. "Could you give this to him?" she asked, setting the package on the sill.

"Sorry, love, but I don't work for him technically, and I don't want to give him any ideas that I do- if you know what I mean. But feel free to walk back through. He won't bite, even though he may sound like it from time to time." She lowered her voice, "He's a bit off, lately..."

Wendy glared at the hand before it retreated as she retrieved the bundle. *That would have been so much easier*, she thought, as she deposited it back in her bag. "Thanks," she muttered as she made for the break in the cardboard wall.

"No problem, love," the receptionist added without looking up from her computer screen.

The hallway matched the bleakness Wendy had observed in the foyer; plain white walls with industrial lighting that seemed to flicker like humming bird wings. The room was dead quiet but for the pecking of the keyboard. *No wonder he'd be off,* Wendy thought, negotiating the boxes. *I would be too if I were cooped up in this place all day.*

She could feel the sweat on her palms as she knocked on the frosted glass door, a grunt answered from the other side. The response brought back memories of being sent to the headmaster's office in secondary school, although that was really not her fault. Taking a deep breath, she pushed the door open, promptly smacking into a stack of boxes identical to those lining the hall. "Umm, hello? Dr. Brown?"

2

"Do we have to go after him now?" Clum asked. Eni looked down the path and then back towards the market, where several dozen people still milled around, including his mother who was talking in Welsh with a gathering of women from the Black Mountains. He knew his father wouldn't be pleased to hear about it, not that that had ever stopped her.

He thought about making a run for the path but knew that with Clum's red hair she would know it was them in an instant. "Let's cut through here," he said, motioning to the woods that stood off from the path.

Clum looked down the trail the man had taken, with its firm footing and gentle grade. "Why not the path?"

"We don't want to be seen," Eni reminded him without looking up, his arms still wrapped around the bundle.

Clum shrugged; they might lose him in the woods, and that would be fine by him.

The coolness of the forest felt good after sitting in the sun for most of the afternoon, but the air was damp here in the cool and shade of the trees and the mud was as slick as axle grease. In spite of the spots of mud, it was not difficult at first; there was enough leaf litter to make for good footing, and the woods were free from fallen limbs since every stick of dead wood for a league had been spirited away by townsfolk for their hearths.

The easy going did not last long; soon they started climbing the western ridge. From clearings they could see both the village and the River Teme that snaked through the valley below. The stream would disappear into a forest only to reappear in open fields with brilliant tufts of white sheep mowing the deep green grass that lined its banks.

These pastoral views, though commonplace, provided a needed

respite from the drudgery of the climb. Walking uphill was much harder without a path, and to Eni and Clum it seemed as though obstacles were deliberately placed to slow their pursuit.

Eni found it difficult to negotiate the constant upward climb and the brambles and low hung branches with his arms wrapped around his bundle, not to mention the tree roots attempting to coil around his feet at every opportunity. The combination left him staggering forward and exhausted, often forcing him down to one knee so as not to fall down the slope they had just conquered. He knew he would have to explain the muddy stains on his leggings later.

Through all this, Clum merely followed behind silently, offering no help or advice as they made their way up the slope, attempting to cut off the wizard's path. He figured that if a fall knocked some sense into the older boy, it would be a fair exchange.

Brother Alfonse always said that a straight line was the shortest distance between two points. Eni knew he was right; the Brother usually was, but the Brother had never had to cut somebody off in the March. With all its hills, vales, streams, and brambles, straight lines were considered more theory than reality.

At one point, a horde of brambles mobbed a forked tree like peasants around a lord handing out alms to the poor. The gathering formed such an impenetrable thicket, the two of them had to circle back down to get around the mass of vegetation before they could be on their way again.

Once they reached the top, Eni wasn't even sure he was going the right direction anymore and Clum's silence only added to his apprehension. *I've ruined it*, he thought, holding on tightly to the bundle as if it could still provide some comfort to him.

He knew this whole idea was wrong, that seeking this man could spell the death of him. He could feel it in his gut as much as read it on Clum's face. But, he had to. If there was any chance, he had to. It was as simple as that.

He struggled up the last rise and stopped to catch his breath. Clum joined him and they stood side by side overlooking the forest as it fell away in every direction. He stared over the expanse, the horizon lost to the grey-green of the early summer wood. He could see nothing, nothing but the trees, and nothing of the wizard. Clum finally broke his silence.

"What about that…" he said, pointing down the hill and to the right. Eni stumbled down the hill, half slipping until he reached the patch of ground. He could see the leaves stirred up by the string of copper pots, the slight indentation of earth under the litter marking a path.

"This is it! Maybe we can still catch him," he called back with a relieved smile to Clum who had held back, reluctant to leave the high ground.

The path was covered by leaves, but Eni was still able to pick up speed with its firmer footing. He led the way until they began to wrap around to the top of a small hillock where they both slowed to let their breath catch up to them. "Listen," Eni said, as both boys struggled to hear over their heavy breathing.

They could just make out the clanking of the copper pots in the distance ahead of them. Although they were high on the ridge that lay south of the village, the trees still lay claim to most of the land and it limited the view of their surroundings.

They ran side by side down the path for a while before Clum's voice broke the cadence of their stride, "What do you think he does with all those pots?"

"He uses them for all his potions and stuff," Eni said in a hushed voice, sensing from the ringing percussion that the man had to be only over the next rise.

The hill proved steeper than they had figured, and Eni feared their heaving chests would give them away as they scampered over a stony outcropping, but once they cleared the hill, there was no sign of the man, and the clanging pots seemed softer and further away.

"Where'd he go?" Clum mumbled in amazement as they both slowed and stared blindly into the woods around them.

Eni stopped and listened. The pots were lightly clinking as if they were nothing more than birds chirping in the broken canopy. He went

10

back up the trail, scanning the ground for any indication of where the man could have gone.

To Clum, it was obvious. The wizard had disappeared altogether from this world with no more than a snap of his fingers. Clum had heard all the stories and expected nothing less from the Wizard of the March.

For all his schooling, Eni was supposed to be the smarter of the two of them, but watching the slender blond boy dashing back and forth along the path looking for the invisible wizard, Clum was beginning to question that.

"On his way back to the devil," Clum said quietly as Eni continued prowling over the path. "He sank right into the ground like it was a stairwell to Hell, he did; that would be my guess." If he squinted hard enough, Clum could see the head of the wizard appear on the ground staring at him only to vanish once his eyes opened again. "We should get out of here."

"Clum!" Eni called out, breaking through the apparition. Clum followed the path back and found Eni crouching under the outcropping they had just conquered.

"He went this way," Eni said as soon as Clum came into view and then divined his way into the brush.

Clum hurried down the hill and noticed the small deer path that dipped under a hawthorn tree. He ducked his head far enough to pass under the inch-long spikes that speckled the grey tree branches. Seeing Eni disappearing over the next rise, Clum stood up too quickly and had to pull free from a barb that hooked onto his matted hair. "Wait uuppp!" he screeched at the disappearing figure pulling free from the thorn but losing a knot of hair in the process.

He had little trouble catching up as the path took a turn up steeper ground since Eni's arms were still bundled around his treasure. The footing here was not much better than when they had cut through the forest. The path was obviously used more by animals than by men.

The wizard and his clanging pots were still out of sight when Clum caught up, but they were unmistakably louder. "What do you think he does with so many pots?" Clum asked.

"Potions," Eni answered again in a terse whisper without looking up from where his foot would next land.

Pots were about the only thing Clum ever saw the man purchase. He must have hundreds of them by this point. Wherever the man was going, it must be flowing with potions. "What do you think they all do?"

"Shh," Eni hissed under his breath as they both slowed to a walk. The man appeared ahead of them as they climbed down the slope into an open meadow. Clum felt his chest tighten as he wondered again why they were doing this.

He let Eni pull ahead of him as the man continued down the path, the pots dragging noisily behind him. When one of the pots caught on a root, the man would hoist his walking stick high over his head like he was swinging a halberd at a bird and the rope tied to its end would swing the pot free. The man would continue on his way without so much as turning around.

Eni edged closer to the man. It took him a few steps to get his nerve up. Taking a deep breath, he started, "If you please sir," but his voice was weaker than he intended and the man continued on.

Clum stopped short, hoping Eni would see it as an omen, but as the man continued, Eni stayed right on his heels. "Sir," he said again, undeterred by the lack of a response.

The man stopped with a jerk and spun around, lifting and pointing his walking stick at the boy like a spear as the pots rattled in protest.

Eni fell back. "I mean no harm, sir," he said, cowering with his bundle.

Rather than a spear head, the stick's end was covered by a canvas stretched and tied off with a leather strap like they would use to cover a jar in the kitchen pantry, but the wizard held it towards Eni menacingly.

"What do you want?" the man asked, taking a step back while pointing the walking stick firmly at him. Eni had never seen the man this close before; nor had he ever been the focus of his attention.

The wizard was always covered by the shroud of his hood at the market regardless of the conditions, but here in the woods his head was uncovered in the afternoon sun and he boasted a stock of dark hair that was streaked with white. His deep hazel eyes bore down on Eni from under his bushy eyebrows that grayed like the mist at daybreak.

The green velvet cloak that typically hid his features at the market was draped over his shoulder in order to escape the heat, but the silver clasp, a medallion with a stone of amber, hung dangling on his chest like a badge.

His clothing was more from the midland than the borderlands of the March, with his shirt of fine white linen, leather boots and silk leggings. His face, though old and weathered like most men of the March, sported a short beard, neatly trimmed to a point, making him look more like an English lord than a Welshman, who tended to let theirs grow long and wild. Though Eni dared not guess his age, he knew it had to be well past two score and ten.

"I...I," Eni stumbled "...my friend and I..." he added, nodding behind him to where Clum was loitering.

The man threw his gaze and the end of his stick towards Clum. "Come here, boy!" he ordered, motioning with his stick for Clum to join ranks with Eni.

Clum could feel his heart tremble. Each beat felt like a boulder ricocheting off a sheet of granite, toward the valley below. He forced himself to take a shaky step forward but all the stories he had ever heard of this strange man, this Wizard of the March, came rushing back to him.

"He knows the future," his uncle had once said at night around the fire. He had heard it from a lad who had worked for the Marcher Lord himself. This lad was a true Welshman, having grown up in the village. He wouldn't make a thing like that up.

Stories abounded that he traveled in the night with an unholy light guiding his way, a light carried aloft by the devil himself. Why, Friar Peter said that he himself heard the bishop wondering why the man hadn't been declared a heretic!

If a bishop, a man of the cloth, was powerless to act against him...

Clum's feet refused to shuffle forward another step. He stood there for a moment seeing the hopelessness of their mission. Then like a deer startled in the forest, he broke and darted away, back down the path from which they came.

A wry smile smoldered on the man's face. "Well," he said, turning his attention back to Eni, "why don't you scamper off like that friend of yours?"

Eni sighed as he looked back and saw last of the red hair disappear back over the hill. He tried to hide his fear as he turned back to the man and his headless spear.

Feeling the weight of the old man's glare, Eni knew how Clum must have felt. He had heard the stories of course- everyone had. It was the reason he came. But even as he tried to fortify his resolve, his legs took an involuntary step backward as if compelled by the wizard's magic.

He thought about springing backward, following Clum back down the path but then looked down at the bundle that still lay wrapped in his arms. The package of hay and fur, the reason he had made this trek. "No!" he said aloud, more to himself than to the man who was ready to dismiss him and make his way home.

"I …I need your help…" Eni said with renewed conviction, offering his bundle to the man before he dropped to his knees to place his treasure on the ground. Its weight had made his arms tingle at the beginning, but they were now numb from the weight as they held tightly to their prize.

The boy looked up hopefully as his arms finally released their cargo onto the mossy path. Among the clumps of hay and straw lay the motionless body of a puppy, its black and white fur strewn with flecks of the dried grass that had cradled it.

"He… he was kicked by a horse in the village this morning as a cart passed through to the market," Eni tried to explain, the weight of his loss beginning to break upon his face. "I tried everything to save him, but I… I couldn't," he added. "Can… can you bring him back?"

"Fool!" the man snapped with his eyes hard and narrow and his thin lips curled up to the side. Eni fell back off his haunches, but caught himself with his hands before he went completely over. "Do I look like God to you, boy?" he roared, casting a dismissive glare at the boy on the ground. "You foolish… Welsh."

Eni sat stunned for a moment. He was not used to being spoken to this way, at least not to his face. He quickly choked down his loss. "See here," he said in as authoritarian a voice as he could muster, "I'm a son of a Norman."

"Then run home to your mama, boy, before I turn you into a toad," The man scoffed and then turned away to the laughter of his pots.

Eni's face was flush as he picked himself up, but his mind was churning as the man continued down the path to the chorus of his pots.

He finally forgot his fear. "NO!" it was loud enough to echo off the rocks of the dell in which they stood.

The man stopped and turned slowly back to the boy, lowering his walking stick to the groaning of his companions. "What did you say?"

Eni sucked down a belly full of air. "I said no." He tried to make his voice firm but could hear the quiver as the words came out. He hoped he had not miscalculated. "I don't believe you can."

The man's face softened, as if Eni's persistence had melted him faintly. The man set the butt of his walking stick down and leaned his weight upon it. "And how did you come to that conclusion, boy?"

The trapped air in Eni's lungs escaped before he started, "You, you indicated that only God can raise the dead, and that you are not he." Eni watched the man intently for his reaction. The man gave away nothing but for a slight nod of his head to go on.

"Since you are not God and you do not have his power, yet you used him as the authority by which you compare…" Eni could feel his heart race. "Since we know of God raising the dead by the Word…"

The man's head inched back on hearing this. "By the word?" he questioned in much the same manner Brother Alfonse would have in Eni's studies.

"According to the priests, of course," Eni corrected hurriedly. Yet the man's unbroken gaze left him unsettled.

They stood in silence as Eni tried again to collect his thoughts,

"…And since the PRIESTS…" he was sure to emphasize, "also tell us that only man has a soul of all God's creatures, then how could you change me into a toad, since a toad has no soul? God would not allow such a thing."

The man dipped his head in acknowledgement, "Well stated, and no… your God would not allow it, nor is it possible by any of the arts that I possess or have knowledge of. But let us keep that our secret, shall we? It is a threat that does clear my path on most occasions," he added with a thin smile. His eyes remained fixed, unchanged, as if they were probing the boy.

Eni felt he was being studied and wondered how he fared in this examination.

The wizard looked up in the sky; "It is getting late, boy, you best make your way home before your friend shares the tale of whom you met out here in the wilds."

Eni knew what he meant; it would not go well with his mother if she found out that he went to find the Wizard of the March. Such things were not condoned by "those right with God."

"Aye," he agreed, and stooped down to pick up the dead dog from the middle of the path.

"Tell me," the man called back as Eni turned to go, "what name do you go by?"

Eni froze. He knew enough about the man to be scared by this question. So he thought for a moment before answering.

"Come, lad, out with it. I mean you no harm," he said as if reading his mind.

"Eni," he answered without the customary acknowledgement of his linage.

The man nodded, fully aware of the omission yet seemingly impressed by its absence. "One more question then, and you may be on your way… Are you the first-born son?"

Eni thought about it. He tried to see a way that this information could endanger him or his family, but he couldn't, nor could he see why the man would care. "I am the third-born," he said, studying the man

16

for a reaction to this news.

"Ah, very well. Good day to you then, young Eni, until we meet again," he added with a hint of a bow.

Eni returned the gesture before turning and running back up the slope. The man watched him until he cleared the ridge. "Third born…" he said to himself musingly, as he hoisted his walking stick and directed the choir of pots back to their melody.

3

Wendy smiled as the man looked up from his desk. He was younger than she expected. She wasn't sure if it was due to the age of her package or just an assumption that the science professor would be an older man wearing tweed and smoking a pipe.

He *was* wearing a tweed sport coat, but that was where the similarities ended. He had an old Genesis t-shirt under his blazer and a grungy week-old beard covering most of his face. His blond hair was from the era of the early Beatles, but his wire rim glasses made him look more like John Denver than John Lennon…well, a scruffy John Denver … and people told her that her history degree had no value.

"Weird," she said under her breath. He couldn't be much older than she was, thirty tops, but she doubted he was even that old. She grew up seeing the package with the name Dr. Brown printed plain enough for a six-year-old to read it. Maybe his father was the Dr. Brown the package referred to. *It's not my problem*, she decided, fortifying herself. She just had to drop it off and she would be done, free from the responsibility, free from the family oath. It would end here and now.

The professor held his gaze, his hand had been on his forehead, holding the front of his hair up like a macaw. "Yeah?" he asked absentmindedly.

"I… I have a package for you," she said, working her way through a gauntlet of boxes, only to have her sandal catch the corner of one. She stumbled in before steadying herself on a pile of boxes.

"What is it?" he asked, dropping his hand from where it was anchored on his forehead and leaving a red impression in its wake. His voice was low and gravelly but he added a belated smile as if to compensate for the unwelcoming sound of his voice.

Wendy gave her foot a quick inspection. "Um, it's from my grand, I mean, my grandmother," she said, reaching into her bag and pulling out the clear plastic bag. "It's a bit late. I was at school and forgot, I'm afraid," she added with a smile as she set the package on the desk. "Only found it again the other day cleaning out my mum's flat."

He shifted his glasses up so as to perch them on his forehead where his hand had been and stared at an old leather pouch inside the clear plastic bag. The color of his face quickly turned to the same hue as the patch on his forehead as he looked up at her, "Is this a joke?"

The body of the pup seemed light when Eni picked it up again, but it gained weight with every step as he retraced his path. His head told him to throw it in the brambles and run back, but he couldn't. He couldn't let it become carrion for the vultures. He would bury it even if it was only a dog; he just needed Clum's help digging the hole.

Eni had just ducked under a hawthorn and turned on to the main path when he saw a head of flaming hair poke out from behind a rowan tree.

"Is that you?" Clum asked, though there was still plenty of light in the shade of the trees.

"… Come help me bury him," Eni said as he hoisted the bundle to his hip to get through the narrow pass where Clum was standing.

"Did he … did he do anything to you?" Clum asked nervously, holding the tree as a shield as Eni moved past him in his search for soft ground in which to dig.

"Don't be foolish," Eni snapped as he moved past the rocky outcropping and numerous tree roots that laced across the ground. They wandered back along the path, Eni weaving back and forth, kicking the earth at random for suitable spots to dig.

Clum followed several steps behind, noting the older boy's every move and ready to fly if he noticed any ill effects from his confrontation with the wizard. Around the evening fires he had heard tales of men growing fangs or wolf-like claws after such encounters with black magic. He was sure to give special attention to Eni's hands for anything unusual.

Eni tried to focus on the task at hand, but Clum's obvious fear of the wizard's reputation only reinforced the thoughts of his own foolishness. His mind wandered back to the wizard mocking him for his hope of resurrecting the pup. He shook his head hoping to lose the thought, and the fear that maybe he was really more Welsh than English.

They were not far into a vale when they came to a clearing. It was in the lowest spot and it was evident from sheep tracks in the dried mud that it had been a popular spot this past winter. The sheep were now gone but they left many reminders of their time there scattered across the pasture.

"Let's do this quickly," Eni called back to Clum, who still loitered some distance away.

The damp soil just below the surface came out easily, but Clum spent more time watching his friend than actually helping. Eni was alternating between using a stick to break up the earth and his hand to scoop it out. After watching for a while, Eni seemed normal enough that Clum began working in earnest.

Clum looked up at the darkening world, the long shadows extended from the tops of the trees, casting the pasture in shadows. "It's getting late."

"Then we must hurry," Eni said wiping the sweat from his brow.

Though he still seemed normal, Clum decided it was a good idea to hurry; in some of the stories the curse didn't take hold until nightfall.

They worked in silence, deepening and widening the hole, but to Clum's dismay, Eni's hands were so black from the soil that they were almost invisible in the fading light. Clum's powerful stroke slowed as he watched his friend.

"What are we going to say?" Clum blurted out, reaching for another clump of earth.

20

Eni looked up, taking a breath as he thought about it. "We tell everyone that my pup died and we went into the wilds to bury it. It is what we are doing, is it not?"

Clum shrugged with half-hearted agreement as he looked up at the deepening shadows that encompassed them. "Still, we should be going."

Eni looked up from his work and drew his forearm across his sweaty brow, leaving a trail of mud in its wake. It amazed him how much darker the world had become in just a few minutes, but looking down, their hole wasn't very deep.

"I'll get some stones. It'll work," Clum reassured him as he got up to search the meadow for suitable rocks.

Eni looked from the hole to the dead figure of the pup, the black and white fur flitting in the breeze. Emotions that he had held back most of the day returned as he placed the body in the hole. It was still so soft, so beautiful.

He would have stayed and stared for a time, but Clum returned bearing three sizable rocks. "We must hurry," he said as the rocks thudded into the ground next to him.

Eni cupped his hand full of the cool moist earth and pushed it into the hole. The soil filled in the voids by the legs as a few scattered black grains of soil came to rest, floating on the white fur.

Eni took in a deep breath. He hated this. He hated saying goodbye, but two more pushes and it was over. The pup was safe in the arms of the earth. Clum returned with more rocks and once the loose dirt was in place, the two boys placed the stones over the earthen mound, hoping it would dissuade predators from vandalizing the grave.

Clum allowed him no time to mourn his loss as they took to a run. Most of the path ran down hill so they kept the pace until Clum broke away on the first fork leaving Eni alone. He continued for awhile along the path before slowing, hoping to make sense of his visit in the wilds and the words of the wizard.

Eni saw nothing of Clum over the next few days. Brother A

kept the lads hard at work on their studies. He was a small man, thin and wiry with a nervous energy that kept his body in constant motion. Even when sitting, his knee would rise and fall like water in a brook. Despite this affliction, he was a scholar who took Latin very seriously and expected his charges to do so as well.

He never would have permitted a day for market, but "when one is in the blessing of a lord, one does the lord's bidding," he would say the next morning, before ladening them with additional work to compensate for the interruption in their schedule.

The Baron was not a rich man by aristocratic standards. The hills and mountains of the borderlands were only good for sheep, not like the fertile flat lands of England to the east that could provide their lords with both financial harvest and political influence in London.

Though a mountain lord was not totally without means, given the revenue from the market and the production from his lands, he was not above using a monk to educate his children when the Abbot presented the offer. The offer, of course, was not done in kindness, but as a means to recruit pledges both for the Abbey and the priesthood.

Eni, as one of the privileged class, was well aware that Brother Alfonse had him in mind for this vocation, and it was common knowledge among the other lads. Brother Alfonse was quick to correct any who would mispronounce "efflagito," but always demanded that Eni be the most exact. Even Philip, the Baron's eldest son and heir was permitted a gaffe on occasion, but Eni was expected to be perfect every time. "How will the people understand if you do not speak it correctly?" he would say, as if it was a foregone conclusion that the preisthood would be Eni's future occupation.

Eni was not totally opposed to this, but the thought of never marrying did not sound as appealing as the Brother tried to make it. "You are married to God. It is a great and glorious thing," he would say, his fist clenched and his eyes closed as if to reaffirm his faith.

The other boys grinned. It was well known that many of the wealthier churchmen took on mistresses and were far from living the life of piety they demanded of others, but the boys were quick to hide their scorn when the Brother's eyes reopened.

Eni knew that at least in the case of Brother Alfonse it was real. The Brother had always been sincere and honest with him whenever they spoke in private. He would share both the blessings and the struggles of the celibate life.

He always thought the Brother was the most righteous man he knew- other than his own father. That was what made it so odd- the two men who best exemplified Christ to him had so little faith in each other.

To the Brother, the Steward was merely the Baron's lackey, a civil official always countering the Abbot's authority with the people of Knighton. He was a problem that had to be managed, and as the Abbot's representative to the village, it was the Brother's job to do so.

For the lord's Steward though, it was a different type of problem and one with far more serious repercussions. Eni's family had always been different, not only because his father was English and his mother Welsh, a pairing that had since been outlawed across the land, but also because they had a secret, one known only to the family and the others of their cause.

It was a secret that Eni had known since he was a wee lad, one that he had been taught to hide from the outside world. Now he was not only being educated by the Brother, but being courted for the priesthood as well. His family was relying on the sixteen-year-old boy to weigh and measure every word with this learned man of the church.

The unspoken fear that rippled through his family and his kin was that if the Brother ever discovered their secret, if he ever learned what they truly were, it would mean death, the same as for any of their kind under the English King, a painful, brutal death.

4

Eni lay on his bed, desperately trying to fall asleep, but the hay mattress was damp and uncomfortable in the humidity of the night. He figured it must be past vespers, but he could hear the dim conversation of his parents in the room below. Their muffled voices were as short and frantic as they had been most of the day.

"Harold, are you sure of this?"

"Yes, it was to be tonight. Go to bed ... I will take care of it."

"But should you get one of the lads to help?"

"No... no, I will take care of ..." his voice trailed off as a horse whinnied down the lane. Eni sat up in his bed and peered out the window. His face was cooled by the moist breeze that had brought the rain earlier that evening. Eni could make out nothing but the dim presence of the old oak tree that guarded the lane. Its leaves were only a darkening shadow against the passing cloud.

The front door swung open and sent a streak of light along the ground, but the shadow of his father filled it as he stepped out. Eni could see him standing below, peering into the darkness. The air was thick and heavy but sweet from the rain that still trickled in solitary drops off the roof and trees.

It was only then that Eni noticed the dogs, or rather the lack of them. They were always the first to hear someone approaching on the lane. Their barks would always identify a trespasser long before braying of a horse. Eni felt a twinge of excitement and thought maybe he should run down and help confront this intruder.

Perhaps that was what his father was looking for as he peered out into the darkness, but he held neither sword nor lantern. "Odd," Eni mumbled under his breath as a chill drove him from the window.

Throwing on a shirt, he returned to his perch. His father was still there, standing in front of the house like a statue. Eni was about to call out to him when the horse snorted again, much closer this time. Eni jumped at the sudden rumble in the silence, searching the shadows that stretched from the open door. His father remained where he was standing, so still it was almost as if he were in hiding. It would have worked save for his shadow reaching out down the lawn before him.

The clumping of hooves on the pebbles of the drive drove Eni's eyes to a darker shadow. He could only tell that it moved if he studied the landscape for a time, its steady progress unhurried in the darkness.

The lord's Steward remained unmoved, but Eni knew his father could see the man approaching. It was the horse the man was leading that Eni noted first. This was no horse of a peddler or even a clergy. Given its size and stature, even in the dead of the night he could tell this was a war horse. It tossed its head in greeting as they came up to the lord's Steward.

As the man pierced the shaft of light, his sword angled a shadow from where it hung on his hip. Eni was about to give a warning, but his father broke his stoic stance and met the stranger with an embrace.

"I wonder…" Eni said under his breath, crouching behind the sill. The men spoke in hushed tones before they began to walk side by side toward the barns. Eni followed their progress until they disappeared from his sight around the corner of the window.

He lay back down on the hay. *Who would come past vespers on such a night?* he thought, as the tempo of the water dripping off the roof seemed to have begun again in earnest. *And wearing a sword…* While they were not uncommon, the weapons of war were forbidden to be in the possession of a Welshman.

"He has to be English," he said to himself, "or a rogue…" Rolling his blanket underneath his body, he tried to drown the disquiet in sleep. Eventually maybe Eni would have drifted off, but for the roll of laughter that came suddenly from the room below him.

25

Still wearing his nightshirt, he crept from his room carefully avoiding the third board from the door which he knew from experience would squeak like an old hen. It was dark in the hall, but Eni could see the flickering light from the hearth as it cast its dancing shadows up the staircase. The mumble of voices, low and earthy, mixed with the crackle of the fading fire in its grate.

Eni made his way slowly down the stairs, moving and halting with the pitch and roll of the conversation, hoping it would conceal his movement. The main hall was awash in the dark orange glow. He thought it appeared empty at first, only to notice the two men camped next to the hearth, where they melted in with the myriad of shadows.

"Just a matter of time…" the stranger said as Eni hurriedly leaned up against the wall, staying in the shadows. The man's voice was deeper than Eni's father's and lacked the Welsh accent most of the local Normans had acquired. "I don't know when, but it is sure to be soon," he added, in a slow and steady cadence drained of emotion.

"I cannot believe the King would allow it," Eni's father said, "after all that you have done."

The man let out an audible sigh, "Aye, I don't know him anymore… he is a different man now that they got their claws into him."

"There is still hope, but you are exhausted. You have been through more than any man should handle alone. We are all indebted to you."

"You are too kind, my friend, but ah… I am tired," the man added with a weak chuckle as he struggled to his feet. "It will be the death of me…"

Sensing the end of their conversion, Eni made his way up the steps as quietly as he had crept down.

"Upstairs, the end chamber has been made ready for you," his father said as they rose.

"How can I thank you…"

"There is no need," his father answered, clasping the man's shoulder. "Is it not written to offer hospitality to the alien outside my gates? How much more would I do so for an old friend?"

Eni had cleared the top step and quickly slid into his room as the man made his way to the steps. "Sleep well, my friend. Here you are as safe from King Henry as you would be from the devil himself."

Eni couldn't believe his ears. It was one thing for the Welsh to say something like that especially after the war, but his father? His father had even once fought with Henry…

The man's soft leather boots shuffled up the stairs, so tired it seemed he lacked the little strength needed to make it up to the next tread. Eni wondered who this man could be. He was an outlaw to be sure. But why would he come to the March, and how did he know his father?

He felt the man's shadow approach and stepped back from the door, only to catch the edge of the squeaky board, which called out its high pitched alert. Eni looked down and quickly moved his foot to find a quieter harbor.

He looked back out the door, seeing a silhouette of the man stationed in the breach.

"Good night to you too," he said and then disappeared from the cavity continuing his way down the hall to his waiting chamber.

Eni tumbled back into bed. The hay, though still damp, felt soft and comforting as he wrapped his blanket about him. He wondered if he could sleep at all after his father's words. How could a righteous, God fearing Norman say such things?

His mind wandered out into the March, wondering if soldiers or the sheriff were out searching for this fugitive. "What would happen if the man were caught here?" Eni questioned. "What would happen to us?"

5

Wendy swallowed hard, "A joke? No... I don't think so. Grand didn't have a sense of humor..." she said with a forced grin, but the professor's stare lingered until her smile melted away. For a moment, she felt as if she were back in primary school. She did a quick mental check list of her appearance: brushed teeth, clean jeans, a decent sweater, which was anything but new, but not overly ratty in her opinion. It was the sudden rush of anxiety as he studied her that caused her to remember her piercing. He wasn't prim and proper himself, but maybe he was one of those nerdy twits who just don't take you seriously with a stud in your nose. *Oh well, sucks to be him*, she thought defiantly, trying to hold her ground.

The professor finally dropped his eyes back to the package, marking the occasion with another grunt. The words had been rewritten on the plastic bag in permanent marker, but the original words, merely a ghost on the old leather pouch still could be made out. He reached into his top drawer and pulled out a magnifying glass from its case.

Dr. Angus Brown
TVR, Suite 75
1001 Bowlsy Rd
London
Deliver in May of 2017

"Humph...It would have been nice to have it back then," he said flatly turning the package over.

"Yeah, sorry about that..."

He studied it for a moment, running the glass across the length of the package before looking back up, "It's well done, I'll give you that... Where did you get this from? Did Hardgow put you up this?"

"Um... no," she said, backing away from the desk. "Sorry, I don't know any Hardgow, sir. My... my grandmother, she said it was old, really old..."

He pulled off his glasses from their perch with one hand and they skated across his desk as he rubbed his eyes. "That's impossible," he whispered.

He stared at the package on his desk for a moment before looking back up at Wendy. "It's impossible," he said again, this time clearly directed at her.

"Listen," Wendy said, "I don't know what you think happened and I don't really care, all I know is what my grand said... She said that the package was always handed down from grandparent to the oldest grandchild. Grand didn't think she would make it, and, well she didn't ...she died a couple of years ago. That's all I know!"

He was about to say something, but stopped. His eyes fell back to the package and he stared.

It was the battle of the roosters that woke Eni the next morning. Constantly crowing in the yard outside, they raced from fence post to cart wheel, making their way around the house as if they were competing at which of them could awaken the most of the household.

Rising from his bed, Eni looked out the window. A low mist hung over the valley where last night's rain met the morning sun. He thought it odd that no one woke him up. Usually Abertha would have him up at the crack of dawn and on his way to town by this time of day.

He pulled his leggings up under his wrinkled tunic then drew his belt around them both. Looking down at himself, he was sure the state of his clothes would generate a comment or two- and not for the first time.

Eni slipped out the door and down the stairs. The house was quiet. Generally, Abertha would be sweeping and washing windows, but there was no one about.

He passed through the hall, enjoying the sunshine that lit up the room. He suddenly stopped as he passed the open door. "Where is everyone?" he said out loud, seeing the deserted side room. His heart leapt as the events of last night resurfaced. What if they came in the middle of the night and took everyone?

He ran back through the house. The door to his parent's chamber was open and their bed was unmade. He couldn't remember ever seeing their bed like that without one of them in it.

Eni could feel his heart pounding as he sprinted up the stairs and down the hall to the room where the stranger had lodged. It too was empty, but the sheet was neatly folded next to the hay mattress. "He probably never even slept there," Eni thought as he raced back down the stairs, fearing the episode was a ruse to entrap his father.

He could feel his heart pounding as he raced outside. The bright morning sunshine did nothing to hold at bay the rising shadow that everything was terribly wrong.

"Iago!" he called out, as he again broke into a run and headed around the house. "Iago!" he could hear the fear in his own voice, but the gardener didn't respond. Eni ran till he reached the stable behind the rear of the house. "Iago?"

There was no answer but for the clucking of chickens at his feet as they scratched for worms that had surfaced from the night's rain. Eni cautiously entered the stable but stopped short at what he saw. He ran back to the yard, and circled around backwards as if in a daze. The carriage… where was the carriage?

Eni stopped and tried to make sense of it. "The stranger's horse is here, two of ours are gone as is the carriage, and there's not a soul here other than me."

It made no sense, why would the stranger leave his horse? Maybe they were all taken in the night and their horses and carriage were confiscated to ferry them away.

Eni's stomach let out a long mournful groan, either churning with confusion or reminding him how hungry he was. Hoping for the latter, he walked through the picketed gate that housed the kitchen garden. The herbs were in flower and bees buzzed about the thyme as if it were their public house.

He thought it was his mind playing a trick on him, a hint of bacon on the air. It was slight at first, like a memory, but it wouldn't go away. He pointed his nose to the air like a hound trying to pick up the scent, and then he turned, slowly sampling the wind for the aroma.

He caught the smell for a moment. He turned back, hoping to pursue it, but it was gone. Eni was about to give up when he noticed a whiff of smoke rise from the chimney above the kitchen shed before disappearing into the morning blue sky.

The stone shack, built on the far end of the kitchen garden from the main house, was set apart to keep any wayward fires from damaging the manor house. It was possible that the cooking fire was still smoldering from the previous night. He couldn't recall eating any bacon, but he never doubted the ability of Abertha to lace it into one of the dishes if she felt the need.

Making his way across the garden, he hoped that she was in there, simply forgetting to wake him, but even if she was not, he could still plunder the kitchen for provisions. The door creaked as he lifted the latch and pulled it open letting the morning light spill into the interior.

A sudden commotion startled him. At first he thought a rat must have beat him in raiding the pantry when a pan went crashing off the table as he poked his head in and called out. "Is that you, Aber ..."

The air left him as a blow struck him hard in the chest and he toppled over backwards. He saw the glint of the steel blade catch the light as a hulk of a man towered over him. *Bandits*, he thought, his chest burned as he tried to take a breath.

In his mind, he knew he should roll away, but the reality was that he was so stunned he could do nothing but look up at his attacker. It didn't make sense though. The man's dark green jacket and embroidered linen shirt were not the typical attire of a brigand. "Who are you?" the man asked in perfect English, the sword held high, ready to fall if the answer failed to satisfy.

Eni tried to answer but his voice failed him, the air refused to fill his deflated lungs. He thought this silence would spell his doom as the man seemed lose patience with his delay.

"Eni!" Shock and confusion greeted him as he saw his father rush to the door. "It's my youngest, John," he explained as he hurried past the outstretched sword to the fallen boy, still muted by the blow.

"Are you all right? You gave us a terrible scare," he said as he reached out, helping Eni to his feet.

The stranger sheathed his blade, but to Eni he looked disappointed at the turn of events. "My apologies, young man," he added with little conviction.

"It is alright, dear," the lord's Steward called as he shouldered his son into the room. "It was only Eni."

"Oh, thank God," his mother sighed, coming out of the shadows with a manuscript gathered in her arms. "What has happened?" she asked, her Welsh accent thickened by the excitement.

"Just got the wind knocked out of him, ain't that right, lad," his father said, helping him to the bench that ran along the table.

"Aye, terribly sorry about that," the man added, as he followed them in, closing the door behind him.

"It's perfectly understandable, Sir John," Eni's mother said with a smile to their guest, waving her hand in the air as if it helped her breathe. Eni stared at her till it drew her attention. "What were you doing here, anyway?" she asked, the vellums still clutched to her bosom. "Why are you not at your studies?"

Eni wanted to scream, but it was a struggle to breathe given the soreness of his ribs. He turned to his father. He was rubbing his beard deep in thought. Seeing Eni's shocked stare, he looked at his wife, who was still clutching the manuscript.

"You might as well put it down, Mali…" the lord's Steward said in answer to his wife's questioning glance.

"I'm sorry, John, we obviously… in the commotion to send our people away, we forgot about someone this morning…"

Eni felt everyone's eyes fall upon him except for his father's, who was studying a barrel of flour in the corner.

Finally finding the strength to speak, he croaked out a weak voice, "Where is everyone?" He saw them share glances, but no one said anything. "Where are the horses… the dogs…? Abertha?"

His parents dropped their gaze to the floor and he heard his mother's breath slowly go out through puckered lips. "Can he be trusted?" the stranger asked. Eni wanted to turn. He wanted to study this intruder to his family but feared he might be hit again.

"Oh, yes," his mother answered immediately.

"Well, we think so…" his father countered. Eni looked up at him, but the lord's Steward avoided his eyes. "There was the incident with Murdoc… the Wizard out in the March."

Eni felt his gut sink; his mother's confidence faded almost as fast as his own. "Yes, well, there was that…" she said weakly and dropped her eyes back to the floor.

"Oh…," the stranger said in a deep voice. It was a simple, one syllable word, but to Eni, it carried both his knowledge of the wizard and his contempt for the man.

"It's not like Eni doesn't know of what we believe," his father started to explain. "He was, of course, raised with the knowledge of the Word, but he is young… and foolish."

"Was any harm done?"

"No," his father said with a sigh. "Not that we know of, but you know the man… and what he is capable of."

"Aye," the stranger answered, and they were all quiet for a moment. Eni felt like they were all examining him. He felt both his mother's hope and his father's concern, but then the man spoke again. "Do you know who I am?" he asked, as he put his hand on Eni's shoulder.

Eni could feel the power in the man's grip, and though it wasn't uncomfortable, he knew it could be if the man wished it so. "I don't know…" he said slowly, "but I could guess."

"And who would you guess I am?"

Eni tried to take a deep breath, but the pain cut it short. He wondered if the answer he would give would bring pain to his shoulder or not. "I would surmise that you are John Oldcastle."

The hand on his shoulder had a slight tremor as Eni spoke, but relaxed as he finished. "And what do you *surmise* your mother is holding?" the man asked, accenting the word as if to mock him.

Eni looked up at her. She still had her arms wrapped around the manuscript, with the papers carefully laid out against her bosom to keep them from being creased. "Is it a Wyclif? …the whole thing?"

"Well, that is it then," his father said with an easy sigh.

"Thank God," his Mother said in relief as she set the bound volume down on the table.

"The boy is rather clever," his father said, as he patted Eni's shoulder.

"He certainly is…" the visitor agreed, "but can he be trusted?" Eni turned to face this man who was still standing behind him. As soon as their eyes met Eni knew that John Oldcastle didn't trust him. "Please understand," the man explained as he turned to Eni's mother, "I have no ill will towards the boy, but we must be certain. Arundel has already murdered countless men over the past twelve years, and his hatred for me in particular would bring a horrible death to whomever might be snared with it."

Eni caught his mother wiping a tear off her cheek as she shook her head in acknowledgement.

"I am not one to walk into a man's house as a guest and tell him what to do with his own offspring, but tread carefully, I beg you…"

"You are right, of course. There are more who are at stake than those in this room," the Steward said, looking over at his wife as she turned away.

"I should like to check my horse," Oldcastle said, breaking the timid silence as he made his way to the door, leaving the family to sort their own. No one spoke as the door shut behind him. Eni looked back

34

and forth between his parents but neither acknowledged him.

"So where is everyone?" Eni asked when the silence got too much for him to take.

"We sent them away for the day so Sir John could come unnoticed," his father said almost flatly, but with his eyes fixed on his wife who turned to tend the cooking fire. "We should have done the same with you, if we had known in time…"

Eni felt his stomach turn. It was not often he was reproached by his father. Being the youngest, he was a quick study of his older brothers' mistakes and always managed to use the lessons to stay in his father's good graces.

"What are we to do?" his mother's voice was drawn and frail but she didn't turn to face them.

The Steward shook his head as if it had been decided, "If he cannot be trusted… we have to send him away."

"But he can be trusted! Can't you, Eni?" his mother cried, turning her head half-way towards them from her station by the hearth.

Eni thought for a moment. What did it mean to be trusted? "I… I would never do anything to harm you… either of you," he said, feeling his way through his thoughts.

"It's not us we are worried about. It is the Word. This…" his father said tapping the manuscript on the table. "This is the Word of God in our people's tongue; this was how God meant it to be…"

Eni said it without thinking, the words just toppled out of his mouth and it wasn't until he heard his mother's shrieks that they ricocheted back to his mind. "How do you know?" It was only a question; it meant nothing, but his father's glare told him they didn't see it that way.

"Oh Eni…" his mother said, with her head still buried in the corner.

"I didn't mean…"

"No, you didn't mean anything by talking to that devil of a wizard either?" his father snapped. "Do you have any idea what that man could do to us? Do you know how many people have died as a result of him and his black arts?"

Eni sat there on the wood bench, its surface stained from countless spills over the years. His hunger had abandoned him as the gnawing fear of what details the wizard may have gathered from their conversation stewed sickeningly in his gut.

"I will make work of finding an apprenticeship..." his father stated as he gathered the manuscript.

Eni said nothing, but his mother interrupted, "He is only a boy..."

"He is no younger than his brothers were when they left, and no less the trouble..." he added, as he made way to the door. "John and I will head to the grove... Fix the boy some food and then join us... alone."

6

Sir John left that evening, disappearing into the darkness as mysteriously as he had come the night before, unseen and unnoticed by anyone except those in the manor house. Eni watched him go from his shuttered window, careful to remain hidden from view lest he be accused of anything else.

It had been a lonely day. His mother had made him breakfast and then departed for the grove to join the others. Eni ended up spending most of day alone in the kitchen, watching the cooking fire dwindle away to ash.

He would have loved to have been at the grove and seen Wyclif's book for himself. His father had spoken of it many times in the privacy of their home, of the work Wyclif had put into it, translating word for word from Latin into the English tongue, so that any educated man could read it for himself. How for twenty years, the Lollards had preached and distributed more and more copies around the countryside.

Then things changed twelve years ago, when King Henry, the usurper, signed a law declaring anyone owning an English copy of the Bible a heretic. Anyone caught with one would be burned alive at the stake.

Several died, but rather than killing the idea, the manuscripts and Lollards went underground. Soon they were known only by winks and whispers along the countryside.

That's what made it so exciting to Eni, being able to read English words and phrases that he had heard in Latin so many times... He had seen bits and pieces, a few chapters and verses, copied and hidden like morsels of forbidden fruit, consumed in private, away from unwelcome eyes. A chapter here and a chapter there, or even a favorite verse kept safe in the hem of a dress or in the lining of a cloak. A whole Wyclif was rare indeed- made all the more so with the burning of every found copy and the possessor as well.

He knew there was danger. He just couldn't understand why his father wouldn't trust him. "I'm his son," Eni muttered. "It is not like I would ever turn over my own father..."

Abertha and all the stable hands returned the next day. While the men had been delivering sheep to a buyer in Hereford, Abertha spent her day in the markets and brought back a small bolt of fabric. She and Eni's mother spent the rest of the day devising how to divide the precious fibers among her wardrobe.

To Eni, it seemed his mother went to extraordinary lengths to bring everything back to normal. She would talk to him in her usual voice, but he could feel a difference. Somehow, it lacked her usual warmth. He couldn't say why, except that she no longer hugged him. Such displays of affection had been typical in their relationship, what with him being the baby of the family.

That was fine with him; after all, he was too old for motherly hugs, but still... He wished he had lessons to occupy his time, but Brother Alfonse had been called back for a planned celebration at the Abbey.

He lingered around the barns for a while, but the stable lads were behind on their chores, and he lacked the motivation to join them in mucking out the vacated paddocks. With his mother busying herself in the parlor and seeing no other requirement for his time, he headed out to the March.

He had not seen Clum since they tracked the wizard the week before, but he was sure it was the red-headed boy who had exposed their activities that day.

The flocks were now higher up in the mountains, trimming the fresh fields finer than the sharpest sickle. Left alone, the grasses in the valley were now long and thick. The wind blew up waves that danced across the green ocean as each blade rose and fell in unison till the wind's fury was lost behind a harbor of trees on the far side.

A dirt path bridged this green sea, the result of a century's worth of carts that had compacted the soil into two parallel depressions, snaking through the grass and exposing the rocks and stones of its mountain core.

It was along this path that Eni traveled, the wind begging him to join the swelling grasses in their dance, but dancing was far from the top of Eni's concerns. What he wanted more than anything right then was to find out why Clum had ratted on him. He knew it had to be him; his loose tongue was always wagging like the tail of a hungry dog.

It was the reason he was forbidden from telling Clum of the Lollards and their forbidden book. "That boy is too simple to be trusted," his father had warned him. Eni's face warmed at the thought of how right he had been.

He could see the settlement above him after passing through the trees. The uneven rock walls and thatched roofs walled off the top of the cliff above the stream, forcing any friend or foe to take the path from the south.

It was more of a hamlet than a village, a small gathering of five huts that followed the bow of the hillock. For generations the Welsh had lived there, raising their sheep on the rich mountain grasses to the west.

At the base of the hill, Eni passed the charred timbers of a barn that once held the shared wealth of the settlement. Its blackened walls still lay on the ground where they had been burned down five years before.

Eni remembered when it had happened. He had been eleven years old when he and Clum watched from behind a boulder above the high meadow as the marauding hordes of Prince Henry's army marched through to stomp out the Welsh rebellion to the west.

Their orders allowed them to take sheep for food, but since these flocks were Welsh, they decimated them, carrying what they could and leaving the rest to rot on the hillside.

Since the villagers' flocks were destroyed, they'd had to till the rocky soil in hopes of coaxing crops from the barren land in order to survive. The only thing that thrived was their hatred for their English lords.

They never said anything to him, but he knew. Whenever he came up the path he could feel it from the way they looked at him for a moment, almost like they wanted revenge for what the English had done that day. Even if he was half Welsh himself, it was the other half that was the problem, his English half.

Heading up the path, Eni was surprised at how empty the place was. There were usually offspring of all ages running about, chasing dogs or being chased by one. Clum had four younger brothers and a sister who could be counted on to make his entrance obvious to their enclave.

Eni looked around, but they were nowhere to be seen. The hamlet was vacant except for a young woman nursing a babe under a rowan tree facing the river valley. "Pardon me?" Eni said hoping it was loud enough to gain her attention yet not wanting to alarm her or the suckling child.

She hastily flung a blanket over her shoulder before turning to face him. Her furrowed brow clearly displayed her annoyance at the disturbance.

She was a relative, a cousin of his mother. They used to play together when they were younger. Though she had a year or two on him he was surprised to see her already with a child. "Oh… hello Mariame. Where is everyone?" Eni asked.

"Haying," she said flatly with barely a nod toward the mountain behind her before turning back to her parental duty.

He could sense her rigidity as she sat there, her back towards him waiting for him to leave before she continued. Eni sighed, wondering why she would treat her kin in such a way.

The path was well trodden and Eni could make out the varied footprints of both adults and barefooted children in the mud of a seasonal stream. He could hear their voices before he broke the tree line. Children were giggling and the women were gathered on one end of the field, layered in conversation as they turned the dried grass to let the sun reach the wet grass underneath. Clum and the men were further up the slope, cutting the standing meadow with sickles. They formed a line, and their long swinging motions looked like a series of windmills as the blades rose high into the air and then fell, disappearing into the

40

green sea. Then, stepping forward in rhythm, their blades would rise and fall, cutting into the next patch.

Eni watched from the edge until Clum's brother Tiago noticed him. "Eni!" he called and a half-dozen children rushed over to him laughing as they raced through the stubble of cut grass.

Eni smiled at their enthusiasm as the entire throng seemed to launch their bodies at him. It took five of them to take him down.

"My, you're getting tall, Tiago. You'll pass your brother one of these days," he teased, since the boy was still about a foot behind his brother. The women looked up from their work of turning the hay and their conversation came to an abrupt end.

"Aye," Eni called over, recognizing Clum's mother, but she merely looked up at him briefly before returning to her work without a word.

He continued throwing the little ones around as they attempted to drop him again and again. Finally tired out, he begged for their mercy.

"Shall we let the English go?" Tiago taunted.

"No!" they all shouted at once and buried Eni under a pile of laughing, playful urchins.

"That is enough!" Clum's mother called from across the field as one of the smaller ones started to cry after being knocked down by a wayward foot. "Let him go now, Tiago!" she added when the boy held his position on top of his prisoner.

"All right," he called back half-heartedly as he slipped off Eni's pinned chest. Tiago and the rest of the swarm made their way into the trees to cool off in the brook.

Eni lay there in the field and watched them go as he waited for his breath to return. He would have dallied longer, but the women seemed to take turns casting glances at him, and while he couldn't make out their conversation, it left him uneasy.

As he got away from the trees and made his way up the open slope, the wind picked up again. "Aye!" he called out, but though a few men looked up, none of them greeted him as was customary.

"What brings you?" Clum's father finally asked after a time of the most unsettling silence. His eyes showed a coldness that Eni had never experienced from him before. And he held his sickle almost as if he would prefer to use it as a weapon than as a tool.

"I…I came to speak with Clum," Eni said with a nod to his friend, who had not met his eyes since he arrived, but had kept his focus on the fallen grass before him.

Clum's father looked at his son, "We have work to do."

"Perhaps I could help?"

"All of our tools are in use. Perhaps some other time," he replied.

Eni stood and watched them for a time but soon turned and made his way back down the hill. His knew his face was red; it burned with each gust of wind that met him. It didn't take much cleverness to understand what had happened or why- even here among the Welsh- he was now an outcast. Such is the result of consorting with the Wizard of the March.

He steered clear of the women but knew they were well aware of his departure, and he could only imagine what was being said about him. He held an even pace and stared stoically ahead until he was well beyond the meadow.

Eni turned south from where he had last seen the urchins splashing in the brook and disappeared into the lush green leaves of the forest.

He walked until he could no longer hear the children or the yelping dogs. He moved deep into a forest valley, the only sound the wind dashing the leaves high above him like waves crashing on the shore.

He looked up at branches dancing, the multiple shades of green intermingled, flexing and frolicking before they sprang back to the trees that mothered them. There was only the briefest of respites before the music returned, but as the romp began again in earnest, a leaf, battered or unwanted, broke free and drifted slowly down through the canopy.

It amazed Eni how gracefully it fell compared to the violence of the dance it was leaving behind. It twirled gently as it floated side to side, as if looking in vain for another to dance with, but it was alone. The leaf continued to search, side to side, until at last it reached the forest floor. There, it fell not on earth, but on the corpses of its comrades, others that were no longer wanted in the dance of the leaves.

7

"Really, that's all I know…" Wendy tried to explain. She remembered back to when she was little, back to when her Grand first showed her the package. She must have been ten or eleven at the time. It was old, and it fascinated her. It still had a smell, the musty leather smell like her great grandfather's leather jacket from the Second World War that hung in the closet. Grand said it was a lot older than the jacket and had seen a lot of history.

Every time she visited her Grand, she would head to the desk and pull open the bottom drawer and stare at it, dreaming about the history it had witnessed, the kings, the queens, the fashions, the lives and deaths since one of her ancestors had first wrapped the leather into its bundle, tied tight with the thin leather strap that still collared the leather edges. It had survived wars and fires, one of which she was told happened during the Civil War and had left a darkened hue on one side where the flames licked the crate that housed it.

At university she wrote a paper giving credit to the package as the reason she chose to major in history. How could it not, a forbidden trinket from a bygone era that she could only admire? It made giving it away even harder, plus the fact that she had forgotten. If her Grand hadn't made such a big deal about it… well, it would still be back home where it belonged.

"Really, my Grandmother said it had been in the family forever and that I was supposed to take it over to you. Sorry that it's late, but you know how it is…" Wendy continued, mostly to keep the silence at bay, but the professor didn't seem to hear her.

She looked around the room. There was a white board with an algebraic equation in the corner. She had taken algebra in school, but the formula was more complicated than any she had ever seen. She shuddered at the memory, mathematics was never her strong suit.

"What are you a professor of?" she asked, breaking the silence again as Dr. Brown continued flipping the package over, staring at every aspect of the wrapping with his glass.

"Huh?" he said looking up. "Experimental physics," he answered belatedly, as if the question had taken a few wrong turns before finally reaching his brain.

He reached into his drawer again, shuffled around before pulling out a tweezers and a letter opener. Wendy watched as he carefully worked the utensils like surgical tools, prying open the Ziploc bag as if it was a surgery.

"So why does a physics professor care about an old leather package?" she asked with her sweetest smile, hoping to compensate for the dour look on the professor's face.

He didn't answer, but leaned over the pouch and took a long sniff as if he were a hound on a scent. "It is old…" he said softly, forgetting she was there. "Real old…Could do a carbon test for age," he added, prodding the leather gently with a letter opener. "Humph, maybe it wasn't a complete failure…but, man, it can't be…"

The rest of the afternoon Eni thought little as he wandered in the wood. The only idea that he held for any length of time was of never going home. It certainly had an appeal, but even at sixteen years old he knew the problems he would face. Dressed as he was in satins and speaking like an educated Englishman, he would be a target for any Welshman who still harbored resentment from the war, and those were not uncommon even among his own kin.

Besides, what would he do? He had no training, other than knowing his letters and a small amount of Latin. He could join the church, but they would not want him either, since it appeared to be well known that he had collaborated with a heretic.

Walking up a small outcropping, he came across a bare rock, blown smooth by the wind that cleaned and weathered the exposed face. He perched on it and scanned the countryside like a hawk seeking prey.

He let a sigh bellow up from deep in his soul. "The curse of the wizard," he said, letting his mind wander to the 'what-ifs': what if he had not been so pigheaded in following the old man into the forest that day?

"Foolish Welshman," he said, shaking his head, blaming his maternal side for his current ills and blocking out the fact that Clum had protested the maneuver at the time. He sighed again, not as deeply, but it felt cleansing all the same. No, he knew his best course of action was to head home and hope his father would find an apprenticeship for him.

He looked out to the horizon, *Someplace in the east*, he thought, imagining what might lay in store for him. He had never been any further into England than Hereford and wondered how he would fit in with the proper English. *The sooner, the better.*

Reaching home that evening, he headed upstairs with little more than a declining groan to Abertha's inquiry of dinner. Though he hadn't eaten since early that morning, his desire to not answer questions outweighed any true need for food.

It seemed like an eternity since Brother Alfonse had left for the Abbey. In that time, Eni had done little but walk the wilds of the mountains and try to avoid any living person who might recognize him.

It was simple for the most part; the sheep would echo throughout the valleys long before any shepherd came into view. Eni would then escape into a nearby woods and wait them out or follow a brook down into the vale since most of the flocks were heading up to feed on the high grasses that were reaching their zenith from the spring rains.

On the eve of the fortnight, Brother Alfonse stopped at the house on his way to Knighton and left a message with Abertha that he expected Eni the next morning. It was the first time he had smiled in a week. He was so relieved; he even broke bread that evening with his parents-though not so much as a word was shared between them.

Eni was up long before Abertha came for him the next morning, and he ran all the way to the village, arriving before most of the town folk had even crossed their thresholds for their morning rituals. He sat cross-legged on the landing with his head against the wood door, waiting for the Brother to arrive that morning.

He tightened his cloak to keep in the heat as he encouraged the inching sun upward and over the nearby wall, allowing the village time to spring to life around him. A clear day with a bright blue sky should have lifted his spirits, but it could not keep the fear from running through his mind - that the Brother had heard of his heretical behavior upon his arrival and would bar him from lessons for evermore.

"Eni!"

He turned with a start to see the Brother bounding up the stairs, his wide smile and stretched out hands bringing instant relief. He pulled the boy to his feet and hugged him as if he were the one in trouble with God, rather than the other way around.

"I think you have grown since we last met," he said, comparing height between the two of them. Eni was still an inch or so shorter than the Brother even with the Brother's shaved tonsure and Eni's bushy hair giving him every benefit.

"How was the Abbey, Brother?"

"Oh Eni, you would not believe the troubles that are stirring in our world..." he said as he opened the door, letting the boy in and then fixed the door open with a rock to let the sweet morning air circulate about the room.

"Really?" Eni answered, somewhat hesitantly.

"One of the King's own lords, an honored knight during the Welsh rebellion no less, is accused of heresy..." the look of horror on Eni's face must have been evident to the Brother. "I could scarcely believe it myself. One could understand a Welshman or a Saxon perhaps, but a Norman lord," he added shaking his head. "What is the world coming to? Obviously the devil's agent, I'll tell you."

46

"Truly amazing," Eni agreed shaking his head. "So what evil did this devil's agent do to be declared a heretic?"

"Eni, really! That would be gossip."

"Oh… right, Brother, I beg your forgiveness."

"Of course boy, but we must be vigilant about such things. We wouldn't want to give the devil a foothold. That being said," he added, with a glance at the door, "he was one of those Lollards. Shh, shh!" he said quickly, before the rest of the boys filed in.

The Brother hopped up to welcome back his charges after their respite from each other, freeing Eni to breathe in relief. Philip and Jestin, the Baron's oldest sons were there, along with Edward, the Sheriff's youngest.

"Glad to have you back, Brother," Philip said with a smirk. "We didn't know what to do with ourselves in your absence."

"I'm sure you got yourself into all kinds of trouble, my young lord. I was just pleased to see the village was still standing on my return," Brother Alfonse shot back in clear reference to a mysterious fire that burned down a barn the year prior when the Brother was also gone.

Jestin laughed, only to get a sharp swat from his older sibling, "I had nothing to do with it, did I, Edward?"

"Not that I recall, my lord," the other boy bluffed. Philip and Edward both had three years on Eni and had been best of friends since they could walk. The fact that not so much as a wheelbarrow of hay could be moved from Knighton to Aserverdy without the permission of one of their fathers gave the boys a tendency to have their revelry go unchallenged. Being that one was the heir to the barony and the other the youngest son of the sheriff, they were rarely held to account except when the good Brother was about.

Brother Alfonse was subject only to the Abbot in Hereford and to the church, and therefore was about the only person who could discipline both boys without suffering some sort of retribution from their fathers, but even he had to be careful.

"Well, let's hope nothing comes to light over the next few days, hmm…?"

"It shan't, Brother. WE have been good and honorable Christians," Philip said in mock humility but gave Eni a wink that made his heart skip a beat.

It was just a matter of time, Eni thought, whenever they need a good laugh, they'll call the Brother over and tell him of the heretic in their midst. Eni could just imagine how the good Brother would react: his face would turn bright red and he would turn and point a shaking finger at him, "You... you... I trusted you." All the while, Philip, Edward and Jestin would only laugh at his fall from grace.

If the bishops were going to execute a man as a heretic for having a copy of God's Word in English, he could only imagine what they would do to someone who sought to collaborate with the Wizard of the March in bringing a dead pup back to life.

8

To Eni's surprise, the day passed with only vague references being aimed in his direction. The closest to the mark was when Philip asked about the spiritual effects on one's soul of associating with an unbeliever; Eni's eyes shot to the floor in humiliation. The Brother gave a lengthy and complicated answer that included the word 'damnation' several times, each of which drove a shiver up Eni's spine and widened Philip's smile. The Brother went on for several more minutes, quoting no less than four Popes in their original Latin, and by the end of his monologue he had bled out the enthusiasm for the subject.

Over the next few days there was little discussion of anything other than the study of vocabulary and church history.

Eni was thankful for the change, even if he was alone in this reaction. Home was becoming unbearable with the forced silence that accompanied every meal. He ended up spending most of the evening by himself going over the memorization for the day, letting the phrases accompany him as he drifted off to sleep.

"So," the Brother started one afternoon, "Which of our Holy Fathers restricted the use of the title 'Papa' to only the Bishop of Rome?"

It may have been a simple question but after spending the last several hours going over the list of the 206 Holy Fathers from Paul in 30 AD to Gregory XII, the numbers and names had long since begun to run together.

"Eni, what is your answer?" the Brother asked, after exhausting the other three.

This was the typical chain of events. Philip was always the first chosen due to his rank as the Baron's heir; if he couldn't answer, it would next fall to Jestin, and then Edward.

There had been times when he was younger that Eni thought this unfair, but he was reminded by his father that he had access to the Brother's lessons due to the Baron's agreement with the Abbot. "...as soon as his lordship's heirs finish their studies, the Abbot will call back the Brother... What would you do then, hmm? Study hard, Eni- this is your chance to improve your station in life."

"Eni?" The Brother asked again, as the other three looked over at the unusual source of silence. It was not often Eni was stumped by any of the Brother's questions.

"Gregory... VII."

A smile slowly came over the Brother's face. "That's Saint Gregory VII. Close, but no," he added triumphantly. "It was Gregory VI who was thirty years earlier in 1045. Saint Gregory is, of course, known for what... Philip?"

The older boy groaned and cast a withering glare at Eni for inspiring the Brother with another question.

"I certainly don't know or care, Brother," Philip said, rubbing his head as if it pained him.

'That is too bad..." the Brother nodded in mock sympathy. "Jestin, can you tell your brother why he should care?"

Jestin was a year younger than Eni, and although he was prone to lord his position over him when given the chance, he did admire Eni's natural abilities. "Can't we just skip to Eni, Brother? It is really the second part of his question after all."

"Here, here," Edward agreed.

"The lords have spoken," Brother Alfonse said, and he clapped his hands together in front of him as if it were an answer to prayer. "Eni, what say you? Why should the future lord Philip know and care what Saint Gregory is known for?"

The three others looked at him wearily, but before Eni could answer, there was a knock at the door.

"Excuse me, Brother." William of Hereford, one of the Baron's squires, appeared in the open doorway. His emerald cloak was wrapped under his left arm and his matching hat clutched in his right.

"What is it, William, that you must disturb our lessons?" Brother asked, as he stepped to the door.

All four boys rose in their seats to catch the exchange of words.

"My pardon, but I'm on the Baron's business. He wishes for young Eni to attend him at once."

Eni suddenly sank back down as the rest of the boys turned toward him with raised eyebrows.

"Perhaps it was Eni who burned the barn down," Edward joked.

In spite of their ribbing, Eni's fear must have been evident on his face, because as he stood to leave, Jestin tugged on his tunic, "Father would never care about that..."

Eni followed William down the wood stairs that creaked under the weight of both of them. William, whom Eni always took as a friendly enough fellow, didn't even turn to wait for him as they made their way across the courtyard to the keep.

The stone walls that ringed the great house had been laid two centuries before but had been reinforced during the last Welsh uprising. The royals were taking no more chances with their unruly neighbors to the west gaining a foothold in the March.

Eni followed silently as they passed under the portcullis and into the courtyard. Looking up, he watched as the flag snapped in the breeze, pointing stiffly east toward the rest of the English Kingdom.

William was half-way up the stone steps that buttressed out from the keep into the courtyard below before he turned to see what was taking his charge so long. It wasn't the first time Eni had visited the keep, but the height and majesty of the structure always amazed him. He could make out a guard helmet atop the turret as it caught the sun and wondered what the view must be like from such a pinnacle.

The mountains may be Welsh, he thought, *but in the walls of Knighton, with its grand stone keep, dancing flags and armored guards, this was England.*

"We must hurry," William called down to him over the din of some sheep being driven into the yard.

Eni nodded as he gave chase, taking two steps at a time as he tried to make up the distance. The doors stood open, but the darkness stunned his eyes as their feet slapped against the slate floor. Eni expected to be led to the great hall, but William passed it by and took him down a narrow passage that lead to a flight of stairs seemingly hollowed out the stone itself.

William hesitated at the landing long enough for Eni to think they were going to head down. He had never been under the keep before but he had heard enough tales of woe to know what went on down there.

The squire merely waited for him till a maid ambled by, and then darted up the winding steps. Eni looked down. He could hear drips of water hitting a puddle in the darkness below.

The stairs coiled around the outer perimeter of the keep like an adder rising step by step, until it finally opened to a narrow passage lined with tapestries.

William led Eni on down the hall till he came to a closed door and rapped lightly with his knuckles.

"Enter," a voice answered, and by its deep baritone Eni knew it was the Baron. He quickly dried his sweaty palms on his tunic as he walked into the room.

An ornate desk dominated the room, but the chair behind it was gone. "Ah yes, Eni, there you are..." the Baron greeted him and shook his hand as if they were great friends after a long absence. "Thank you, William, that will be all," he added, dismissing the squire.

William nodded reluctantly before turning to leave. The Baron waited until the door thudded shut. "You have been the topic of our discussion, my boy..." the Baron said as he put his arm around Eni's shoulder to walk him to his desk. It was only then that Eni noticed the two others in the room.

The sight of them together made Eni freeze mid-stride. His father stood in the corner behind the door he had just entered. He looked small and was paler then Eni had ever seen him, as if the blood had drained clear out of his body.

52

Eni caught the look of fear as their eyes met briefly before his father turned away, dropping his gaze to the floor.

In the other corner, sitting comfortably on the Baron's chair, was the Wizard of the March. His linen shirt, tailored and white, would have cost a month's wages and seemed to catch the light that poured in from the window across the room. It was all the more brilliant for being framed by his dark green cloak that was flung behind him.

Eni's mind raced as he tried to decipher what was happening, but before he could make sense of anything, his lordship muddled his thoughts. "You know everyone here, I believe…" he said in a chipper voice, as if trying to overcome Eni's father's bleak appearance.

"Aye," Eni said weakly with a nod to the Wizard, as was customary, who returned it accordingly. His father said nothing, casting a glare toward the wizard who apparently took no notice of it.

"Well, Eni," the Baron said, turning him by his shoulder away from his father to the desk in the center of the room. "Your father has informed me that he has been seeking an apprenticeship for you," the Baron said with a smile that diminished once he rounded his desk and reached for his missing chair.

Eni followed the Baron's gaze toward the Wizard in the corner who seemed not to notice the lord's displeasure.

"Anyway," his lordship continued, shifting uncomfortably behind the wooden desk, "Murdoc here has decided to take you on as an apprentice. It must be a divine intervention…"

"My lord, please," Eni's father gasped.

"Well, Harold, it seems quite miraculous to me."

Eni's father sighed, "I dare say it was a bit more earthly than that."

The Baron took no notice of his Steward but continued speaking to Eni, "There are few more powerful men in all of England than Murdoc. I've heard it said he even has the ear of our new king…"

"You are too kind, my lord," Murdoc cut in with a nod of his head as if it were a bow. Eni could not remember ever seeing a commoner speak to the Baron who didn't at least stand before him, much less pilfer his chair.

"Young man," Murdoc addressed him. He was tall even in the chair and his dress was so fine Eni doubted that the Baron could afford its equal. "We have come to an agreement, though not unanimous I'm afraid, that you should accompany me and I will teach you the art of council. I am not getting any younger, and it is time to pass on the knowledge of my trade to the next generation."

The 'art of council' does sound impressive, Eni thought.

"It is a wonderful opportunity," the Baron agreed as he bounced up and down on the balls of his feet. "You could do so much for the Kingdom, and of course you would always be welcome here in Knighton and the March."

Eni could see himself riding into the castle gates, dressed in such finery that the girls would gaze at him from afar hoping to catch his eye. He would have his pick of all the prettiest lasses.

"That is true," Murdoc added with another nod to the Baron. "Wise council is always welcomed in the halls of power…"

"…Or despised by the God-fearing commoner." Eni had almost forgotten his father was in the room, but the bite of his words cleared his head like a pinch of smelling salts.

"Harold, he's our guest!" the Baron scolded.

"It is all right, my lord," Murdoc said, with none of the emotion that Eni's father had shown. "The Steward is quite right. To the uneducated and the Welsh in particular, the art of council is not held in high esteem."

"Indeed," Eni heard his father mutter under his breath.

"But I can assure you, my boy, that the benefits of my position far exceed the minor inconvenience of my reputation with some of the commoners as you already know."

Eni felt his chest tighten and could feel his father's eyes bore through him. The Baron must have feared Eni's father was about to insult his guest again and added a quick "How true, how true." It made Eni wonder how much of the tale the Baron knew.

"I must soon be off, my lord," Murdoc said, straightening out his cloak. "I will return in a fortnight for the boy, thereby giving the

Steward and his family time to say their farewells."

"That is very kind of you, councilor," the Baron said quickly, to cover up the bitter silence from Eni's father.

"It would please me if you have him ready to travel at that time," Murdoc said coolly, turning to Eni's father for the first time since the boy had walked into the room.

In the brief silence that followed, Eni worried how his father would answer. It seemed to take forever, especially with the Baron struggling to remain calm as he shuffled his feet back and forth behind his desk.

The Steward finally cleared his throat. But his words were still choked with emotion, "It will be as you wish, my lord."

9

"What is this about…Dr. Brown?" Wendy asked, after watching the professor examine the leather pouch from every angle still inside its plastic nest. The tweezers and letter opener were placed on either side like a fork and knife to a dinner plate.

The professor leaned back in his chair. It offered a squeak with the change of position. A squeaky chair like that would drive her nuts, but the Professor didn't seem to notice it. He brought his hands together at the tips creating an arch with his fingers like the ruins of an old cathedral as he stared at the pouch on his desk.

"How long did you say it was in your family?"

"Umm, I don't know," Wendy started. "Generations, was what my grandmother always said."

"How many… three, four?" he asked with eyebrows raised.

"Well, I got the impression she meant like, hundreds of years…" Wendy offered, hoping that she was not coming across as being completely off.

The professor shook his head. "Can't be," he muttered, still staring at the item as if it had him in a trance. "No…no, it could never make it that far." He stared at it again saying nothing and only occasionally shaking his head. Suddenly he looked up at her, "I don't see how that is possible…"

She gave a relieved smile, "I know… Grand said she thought her grandfather was off his rocker when he passed it on to her right after the big war, you know WWII. I mean, how could it be addressed to somebody seventy years in the future, right? That was my whole thinking …" she said, adjusting her shoulder bag, "…motoring over

here, but I get here, and low and behold, there really is a Dr. Brown…
It makes no bloody sense, does it?"

The professor glanced up. He looked directly into her eyes for the first time. She saw that his stone exterior was gone and for a second she saw what she thought was fear before he dropped his gaze back to the package. "No, it shouldn't…" he agreed, "unless…."

Eni headed out after the meeting, thankful for the long walk home, made even longer by his wandering along the River Teme. But in spite of the distance he traveled, he couldn't escape the image of his father as he was ushered from the Baron's study that afternoon.

Seeing the Steward standing silently in the corner reminded Eni of when his sister Sara had died two years before, but his father's hollowed cheeks and reddened eyes had some furiousness this time as well.

Eni's hands tingled as he climbed a wooded slope, dappled in sunshine under the oak trees. Reaching the peak, he saw that a fallen tree had torn through the canopy. The resulting gap offered a view of the river as it cut through the valley.

It was a cloudless day, and the sun lit the vibrant greens of late May. But even the magic and beauty of the countryside couldn't break the spell of his father's anger and despair. The vision haunted him and he wasn't anxious to relive the experience at home.

He wandered the hills and meadows for hours until the sun faded behind the mountains and the long shadows crept over the hills. He would have continued drifting but for the hunger pangs that finally drove him home.

Darkness had fallen by the time he reached the hedge line that encompassed the manor's western flank. Eni walked until he reached a slotted gate that kept the bearing ewes and young lambs from breaking away up into the hills with the rest of the flock.

The sheep took little notice of him as he secured the gate behind him and made for the light that flickered restlessly in the kitchen. Eni hoped that Abertha would still have some biscuits left.

As he cleared the barnyard and reached for the latch, he froze at the sound of his mother's voice.

"It cannot be, Harold," she said, with as commanding a voice as she could muster through her tears. "I will not permit it!"

"We have no choice," his father answered as if all the energy had been sucked out of him. "It is the Baron's will…"

"The Baron… the Baron; that pompous little man," she hesitated so as to keep herself from breaking into Welsh and swearing. "We are free. Eni is a free Englishman - does it not mean anything?"

Eni pressed against the door at the mention of his name, but the voices were still until he heard his father's voice, "Sometimes none of us are truly free."

"Harold, it is his soul we are talking about. You are sentencing your son to hell if you send him with that… that man."

His father said nothing, but Eni could hear the air escape as he sighed. He could imagine seeing his father with his head cupped in both hands, shaking his head as if trying to free himself from their grip.

"Just tell me why… Why does this devil want my son and why is the Baron forcing him to go?"

It was a question Eni had not thought to ask. He was more concerned with what Brother Alfonse would think of him than the reason why. Striving to listen, Eni pinched his other ear, trying to deaden the frogs in their nighttime frolicking by a meadow pond.

"Politics…" his father said hopelessly, "same as everything else in England."

"You have to do better than that," his mother said tersely.

"Murdoc has great influence at the courts of the lords, not just our Baron, but all the lords, even the Marcher Lord himself.

"And your King…"

"You mean our King, Mali," he corrected her.

"Yes, of course I do," she said cheaply. While this was typical banter between his parents, Eni wished they would stop and get to the point.

"So they say..." the Steward continued. "But the Baron sees this as an opportunity of raising himself up. If Eni becomes the next Wizard of the March..."

"You mean footman to the devil."

"Aye... well, the influence the Baron might command would be substantial, especially if I were still the Steward to his lordship."

"You English..." his mother muttered.

"Yes, yes and you know that a Welsh lord would act the same. Politics is the one constant on either side of the March."

The conversation died and Eni heard a popping ember from the fading hearth fire. He was about to take his leave when his mother spoke up, "What about the Bishop?"

"The Bishop?" his father's voice mocked. "As if he would help..."

"He is of the church. Clearly he would intervene if a boy was about to lose his soul."

"Mali, the Bishop is far more interested in persecuting peasants with English Bibles. He has known of this man for years and has never stood in his way. Why? Because it was not profitable to do so. Even in Rome, it still comes down to politics." Eni could tell his father was measuring his words.

"But a boy's soul is at stake... *my* boy's soul is at stake."

"If the Bishop could be persuaded to our side, what then? There is too much to be gained for even a Bishop to affect the outcome.

"So it's done then... nothing can save my son from this doom."

"There is always hope, Mali. He's a smart boy. Pray, pray he will have the wisdom to see past this wizard's dark arts. That is all the hope we have left, however distant it may appear tonight."

10

Over the next few days, Eni couldn't decide if he felt like royalty or one condemned. Abertha made all his favorite dishes- even butchering a cockerel that would have dressed much larger had they waited till fall. Honey cakes, jam and even the last of the stores of spices graced his meals over the next week.

He would have enjoyed these delicacies more if not for his mother. While she darned his socks and mended both of his britches she could hardly look at him without getting weepy.

The roasted duck, biscuits and bread pudding almost caused him indigestion with his father wordlessly picking at his food and his mother staring at hers, only to be interrupted with an occasional dab of her handkerchief whenever her eyes ventured in his direction.

In spite of his parents' trepidation, Eni was looking forward to the summer solstice, not that he would have dared mentioning it to them. He didn't think he could bear another week of the silence that reined over the manor, despite how good the food was.

The day before Eni was to depart was much like the ones that preceded it. His mother would have woven him a blanket with gold thread if she thought it would have kept him warm; it became her overarching concern. She could not say a word to him those last few days unless it dealt with staying warm and healthy on his travels.

Evening supper started much like others - the saying of grace and a delectable, but quiet, meal - but as the platter emptied and Eni drained the last of his cup, his father reached out taking his arm and said, "A word, my boy…"

He could feel the tension in his father's grip and cast a glance between his parents. His mother, on cue, got up from her seat and began clearing the table. But his father met his gaze and Eni saw something he had never seen him express openly before… Fear.

"Your mother and I have shared many sleepless nights lately, Eni," his father said, letting his hand fall from the boy's wrist. "This man… Murdoc, is not one of the chosen."

"He is of the Devil, Eni!" his mother blurted out from the wash bowl in her thickest Welsh accent. She stared at her youngest son and for the first time in weeks she held her gaze and let the tears fall unhindered. "He comes from the depths of Hell, that man and his strange powers. There's no other explanation."

"What your mother means to say," his father continued in measured tones, "is that although you must go with him, be discerning, always questioning what is of God and what is of the devil. This is why we raised you with the Word. Don't fall into the trap, Eni. Your soul depends on it."

The next day was clear and bright and Eni could not deny the excitement that raced through him like a hound giving chase to a rabbit on a spring day. Though, for the sake of his family, he did try to hide it the best he could.

He walked with his father down the road until the city walls came into view. Eni wanted to sprint ahead but forced himself to walk behind the Steward as was his place. To Eni, it seemed his father was slowing as they approached the gates. "Enjoy this, Eni," he said, turning to him with a pondering glance. "This may be the last time you come here through the main gates."

Eni stopped, "Why shan't I always enter this way?"

The Steward shook his head. "You have much to learn, boy. I will leave that to your new… master."

Eni started walking again. "He's not my master… I'm a Norman. I'm free," he said under his breath.

His father looked back at him, amused. "We shall see," he said, trying to sound cheerful, but his face lacked any emotion.

The bright red banners fluttered over the stone buildings shining in the blue sky like spears in the sun as they passed under the portcullis and into the courtyard. The sheep penned into a corner made their presence known by their smell as much as by their baa-ing.

Several of the guards snapped to attention as his father passed the gate house. "Morning, Steward," one them greeted. He nodded to them in return. Eni took a deep breath as he stepped inside. He could imagine that they would greet him like that soon.

"Come Eni," his father beckoned, dragging him back to reality. They made their way up the steps, but again, rather than going into the great hall, he followed his father to the back stairs, the same way William had led him up the first time.

"Wait here," his father said, pointing to a bench that guarded the landing above the stairs.

Eni plopped down on the hard wood seat, sticking his feet out across the hall as if they were a gate. He hated waiting. He hated the fact that they were in there, deep in discussion and he had to sit alone in an empty passage. *Someday*, he thought, *someday I'll be the one on the inside*.

He wasn't sure how long he sat there, but it was long enough that the excitement of the day melted into boredom. The passageway was empty but for the lone wood bench. The long corridor reached out past the Baron's study until it turned a corner and ran to the left. After running his eyes first up and down and then across the joint lines of the stone walls for what seemed like eternity, Eni discovered two lines of ants that were passing back and forth from the edge of the steps.

The competing caravans both ran along a joint of mortar that bordered the slate floor to stone wall as they ran to and fro. Eni followed their progress as they ran under his bench and then made a sharp turn at its back right leg. The port of arrival and departures was a crumb of bread that must have fallen from a former tenant of the bench.

Eni cantilevered over the wooden arm like a gargoyle, and he studied the ants as they arrived and carved free a morsel to ferry back to their harbor by the step. He wondered how many there were, and if they simply dropped their cargo and returned, or if they took leave from the procession once they made it back to their nest.

He was so captivated with their activities that he failed to notice the swooshing of leather on the stone steps below him. It wasn't until a head appeared above the coiling stairs and bellowed at him, "One must have better posture when at court, master Eni."

He jumped at Murdoc's thundering voice and quickly took a stance that would have pleased the pope.

"Much better," the man said coolly as he walked past, his forest green cape flowing behind him as if it were a single wing. He rapped once on the door and entered without waiting for a response.

Eni held his pose for a time before the activity of the ants pulled him back over the edge of the chair. He studied their comings and goings but remained watchful of the door to his right. He could hear their voices from the room, low, almost murmurs, but they increased steadily.

He pulled himself away from the procession of ants and focused on the wooden door. It amazed him that the sound could so easily penetrate the massive slab of wood. Striving to make out the words, he rose from his seat and inched toward the chamber.

"I will not!" He could tell it was his father's voice. "You come and steal my son and then expect to have me pay you?"

"The boy will be receiving the finest education in the kingdom…"

"You will be making him an outcast among his own people!"

"Gentlemen, enough!" Eni recognized the Baron's shriller voice attempting to take command. "Steward, you have to admit that Murdoc has a point. Is it not common for the family of an apprentice to pay for the tutoring?"

"My lord, it was not I who insisted on this arrangement. I begged you no, but you commanded it. Not for the good of my son, I might add, but for benefits that you hope to render from it." To Eni it reminded him of over-hearing his father that night in the kitchen. He was using the same measured tones as he did speaking to his mother.

"I have paid this man enough," he said with finality. "My very flesh and blood- if there is a remittance owed, it is to me and mine."

63

"I can certainly find another apprentice, if that is your wish, my l-" Murdoc offered.

"No! ...no," the Baron hastily interrupted before Murdoc could finish. "I will see to it you are compensated for your tutelage."

"That is very kind of you, my lord," Murdoc replied. Eni noticed the door flex on it hinges and he quickly returned to his seat, his perfect posture intact.

"... shall take my leave then, my lord," the voice became full and rich as the door swung open. "I trust you will fund this expenditure with all due haste?"

"Yes, yes of course, Murdoc. I will have it for you within a fortnight." The Baron replied with paled acceptance at being outmaneuvered. "Just take good care of that boy... I expect a return on my investment."

Murdoc dipped his head in acknowledgement. "I shall do my best." He turned from the door toward Eni who held his perfect pose staring at the stone wall ahead of him. "Come along, lad," he said as he passed him by, walking toward the stairs.

Eni looked back at the door, hoping at least to bid farewell to his father, but the door remained closed and the wizard was already circling out of sight. He took one last look back before following behind the descending Wizard of the March.

11

Eni raced down the stairs after the old man, but instead of heading through the great hall, they cut back through the service entry, past the slaves and servants weighed down with casks of ale and sacks of flour as they made their way to the larder. Once outside, the two of them rounded the back of the keep until they came to a small opening in the great stone wall.

Murdoc moved quickly as he ducked through the opening, but rather than follow the road that ran parallel to the river, he took a foot path that ran southwest to the base of the hill.

The village and the river Teme were nestled between the two great hills. The valley they formed was considered a gateway to central Wales and the road that ran along the river carried most of the travelers who made their way to the village and beyond. Eni knew that the old man rarely took the road, but as Murdoc, his walking stick in hand, started up the hill path, he wondered why that was.

They moved in silence. The forest engulfed them and the sounds of the village faded into the trees behind them. The hill was too steep for a direct conquest so the makers of this path cut the slope on an angle by running along the sides of the hill to a point higher up and then doubling back to a point higher still. This continued until the crest was reached. These switchbacks, as they were called, allowed even an old man to master the climb.

Murdoc moved gracefully in the valley with its flat open land and level terrain, so much so that Eni had struggled to keep up, but once they began to climb, the old man slowed drastically so that he had to use his walking stick for support. Eni eased up so as not to pass him. Although he was new to being an apprentice, he knew that one was expected to show respect to his mentor. This meant to follow behind at a respectable distance.

Murdoc glanced to his side and grunted at the sight of the boy's uncomfortable gait. "So," he finally said. "What have you learned?"

Eni studied the man for a moment before answering, "I suppose that you are out of sorts, since you can move quickly on level ground but you seem to struggle when you climb."

From behind, walking in Murdoc's wake, all Eni could see of the man's face was the edge of his graying beard, which gave no clues as to whether his answer was correct. Murdoc only continued on in silence. As they reached a cutback where the path turned sharply, Eni could see the old man's face was contorted by the struggles of his climb. He continued slugging up the slope, breathing heavily and relying more and more on a staff that looked too thin for such a load. It held, not even flexing under its master's weight as they passed the last tree and made their way up the barren ridge.

"Can I be of service?" Eni offered as the pace slowed to a point that it was a struggle for him to keep forward momentum without running into the back of the old man.

There was no answer. Eni hoped it was due to Murdoc's shortness of breath but wondered if he was just ignoring the proposal. The old man continued to toil until he finally topped the hill then heaved a sigh, swabbing his brow with his hand. He poled himself to a well-worn rock on the side of the path.

"Ohh,' he groaned as he lowered himself to his stone bench and wiped his brow again, spraying a dribble of sweat. Eni stood at the peak feeling awkward, not knowing if he should sit as well or if he was expected to continue standing.

Murdoc looked up at him once his breathing slowed. "Sit," he said with a flick of hand. Eni looked around, but followed Murdoc's gaze and dropped to the ground right there in the middle of the path.

The ridge rose above the tree line and provided a vista that stretched far into England in the east. The deep greens of summer faded in the distance to a hazy purple where the horizon greeted it. Above, the blue sky was empty but for a pair of vultures who rode the currents of the hills and western mountains, circling high above them.

"Your prognosis was correct," Murdoc said at last, staring out into the east. "Though that was not the answer I was searching for. What I meant to have asked was concerning the events in the Baron's study."

"Oh, sorry," Eni said, dropping his eyes guiltily.

"It was my error entirely," Murdoc admitted freely, "but now to my question?"

"What did I learn in the the Baron's study?" Eni repeated the question as if it held the answer.

"Surely you left the bench to overhear the conversation."

"Only a piece, my lord, the part where you tried to get my father to pay for my education..."

Murdoc interrupted him with a laugh that surprised Eni. The man's face did not look to be one to which laughter came easily. "Your father was in no danger of losing so much as a pence, I assure you; he's far too astute for that."

Eni didn't know how to react to this compliment. The old man seemed sincere enough, but Eni knew his father would not have reciprocated so kindly.

"But you are right," Murdoc continued, as he rested in the cool mountain breeze. "In many ways I... or, as I must now say, we, are no different than the peddler or the silversmith. Everything we do, we must be paid for... by someone. Just as every strand of fabric or ingot of silver is paid for before it leaves a shop, so too must we account for our wares."

"Wares?" Eni questioned, "I thought you... or we were councilors."

"Aye, that we are, but rather than peddling cloth or metalwork we offer something far more valuable. Knowledge."

"Knowledge... Knowledge of what?"

"Tell me, lad, how much would you pay to know if it will rain tomorrow?"

"Nothing," Eni answered without thinking about it.

"Nothing," Murdoc repeated as if this surprised him.

"Well no… who would?" he shrugged. "It will rain whether I know it or not."

"Yes, yes, it would, but let us raise the stakes. What if you were going to cut hay today? Do you think a landowner would like to know if it would be rained on for the next fortnight and ruined?"

"I suppose so," Eni answered, eyeing the ground before him.

"Of course he would. The loss would more than compensate the fee he would pay for such knowledge." Murdoc took a deep breath and scanned the horizon with all the conviction of a sailor. "If a land owner would pay for that simple information, you can imagine what a King would pay if his own life were at stake."

Eni thought about it for a time; he agreed it made sense in such a case, but how could they know something would happen before it actually occurred? It was impossible, unless… unless the old man really was in league with the devil.

Eni eyed the old man as he yawned and sucked down a chest full of air. "I think I have my second wind," Murdoc said after a time, patting his chest. "We should be off."

It took Murdoc a moment to straighten back up. Eni watched as he worked out the kinks in his back with his first few steps. "Come along," he added, as he set off slowly down the path.

If he really were in league with the devil, Eni thought, *he wouldn't have the problems he has been having.*

Eni took off after him as the old man began to pole his descent off the crag. "So is it?" Eni asked once he caught up.

"Is what?"

"Is it going to rain tomorrow?"

"Oh, I have no idea…" the old man smiled. "But if I did, I would reap as many shillings from as many people as I could manage. That is for sure."

12

They spoke little as they moved along the path, following it southwest over the hills of eastern Wales. Murdoc walked without resting, but still slowed to negotiate even the smallest of rises.

Eni followed closely and saw little of the countryside but for the bobbing shoulders of the old man as he labored ahead of him until they came upon the path where he first intercepted the wizard a month before.

The now long grasses waved bouquets of wild flowers at the wind as it raced up the hillside, before it roared into the forest, shaking the darker green leaves of midsummer.

The path rose and fell on the foothills until they finally cleared a cluster of trees that overlooked a small valley wrapped in the arms of a mountain.

"There it is," Murdoc said, raising the end of his walking stick. Eni looked down the valley that stretched out before them. He first noticed the small flocks of sheep scattered across the valley floor like the clouds in the sky. On the far side clustered around the mountain's base, Eni could see a few earthen huts dug into the slope. To their left, a path snaked up the mountainside before branching back to the top of the crag. A stone keep lodged there was all that remained of a fortress that once lorded over the valley.

Eni stared at the scene before him. He didn't know what to expect Murdoc's home to look like, but this… Murdoc took no notice of the boy's reaction, but started down the path using his stick for support in slowing his descent.

Eni looked back down the path they had traveled. Its meandering course wound back through the hills before dropping out of sight to the north. "Is this Wales or England?" he called out ahead, as he trotted down after the old man.

"It's England- all England, and always will be!" Murdoc called out cheerfully as he met the open valley. Eni questioned the truth of that; he didn't notice crossing Offa's Dike since they left Knighton, but he didn't really know if it ran this far to the south either.

Murdoc picked up speed again as the valley flattened into an open meadow. The sheep parted before them as they crossed the grass, and the stone face of the north arm rose before them.

The few peasants tending the flock took no notice of them, which struck Eni as odd. The tenants of his father's farm would doff their caps and extol the virtues of the day whenever he would pass.

"Morning," Eni said in a voice as chipper as a gold finch. The girl closest to him looked up and smiled. She was about his age and wore a smudge of dirt across her cheek from her toils, but her eyes were mesmerizing. They were as clear and green as the patch of grass behind her. Eni unconsciously slowed and may have had his mouth open, but the man beside her glared as if he had been insulted. Eni quickened his pace, catching back up to his mentor. Murdoc, who took no notice of this exchange, kept his focus on the vein of a path that rose ahead of them.

Eni came within a stride of the old man. "Friendly lot you got around here," he said, looking back at the peasants who had resumed their work.

Murdoc looked down at him blankly before turning back to the path. "We have a mutual agreement. I ignore them and they reciprocate the gesture," he said flatly.

Eni fell back, following at a respectable distance until they reached the place where the path pivoted up the arm of the mountain. Murdoc again slowed and sighed as if to gather his strength for the final assent. "One of these days I'm going to have to add a lift," he added as he struggled to negotiate a pile of logs that had been left at the base of the path.

70

Eni had no idea what a 'lift' was, but he was just as confused by the impromptu barricade on the path. "Just consider it the front gate," Murdoc said in response to his puzzled gaze and then began again to pole his way up the slope once he had conquered the last of the branches.

The way was slow and Eni kept his distance behind his new master. His eyes wandered to the rock wall beside him and the myriad of marks cut into the stone. Most had moss and lichens nestled deep to their core. He ran his hands over the surface and was surprised by how smooth it felt.

"This road was cut out of the rock," Murdoc explained as he rested a ways ahead him. "It was probably nothing more than a ledge at a one time. One can only imagine the number of men and picks needed to carve this road out of the solid stone."

Eni tried to imagine how hard it would be just to muster a chip out of the rock face, much less make it wide enough for a cart and ox. "Who made this? Was it the Welsh?"

"The Welsh," Murdoc mocked. "More than likely it was made to keep the dirty buggers locked up in their mountains, but by whom... Well, that is one of the few questions you will find that I cannot answer. It may have been the Romans or even the Saxons, but it was long ago and there's no longer a record of it... A pity really."

Eni ran his hand over it again. It was warmed by the sun and there was not a chip or an edge that would even crease his skin. "How old do think it is?"

"Not less than three hundred years. Maybe closer to a thousand, but we have no way of knowing." He let Eni puzzle over it until he caught his wind. "Let's be on with it. The place is old, but it has the freshest water in all of England."

When they reached the crest, Eni got his first real look at the wizard's keep. What from across the valley looked impressive, up close looked like a battlefield. The once massive wall had been leveled, with upper stones sent over the edge. The only thing left intact was the keep itself, a stone structure as big and wide as a barn and thrice its height. It would look massive in a meadow but here it was dwarfed by the mountain that rose around it.

A woman came out to greet them as they crossed the barren yard. "Master," she called from the veranda, hobbling down the steps to them. Eni couldn't decide who looked older. The lady's unmeasured gait looked as if she had greater need of the walking stick than Murdoc did. "There was a message sent for you from the young Marcher Lord," she said breathlessly.

"Ah, yes," Murdoc replied. "Good. I assume it is in my study then?"

"Of course, master," she said, as if the answer could not be any other.

"Ingous, this is our apprentice, Eni."

"It's a pleasure, young master," she said, with a curtsy that showed more of her leg than Eni thought proper. Ingous's hair was gray and matted, accented with a front tooth missing from her smile; there was little doubt that she was Welsh born.

"Show him to the upper room."

"As you wish, master," she said, with a much more modest curtsy.

"I bid you farewell for now, lad," Murdoc said, turning to Eni. "Ingous will show you about and you may rest till we sup."

Eni looked at the towering hulk before him that was to be his new residence. It was not what he expected, to be sure. In the light of day, it looked much like the mountain from which it was hewn- old, white, and wild.

He looked back across the valley and thought of his mother. The old keep didn't feel like it was the devil's den that she had feared, but then, he had yet to be inside.

"Come along, lad," the old lady beckoned from the top of the steps with a welcoming smile. He hoisted his sack back over his shoulder and headed up the stairs.

"Don't let it worry you, lad," she reassured him as he peered into the darkness. "In a couple of days it will be just like home."

13

He stared at it for a while before looking up, "Come on, level with me," the professor smiled. "Someone had to have put you up to this." Wendy was startled by the abrupt change in his demeanor. It was as if he waved his hand over his face and his sense of worry was wiped away like it was the morning dew on the windscreen. "Tell me, who was it?" he coaxed. Perhaps it was nerves, or maybe he just lacked the confidence to pull off a theatrical ruse, but he added a "Please…" that lacked the spit and polish of his earlier words. It suffered a mild break mid-word that left the end of it quivering.

Wendy had heard lines before. After all, she had been in university the last four years. But these science types were not as skilled in the art as the English majors she used to hang out with. How could they be? The science geeks spent all day with formulas and theories, while her friends were coupled with Shakespeare and Chaucer.

To be honest, she wasn't exactly sure where he was going with his line of questioning. She just knew he doubted her, and that was enough.

She always thought she had a good sense of humor; she even let her younger brothers get away with hanging her bra from the flag pole in the front garden the night she was waiting for her first date to pick her up. They deserved so much more than what they got, but it was funny; she could even laugh about it now. But this, this set her off.

Maybe it was just the package. It was weird enough having to bring this thing up to London. Maybe it should just have stayed in the dusty cabinet that had been its home for years on end. She certainly dreaded taking it. And now this. *He thinks I'm lying!* her head screamed.

Wendy thought for a moment as she looked at the package there on the desk. To say it meant nothing to her would be a lie. She had made up stories about it as far back as she could remember. In several it was a treasure map, in others a jewel from the royal crown. She even dreamed it was evidence that she was the rightful heir to the British throne, she'd used this made-up tale more than once over the years when she had had a hard time falling to sleep, and to be honest it was still her favorite.

The professor stared at her as if hoping his ploy still had some chance of working. She thought she could even detect a subtle nod as if he was egging her on. With all the thoughts running through her head she had to remind herself of his question. "Just my Grandmoth…"

"No," he snapped. His smile gone as quickly as it had appeared. "It can't be…"

"Listen, what I said is the honest truth," she countered. "Maybe I better leave…" Wendy said, backing to the door as the professor's eyes dropped back down to the package.

She took a few steps to the door, but stopped. "Since you think it's all a lie," she said stepping back to his desk, "I'll take my package with me…"

Eni knew the smell of keeps, even though the one in Knighton was the only one he had experienced first-hand. It was well known that the stone fortresses were equally as good at letting water seep through their porous rock as they were at keeping out invaders. These fluid interlopers would leech through stone and mortar till the interior smelled more like a cave than the residence of the richest and most powerful men in Europe. It was a fact proclaimed in both song and verse from every inn along the March.

His lordship has his damp old stone
I stay in my little thatched home
It keeps me dry

74

It keeps me warm

But Lord protect me when the brigands swarm

This was one that he had heard in many a pub. It was easy to sing ... not that he was allowed to utter such a vulgar song given his father's position. The song, like many pub songs, failed to hold the lordship in very high regard.

It was this damp aroma that Eni expected as the wooden door screeched closed on its iron hinges. He sniffed the air as he followed the old woman up to the first landing.

The air was still but dry. He looked down into the great hall below the landing. The breadth of the room was filled not with trophies of war or ornaments of wealth, but large rough tables, weighed down with all manner of metal and fiber. Tin, copper, iron, wool, and leather were laid out by their kinds.

Tools that looked more at home with a blacksmith were hung by the hearth, complete with an anvil and a bellow directing its fury towards one end of the fire box.

Eni stopped to take it all in; the high market at Hereford would have nothing on this venue. Each table sported tools and contraptions, many he had never seen before. "The master's toys..." the old woman said, her voice breaking the magic of the sight.

Eni turned back to her; she wore her smile proudly. "He likes to tinker," she said warmly. Eni tried to imagine Murdoc, dressed in his usual finery, working with the dirt and grime for which blacksmiths were known. It was not a vision that came naturally to him.

"Not a typical lord of a tower is old Murdoc," she said with a chuckle. "Come let us find your room, lad. There be time enough for this later..."

Eni took one last study of the room. The tables were placed every several feet. Each was host to artisan's tools of the trade. The closest had piles of leather with shears and punches of varied sizes that would make any but the most established cobbler drool with envy.

Eni sighed as he heard her steps on the stairs beckoning him onward. He hoisted the pack to his shoulder and headed up after her.

Eni's room had four walls of stone with a door in the midst of one of them. A bed with a turned over crate next to it were the extent of its furnishings. He sighed as he set the pack down, taking in the entirety of his habitat. It was a small room, and he already missed his bedroom window. From this room, an army could take position in the courtyard below and it would go unnoticed.

The next morning after dressing, as Eni made his way down for the breaking of the fast, he was stopped before he could reach the stairs. "You will be working with the master at the tables," Ingous said as she was coming up the steps. "Save your fine clothes for the days they're needed."

Eni looked at his linen shirt. "It's all I have... my other is the same."

The old woman shook her head, "You Normans..." She grabbed the shirt by the collar and rubbed it between her fingers. "It would be a waste to wear such fine clothes especially if he has you working the potions- they stain something furious."

"Potions?"

"Aye, lad, the master loves to mix things together. Scares me, I'll tell you. Some do a powerful number on clothes- I'd better pick up something more suitable in the village for ya."

"The village? You mean the huts?" he said, looking down at the floor as if they were right below the planks.

"Aye, they don't have much there, but wool handles the potions better than your finery would, that I'm certain of... Hurry along now. There is porridge in the kettle."

Eni followed the winding stairs down to the great room where he found the porridge bubbling contently in its pot on the edge of the hearth. A couple of bowls and two quarter loaves of bread waited on the table nearby. Eni started eating alone, staring at the assortment of equipment gathered nearby.

The closest to the fire bore crocks and jars of varied sizes each

76

covered with a flat flap of leather to seal the contents and tied down in much the same manner as Murdoc's staff had been capped off. "Potions," Eni said aloud, broadcasting crumbs on the table in front of him. With his bread in hand, he stepped over to the table, picking up the closest crock and shook it so as to get a sense of its contents. The rattle that answered sounded like dried peas.

He slid off the leather lid to peer inside when a voice boomed behind him, "I have no use for a blind apprentice." Eni stopped, slid the leather cap back over and gently set the jar down on the table. "Good lad."

Eni turned toward Murdoc, who had walked over to the kettle, helping himself to the porridge. The old man looked like a commoner without his typical finery. His wool tunic was stained and soiled, making him look like a peasant as he spooned some of the cooked grains into his waiting bowl.

"Sorry," Eni said as Murdoc sat at the table closest to the hearth, "but they sounded like peas."

The old man looked back, taking inventory of the table in question, "In that case they were peas... but it could just as easily be an acid that would burn the skin right off your face," he added, tearing off a chunk of bread. "First rule - never sniff or look into an unknown container, as you attempted. Each is numbered and noted in the ledger as to its contents."

Eni hoped Ingous would return soon. He felt conspicuous, being dressed more finely than his better, but Murdoc appeared to take no notice.

"There is a pile of firewood behind the keep," he said, with his spoon in hand. "I paid much too steep a price, but still... it is one of the few necessities the mountain does not provide us," he added, as he stirred his porridge. "Split them to the thickness of your arm." He looked up from his food at the boy as if measuring him, "make that your leg; otherwise you will be chopping all day."

"Yes sir," Eni answered, dropping his arms down to his sides.

"Drop them down the chute - at the base of the keep – you can stack them later," he added, blowing on the steaming grains.

Eni thought for a moment "A chute, Sir?"

"Yes, a chute, a slide, a ramp, a downward slope even. You'll see it; it is behind the wicket under the thatched roof."

The day brought forth a blue sky with large white clouds that raced over the mountain. They were too high and light for carrying rain, but their billowed forms sent shadows leaping off the cliffs to the valley below. Eni raced one from the keep to the outer edge - he lost, but looking out over the vast green plain below him, he could see the figures of peasants in miniature working in the fields as the silhouettes raced over them.

He wondered if the green-eyed girl was there working in the shadow of her father, but from the height of the keep, he couldn't tell. From here there were neither dresses nor leggings, hair nor hats; all individuality was lost. They were no more unique than the dots of sheep that grazed beyond.

Eni turned from the vista and walked behind the keep. The thatched roof stuck out oddly from the back of it. It was crudely built and would only last a season or two, assuming the snows were light. The firewood had been dumped by an ox cart and was strewn about with little rhyme or reason.

He was sure one of the peasants from the valley hurriedly dumped it, but in imaging the episode, Clum's face and wild eyes from that day in the wood played the part. Of course, not every peasant shared Clum's particular fear, but the thought still made him smile.

He wondered how Clum was getting on and if he had been forgiven or sent away for the deed like Eni had. Not that it worked out the way his parents had intended, considering where he ended up.

Setting to work, he split a score and quartered a dozen more before sectioning the rest into eighths. Wiping his forehead, he looked for the chute. The wicket, pond reeds woven through a willow frame, was set behind two stones that held it tight against the wall under the thatched roof. Eni kicked these aside and pulled the wicket from its moorings.

A blast of hot air shot out the opening like the devil himself was escaping. "That is not right. It should be cool," he said out loud, his voice echoing off the stone wall. Eni sat for a moment. Cellars and dungeons were always cool and damp, slimy even, given the stories the bards tell. Shaking his head, he crept toward the hole. Seeing nothing, he leaned in, peering into the darkness.

Everything was black, but as his eyes adjusted, he could see a glow. Just a tinge at first, there was a speck of orange like the first cut of the sun in morning sky, but as he blinked it got darker and redder. He blinked continually, hoping to see what evil lurked in the foundations of the keep. It was big, that he knew. He heard the low deep rumble before seeing the blood-red glow reflected off the stone walls, but the light died against the blackness of its mass. Eni leaned a little farther into the chute to see.

Then it snorted. So loud, so powerful, Eni covered his ears. It was how he had imagined a minotaur would have sounded, when the Brother once read the stories of the Greeks - a monster, mad with fury.

He should have escaped. That is what his heart told him to do. It pounded in his chest like a blacksmith's hammer. *Run! Get off this mountain, run back to the safety of Knighton, back to the safety of home.*

He did not know why he moved forward, but he eased his foot onto the ramp, keeping the right one back, just in case. He knew he was too curious- he always had been. Abertha used to say it would be the death of him. "Lad, you are always sticking your nose into places it has no business being…"

The hot steam showered from the beast's nostrils, choking the air with fumes. Eni could feel the sweat pour off his body like rain as the curling vapors vented past him. He leaned further, arching his neck to see when a shadow suddenly moved below him.

The beast's mouth opened and fire leaped out into the darkness. There in glow of hell, the wizard appeared, bathed in red as the roar of flames filled the dungeon. His mother's words rang in his ears, "That man is of the devil. He comes from the depths of Hell, that man and his strange powers..."

Eni jumped back, trying to escape, but as he turned to the light, his leather boot slipped on the chute as he leapt, and his leg gave way. He felt heat rising as he slid down... down... down to the belly of the beast.

14

The beast snorted as Eni came to rest among the pieces of firewood on the dungeon floor. The walls danced to the blood-red music of the flames. He half-expected to have a bite taken out of him by this point, but feeling all in one piece, he turned from his belly to see the belching creature before him.

Above him, its arms reached up to a long narrow log complete with iron fittings to keep it from being torn apart. With each breath the beast spun the log like it was a twig. The beast drew its breaths faster now, and its arms and the log quickened their pace accordingly. Eni lay there, mesmerized as the arms soon whirled in their mission.

Eni sat up and looked at the room before him. The beast took up most of it, but standing in the red glow of its mouth stood Murdoc. He looked down on Eni with what may have been a smile behind his fire-stained beard.

"It only feeds on wood - unless you are offering yourself, of course," he yelled over the roar of the beast.

Eni looked up in utter fear at the old man, who shook his head and pointed to the chute. "Get the wood!"

Eni sprang from the floor and clambered up the ramp. He slipped now and again, but reached the opening, and once outside looked up at the passing clouds, thankful to see the light of day.

"Wood!" the old man called from the pit. Eni snapped out of his trance and began tossing wood into the hole. He worked in silence, listening to the rhythm of the beast. It increased till Eni could not even mimic the rate of its 'pop, pop, pop.' It held that tempo so fast and steady Eni wondered how it could even take a breath.

Tossing in the last of the logs, Eni stood above the pit and watched.

Heat and steam poured out of the opening, still shrouded in darkness. He stepped away to find relief from the heat and flung himself gratefully on the ground in the shadow of the keep.

Resting there, he would have sworn he could feel the earth itself vibrating with the beast's every move. He was wondering if there was a way of telling for sure when Ingous appeared from around the keep.

He lifted a hand in greeting but she scowled a reply.

"What have you done?" she said, shaking her head in dismay. "Why is it so hard for a boy to remain clean and it's not even noon yet?"

Eni attempted to brush of the bits of bark that clung to him only to see the front of his shirt bore a black smear of soot from the ride down the chute, "Ohh."

"How will that come out? And after spending three shekels on a wool shirt in village, the master will not be pleased." She continued, "You best get in there, he is waiting for you."

"Yes, mum," he said, getting to his feet. "I didn't intend to soil it...but what is that down there?"

"It is the master's... his creation." She said rolling her eyes. "He can explain it much better than I. Now hurry along but change first, and I'll see what I can do about that," she added, pointing to his shirt.

In the great hall, Eni was surprised by the noise. A hum sounded from along the wall as an iron bar that ran the length of the room whirled around like the twirling beam below. Looking at it, Eni figured that it must be right above the one in the dungeon.

Murdoc looked up from his work in the far corner and watched him piece things together. "So," he said above the whirling hum. "What are your thoughts?" Eni looked about the room uncommitted. "Come," Murdoc beckoned. "I wish to show you something."

Eni walked slowly toward the hearth, watching the spinning pipe that spanned the length of the room. Above each table hanging from the iron pipe, a strap of leather bounced and shimmered as it rode the rotating bar, but was too loose to match its movement.

Along the length of the bar however, there were four straps that were tight and spinning. Three of them were spaced evenly across the room and were wider than the rest. They ran through holes in the floor and circled back up around the iron bar. Eni could see the seam where the leather belt had been joined disappear beneath the floor only to reappear coming up on the other side.

The fourth strap running this race was shorter, ending at the table where Murdoc sat waiting. The leather twisted to a larger wheel in front of him. "Behold," the old man said. He pulled a lever. The belt tightened on the wheel, and a larger iron drum began to turn. Murdoc dropped copper medallions under the heavy wheel and the copper emerged from the other end, pressed and elongated. "A Welshman would say the press was turned by a demon. What say you?"

Eni looked the whole process over again. "It is turned by the leather straps and that iron rod," he said, pointing up along the wall. "Those straps there, they run through the floor to that big wooden pole that is spinning in the dungeon which… is powered by the beast?" he said as matter-of-factly as he could muster.

"Ah… the beast?"

Eni shrugged.

"And where do suppose the beast is from?"

"Hell?"

The old man sighed, "We must get that Welsh blood out of you." He released the lever, allowing the leather belt to slacken. "Come, it is time for you to properly meet this beast."

15

Even though the wizard's keep looked like its ramparts and walls had fallen into ruin before the keep at Knighton had been built, they shared a similar method of construction. The stone was different. This one was quarried from the mountain behind it, but the design was nearly identical, with a great hall opening to the front and a passage to the rear that ended in a coiled stairway.

The apprehension of the previous day flooded back as Eni reached the landing. This time, instead of heading up to his room, he followed the serpent's scales of the stairs down to the dungeon. Rather than opening to a wooden landing like the one overlooking the great hall, these stairs continued to twist around the outer edge into the pit of darkness.

It was as his mother had predicted, Eni thought as the old man faded from his sight. His first full day in the service of the Wizard of the March, and here he was, off to learn how to feed a beast from hell. He could think of little else, until he was greeted by the sudden heat and rhythmic beat of the beast.

In the dim light he could just make out Murdoc as he floated away gracefully. Eni landed awkwardly as he reached for a nonexistent next step. The floor was a mix of stone and dirt compacted to form an uneven surface. It reminded Eni of a cave, a very hot and dry cave.

Taking a deep breath of heated air, he followed Murdoc, who had rounded the stone wall. The old man stood there gazing at the glowing machine before him. "Here is your beast," he said, waving his arms like the bard in front of a gathered crowd at the market, but with a voice that lacked none of his customary sarcasm.

Eni could feel his ears burn as he took in the sight before him. The fire still burned in its grate, but the red glow was washed out by the light pouring in from the open hatch before them.

"Are you trembling in fear?" Murdoc continued, striking the beast with a stick. The resulting noise merely echoed around the dungeon, sounding more like a half empty kettle of soup than a creature from hell. "It is so dreadful!" he exclaimed, only to howl with laughter at his own words.

The spinning wheel and the whirling arms worked in unison, turning the rotating beam. The creaks, pops and whistles of escaping steam together formed a cacophony of sound that groaned and wailed like a chicken coop during a night visit from a fox.

The beast seemed different, less dreadful than his prior encounter. Perhaps it was the sunlight from the open hatch or the mockery in Murdoc's voice.

To Eni, it was like the day in the wilds carrying the dead pup. "Foolish Welsh," he said to himself. The words still held their venom.

The hum of the machine filled the air as he watched. A breath of steam puffed from a cylinder as the two arms circled in their orbits. It happened so quickly, he wondered which one was the cause and which was the effect.

"What is it?" he finally asked.

"My greatest creation," Murdoc answered, his voice suddenly reflective. "I have spent the majority of my life building it," he said, admiring its movement as if it were a beautiful woman. "There will be nothing like it for another three hundred years. It is called a steam engine."

Eni looked up at him quizzically but said nothing, lest Murdoc unleash another rant against his Welsh blood.

The beast sustained its velocity as it churned its arms, ignoring their conversation. "It is really nothing more than a pot of water boiling over a fire. I am just harnessing the steam that is produced," he added proudly. "Look here," Murdoc pointed to the top of the boiler. "This is the most vital instrument," he said, tapping a cylinder that rose from the surface.

Eni could see a copper flag no bigger than a thimble floating midway up the front of the cylinder. "What is that?"

"This is a gauge. It shows how much pressure is in the boiler, how much power it is producing," he added, waiting to see if the boy understood.

Eni nodded, fearing how a question would fare.

"The more pressure, the more power the steam engine produces, but only to a point. The standard should never rise above this mark…" he said pointing to a notch two-thirds up.

"What would happen then?"

Murdoc shrugged, "It will make too much steam, too much pressure. If not released, the whole thing would blow up like a volcano, taking the keep along with it, I would wager…"

"Oh," Eni said backing away. He had no idea what a volcano was, but it seemed the sensible thing to do nonetheless.

"It would take a great deal of wood to get to that point, mind you. But you should be aware of it…"

His voice trailed off as he watched it. Eni said nothing, but watched his master and his creation. He had to admit this machine was impressive, the way it moved, spinning the pole like a jester at the market can spin a plate on the stick.

"In some ways," Murdoc interrupted his thoughts, "this is a beast." He looked back to his creation. "Instead of hay and oats, we feed it wood and it produces work, of course far more work than an ox. But like an ox, it must be tamed and controlled to get any work out of it, and that, lad, is your job. I do hereby anoint you as the beast driver." Murdoc bowed to him, and Eni caught a smile emerging through his fire-lit beard.

16

If that was the only work to be done around Murdoc's keep, it would not have been so bad, but as Ingous had suggested, the lord of the manor had many such interests. "After chores, today you will start at the middle table..." Murdoc cheerfully informed him the following morning, waving his hand toward the center of the great hall.

So after the morning of splitting firewood and feeding the beast, he spent the rest of the day as a coppersmith. It wasn't hard work, but his bottom wasn't used to sitting so much in one spot.

He was excited at first, wishing he could tell Clum that he had the answer to the riddle of why the wizard used so many copper pots, and it had nothing to do with potions.

Murdoc had taken pots and pans, anything that had the burnt green patina of copper and cast them into a large iron pot that glowed red on the smith's furnace. He heated them until they lost all hint of their prior form. Then he ladled the molten copper into molds, reforming it into small flat copper ingots.

It seemed like a waste to Eni. Most of the utensils were perfectly fine. Some had a small dent that could easily be repaired, but Murdoc showed no interest in this. He melted it all. A barrel with the finished ingots stood next to the table waiting for the apprentice.

Eni would sit at the table and supply the rolling press a steady ration of the copper pieces. The press rose and fell powered by the spinning rod overhead. The hum of the beast was dwarfed by the crash the press made as it flattened and elongated the copper into long narrow strips.

By overlapping the next ingot before the first one was finished, the two pieces would merge into one. Repeating this over and over formed a coil of thin flat copper wire. The wire then had to be wrapped in burlap, dipped in hot wax, and wound around a board like a bobbin with a heavy wool thread.

It made little sense to Eni why useful pots and pans should be deformed like this, and Murdoc gave no indication but for a gleeful grin under his beard while inspecting the finished spool.

"I have something for you," Murdoc announced when their work was finished for the day. He had been working on the hearth since the morning but kept his back to Eni as if his project was secret. All the boy could see of his activity was the sparks from molten metal as it was poured into a mold.

Murdoc had sent Ingous home early that day to gather supplies from the village, so the two of them took a loaf of bread and the salted pork she had left them, with the intention of eating in the courtyard.

The clouds hung low on the mountain, blocking out both the sun and shadow of the coming night. "Come, let us sit on that rock," the old man motioned to Eni, who was carrying the components of their dinner. The cool breeze was welcome after spending the day next to a fire in the hearth and the steaming beast below.

They broke the loaf with no blessing, dividing it between them, and ate in silence. Eni would have preferred to sit on the wall and watch the comings and goings of the village, but Murdoc had no such interest. He liked to be far from the edge, far from the eyes of peasants below.

"Here," he said, once he had eaten his fill. He pulled from his cloak an iron key. It was the size of a spoon but weighed five-fold more. A leather cord looped through the end, long enough to fit easily over his head.

"What is it for?" he asked, taking the key. It was still warm from its creation.

"You will know when the time comes, but you must promise me..."

Eni looked up, waiting for him to finish, but the old man was staring at the ancient keep. He let his eyes run up and down the old structure that had stood for hundreds of years and could stand for hundreds more.

88

"Promise you… my lord?" Eni prompted.

"Oh, yes, you must promise to never let it out of your sight. It is for you only, Eni. No others. Understand?"

"Of course, my lord," Eni answered, placing it around his neck. Sitting there, feeling both weight and warmth against his chest he could not be more pleased. He wasn't sure why it gave him such pleasure. Maybe it was the thought of being able open something, even if he had no idea what it was, or maybe it was something more.

He had always been a child at home and had been treated so by parents and household staff alike. Even as a student, he was an outsider, sitting in on the classes that were meant for his betters. But here, in the wizard's fortress, he was given a key. For the first time, he could feel the weight of adulthood press against him.

It was sheer delight to escape the table one afternoon after spending another morning at the copper press. He had seen little of the surrounding area but for the courtyard and the wood pile, so it was with a renewed sense of freedom that after lunch he fled to the outdoors.

The August day was bright and warm in the sunshine that ebbed and flowed under passing clouds, but the mountain breeze was like a quick-running stream as it circled the peak, forcing him to wrap his cloak tight when it struck him head on.

Though his latest chore lay uphill of the keep, Eni couldn't resist a stroll by the edge of the cliff to view the valley below.

The bright green fields of June had yellowed and dried under the August sun. The sheep that had grazed the succulent grasses were gone. "Up in the hills," Eni reckoned, but a summer haze had dimmed the view beyond the near valley.

He wondered if the green-eyed girl was in the village below or if she had joined the sheep herders. At home, women would have stayed in the village, but here he didn't know… Ingous would know. She seemed to know everything about life in the village below.

Seeing nothing that held his interest, Eni turned back to his task. "Stir up the barrels," Murdoc had told him. "They are in the cave up behind the keep."

These were not exactly detailed directions. He had not been to this cave and did not have much of an idea where it lay, other than that it was by a 'singing pond.' Murdoc was like that sometimes, leaving his quest for reason and profit and going all 'poetic' on him.

A path broke from the courtyard and meandered up the mountain. It was overgrown and required Eni to wade through a river of goldenrod and grasses. Yellow pollen clouded the air, as bees broke from their moorings to avoid his wake.

The path rose quickly and Eni wondered if this was the task that convinced Murdoc he needed an apprentice. He doubted the old man could make the climb in his present state.

The path leveled for a stretch on a ridge, so Eni could look down to see the keep shrinking below him with the valley in the distance as its backdrop. The pass that led up to the fortress ran directly below him.

Eni could imagine sending boulders and logs cascading down the sheer cliff at an incoming army. He could almost hear their shouts and screams as the legion fell from the onslaught.

"Somehow they got through…" he said to himself, looking back at the scattered rocks that had once guarded the keep. Not a stone remained where it had been placed by its builders; not one could now offer the protection for which it been designed. "I wonder how they did it."

He continued his climb, following the path as it ran up into the mountain's interior, into a ravine that narrowed until stone walls formed a dead end.

He thought he had taken a wrong turn as he looked up, listening to the wind ricocheting off the granite face above him. It seemed to lose all its force as it circled down through the ravine. He could feel nothing of its power standing there under the wall of stone, but if he listened, he could hear it, a high pitched whistle coming from a hollow of reeds that ringed a lonely pool of water.

It was little more than a puddle, really, and he would have missed it completely but for the trickle of water that fell from an upper cliff. It beat the surface like a drunken drummer as the wind sprayed the falling drops across the pond.

This odd duet of fife and drum echoed across the ravine, back and forth between the stone walls to join a harmony of chaos.

Eni listened for a moment and smiled. "The singing pond," he said. His words seemed over-loud and destroyed the quiet magic of the music, not that he cared; he had work to do.

He found the cave along the western wall behind the pond. A stone sill of broken rocks had been placed in front, lifting the entry several inches above the hollow and a branch of dried bracken that had been set against the entry to hide it.

Its opening was nothing more than a fissure in the rock so narrow Eni wondered how Murdoc even got barrels into it.

Murdoc had forbidden a torch and as Eni squeezed through the dark hole he wondered how he would see anything. "Why store barrels so far away?" he wondered. "I will store them in the cellar…" he added, as he walked blindly forward, his hands running along the wall for guidance.

He felt something give way as he shuffled in; he heard it scrape the stone wall before crashing to the ground, its uneven bounces echoing in the stillness. Eni reached down, his hand fanning out back and forth until he found the long wooden shaft of the stirring stick.

With the staff in hand, he moved forward like a blind man, probing the darkness until the pole struck something with a satisfying thud. He quickly sized up the three barrels and pulled the lid from the first.

"Agh…" he cried out, doubling over as the stench overwhelmed him. "What is in there?" he wondered, wiping away tears as he sought refuge deeper into the cave.

He stumbled in several feet till he could breathe again. Looking back, the barrels were silhouetted against the bright opening that leaked into the darkness. He felt cool air rush past him not from the opening, but from the blackness below.

It was not quick or without suffering. He would make forays to the barrels and quickly muscle the contents around before being forced to retreat back to the depths where he again could breathe in the cool air that raced up from below.

There was not enough light to see what he was stirring. The stick slid in easily enough but would splash and sputter as he struggled to get the concoction to rotate in its cask. The drops felt cool as they sprang up, striking his bare arms as he pushed and pulled the mixture around.

Three barrels later he finally emerged. The shadows had laid claim to the ravine for the evening as Eni headed down the path. Every so often, he caught a putrid whiff of the barrels. At first he thought it was his imagination, but as he continued, he would have vowed that the odor shadowed him like a ghost as he made his way down.

It was not until the wind joined him on his trek along the upper trail that he thought he had lost his pursuer. He stood for a moment as his clothes fluttered in the breeze just to be sure.

The mountain's shadow reached far into the valley when Eni reached the courtyard. The open sky was now cloudless with only the silhouette of Murdoc gazing over the vista to break up the blue tapestry.

"Ah, you are back. They are mixed then?" Murdoc asked, turning when the boy approached.

"Yes sire, they are," he said as he walked over to his mentor, who had taken a step back. "I was wondering what is in them to make them reek as they do."

Murdoc inched away before looking down at the receding edge and then back up at his oncoming protégée.

"Lad, you did notice the pond, did you not?"

"Aye, that is how I found them."

Murdoc turned aside. Taking a breath, he continued, "The purpose of the pond is twofold- to mark its location but also to bathe in afterwards."

Eni stood for a moment "Bathe in... oh... you mean..." he said before sniffing at his tunic.

"Indeed. Go back and do so immediately, fully clothed if you please," he added, sweeping him away with hand, "lest you enter the

92

keep with that stench."

The water of the pond was deeper than he had expected, but the bottom was soft and his toes sank into the mud, turning up brown squalls that billowed through his tunic. He took a breath and sank under the surface, rubbing his head in the cold water, hoping to free the last remnants of his occupation.

Wading deeper, he stood under the falling stream of water from on high. It was little more than a trickle in late summer, but he figured it was a torrent in the early spring.

It was only after taking note of this that Eni saw the small stream meander towards the cliff edge.

He followed its flow like a giant carp with its fins cutting through the surface, his belly scraping along the sandy bottom. It was no more than three feet wide and a foot deep at any point of its travels through the underbrush, and then it fell away suddenly.

His hands locked on to nearby rocks as he braced himself against the flow. The water pooled briefly behind his human dam before discovering paths around him and continuing its journey. Allowing himself to ease forward, he peered over the edge, expecting to see it fall.

To his surprise, just below the edge, a hollowed out log transported the water thirty feet down the hillside. There it released the water above a small wooden wheel. Eni was familiar with water wheels, they were used to powered flour mills throughout the kingdom, but this was much smaller and spun faster, like a child's toy in the wind.

He pulled himself from the stream and eased his way down the slope, as dripping water traced his path to the spinning dervish. A small axle held the water wheel in place and transferred the power into a wooden box next to it.

He searched in vain to find an opening in the box, wondering how the grain could be poured in or retrieved after milling, but it was sealed tight.

"That is odd," he said staring at the crate. Even the cracks were sealed up with pitch. "Don't see much good it could do." He studied it for a moment, but his wet clothes brought a sudden chill, forcing him to give up on his investigation.

It was only after stepping away that he noticed it. He dropped to his knees and cleared away some sod. There, in the soil and grass, lay two strips of brown waxed cords nestled in the roots of the vegetation. He sighed, as all his questions had been answered by a single word, "Murdoc."

17

She expected that he would argue. After all, it did have his name on it. But it was hers, or at least her family's. It was a remarkable feat passing it from generation to generation like they had for who knows how many years. That would give them some standing, legal or otherwise she thought. But as she approached his desk, he pulled his hands back with his palms up like he was offering an award on a game show.

"Go ahead…" he said, with a smug look that to Wendy only confirmed that he was a complete jerk. She was out the door in a heartbeat with the package under one arm and her bag slung over the other. She passed the receptionist without a word and was in the car park as the door buzzer hummed its alarm in the background.

It would have been nice to walk into sunshine, but the sky maintained its heavy clouds and matched her mood. Part of her wanted to cry, but she was too bloody mad for that. She wasn't exactly sure why. Perhaps it confirmed that this was a complete waste of time, or maybe she was just hoping for validation that she was not the last in a long line of nutters.

She reached for the keys in her bag. She pulled them free from their nest, but they took flight as they cleared the rim and fell with a clang to the wet tarmac.

"Damn it," she breathed, as she readjusted her load so as to pick them up. As she reached for them, she heard footsteps race up to her. "What do you want?"

Dr. Brown let out a deep sigh as he slowed from his run, "Please wait…I'm, I'm sorry. You must think I'm a jerk. It's just that… Well, this hasn't gone well and this…" he waved his hand over the package, "is just, well…unexpected to say the least."

Wendy simply rolled her eyes as she gathered the keys off the pavement and turned back to her car. A light drizzle had started up again, much the way it had been falling on her drive in that morning.

Please…" he said again. It was more begging than asking. "You and I have this… this package in common. If this is real, it represents my life's work. Everything," his voice started to quake as he spoke. "If this is real… I'm sorry I accused you, but, you see, I have been the butt of more jokes than I can count, and if this is real… well then, maybe I will have something to smile about for the first time in a very long while."

Wendy waited as she held the key to the car door.

"Please…There's a shop just around the corner," he continued. "Let me buy you a coffee. We can get out of the rain and I'll tell you why I think my name is on that package."

For late August, the weather was unusually warm in the March. The winds that typically ruled the realm had been taken hostage somewhere in the west, leaving the mountain surprisingly quiet above the wizard's keep. Eni had learned to appreciate his abode in the inner room.

Cloudless days were rare enough in Wales where it was well known rainy days outnumbered the dry ones by a wide margin. But with no wind washing over the mountain, the heat of late summer seemed to boil up from the valley steaming the keep in the still air.

By the end of the week, the stones of the keep had heated up like a kettle over the fire. The outer walls were the worst, radiating heat as if they ringed the fires of hell itself, but even the walls of his inner room radiated with heat. Murdoc said the keep was acting as a 'thermal sink.' Eni had no idea what the term meant, but it made it difficult to sleep all the same.

It was one of these sleeps, one that included tossing and turning and sweating through his shirt, from which Ingous tried to rouse him. "Eni... Eni come quickly, I cannot raise the master."

Eni staggered out of bed, his night-shirt still damp from his slumber, and followed the old woman up the stairs. "I cannot..." she said breathing heavily, "...wake him."

The winding stairs opened to the massive wood door designed to be the last defense of the lord of the keep.

Ingous pounded on the door that barred them from Murdoc's inner sanctum, but the dull thuds seemed to dissipate against the wood, "Master... Master..." she called again, but to no answer. "You see," she said, massaging her knuckles with her other hand. "Somethin' wrong. He's up with the sound of me up the steps..."

Eni joined in, hitting the door hard with his fist, but it too seemed to lose its fury on the slab of solid oak that barred them. "Murdoc!" he called, but he was greeted with the same silence.

"What do we do?"

Eni inspected the door. There were no exposed hinges, nothing that he could pry open but for the wood door itself. His mind raced over tools from the great room, trying to think of something that would work.

"He's always locking the door," Ingous said, hitting the door bitterly. "The man is more worried about squirrels raiding his treasures than thinking about safety."

"I could get an axe."

"Nay lad, the master has traps set on the door, breaking it down would unleash all kinds of mayhem." She shook her head, "We need the key."

"Key..."

"Aye... do you know where it is?" she asked urgently when she saw his face, her voice almost giving out on her.

Eni reached into his night shirt, pulling out the iron key and its leather cord from around his neck. "Is this it? He never said what it was for."

"Quickly, lad!"

He inserted the key in the narrow opening. It fit, but he found it hard to turn. Eni thought perhaps it was the wrong one, but he gripped it harder, getting several fingers around the large flat bow. With some effort, he could feel the tumbler turn until the wards finally clicked and the door swung open to greet them.

"Praise God!" Ingous exclaimed as she rushed in past him. Eni followed, his eyes racing around the interior of the room, until he saw the old woman crouching by the bed along the far wall. Murdoc was covered by a wool blanket with only his bearded head protruding from the folds. The fact that he could see the blanket rise and fall with each breath brought some relief.

"He's burning hot, he is," Ingous said in answer to the boy's blank stare. He put the back of his hand to Murdoc's forehead like his mother had done so many times to him as a lad.

It felt like the fire box of the beast soon after the fire had started in the morning. Of course, the beast would then get so hot that spit would ricochet, leaving nothing more than a sizzling pop echoing in the dungeon.

"Aye…" he started, but didn't know what to say. "Should I run to Knighton for the Brother?"

Ingous stared at him for moment. Her eyes drifted behind him and hesitated before dropping her gaze back to the old man. "No," she said, stroking his thinning hair. "You are his apprentice; the future Wizard of the March. If anyone can heal him, then it be you."

"Me? I know nothing of his art. I bring wood and stir barrels of his putrid stew."

"Then it is time you learn," she answered, dropping her hands back to her hips. She was not a big woman but made up for the lack of stature with the steel in her eye.

At first he thought she was pointing at him. "There must somethin' in them that would be of use."

Eni turned. There, protruding from the wall, a wood shelf cantilevered over a wide oak desk. The board was wide and rough as if it came right from the forest for this purpose.

His eyes widened as he realized what it held. His mouth dropped and he stared in amazement as if he was taking in one of the wonders of the world. Even though he was only a lad from the March, he knew well enough that few men in the entire world would behold the likes of these.

"Books," he said as if the spoken word alone would help him believe that they were real.

"Aye," Ingous nodded, "The Devil's books."

Eni spun back to face her. There were mixed emotions in her words as she stroked her master's head. "They say it is the source of all his black magic... a gift from the devil himself... such a foolish old man to get mixed up in such things."

They were indeed like nothing he had ever seen before. There were eight volumes in two groups of four that stood at attention on the shelf. Their spines were of darkened leather, but each held a blue shield and above this crest there were embossed gold letters as if each fought under a different banner.

Eni was about to reach for one when he noticed their missing comrade on the desk below. It lay open, beckoning him to its pages like a spell. They were unlike anything Eni had ever seen before. Not that he had seen many bound volumes, in fact there had only been two; the Abbot's copy of the Latin Bible and the illegal English Wyclif.

This was unlike either of them. The lettering in both bibles was beautiful. The scripts were flowing and elegant. The Latin copy also had pictures made from crushed shells or berries. The colors ranged from blues and reds to greens and yellows and resulted in rich artwork of flowers or creatures that monks had painstakingly applied to show their devotion to God.

Even an illiterate deputy would know that such finery had no business in the possession of a commoner. It was a death sentence, so the English version had no such adornments. They were simply lettered, but in the language of the peasants, easy to read and just as easy to hide.

The book before him was entirely different. The letters were small and uniform and lined the page like ants going to war. He could not see how a hand could reproduce the tiny letters with such perfection; they were close to one another and yet spaced to form the words which the eye could read. There were two columns on each page, and so many letters it was almost overwhelming.

The pages were framed by a ring of black soot that lined their outer edge and rounded the corners like a log rescued from the fire. Each page was as thin as smoke; dried and pressed by the hundreds to form the bound volume before him.

Eni had little doubt where his father would say this manuscript was from and looking upon its unearthly design he would readily agree… *"The Devil's book,"* he said to himself.

"What does it tell you?" Ingous interrupted, looking over his shoulder at the book.

"Umm," Eni mumbled as he returned to the text. The words were different. At first he thought it was a foreign tongue, but he could make sense of most of the words. They were far more like English than Latin. The other marks though, dots and dashes and the like, scattered over the page, he had no idea what they might mean.

"Can you help him?"

"I do not know yet…it is not that easy," Eni tried to explain. "They're different… the words."

"But you do know them, right? These words… you understand them?" she asked, tapping the page with her finger.

"I … I need some time to figure it out, but I will."

Ingous sighed as she moved back to Murdoc's bedside.

Eni watched her for a moment as she caressed his forehead with a damp cloth before he returned his attention to the desk and the open page.

The top of each paragraph had words darker and bolder than the rest of them. As he scanned the page most of the topics were either places or people but as he studied each one it confused him. He turned the page and a drawing leapt out at him. It was unlike anything he had ever seen before. It was as if the person's every detail were inked on to

100

the page.

Most were colored in the same ink as the script, but a river scene looked as if one were seeing an actual river from a hillside. Eni ran his finger over the page to see if the water would wet his touch, but the page was smooth and with no perceptible difference in elevation from the lettering to the pictures.

He turned the pages, looking for a name or a place that was familiar to him. All of them started with the same letter "L", but after several pages the book ran out of L words and started into "M" words. The pages slipped through his fingers as he scanned the words for one that made sense to him, but as a sheet rolled over he stopped suddenly. Slamming the page down, he stared at the words before him. "March, Edmund Mortimer, 5th earl of..." and he stopped short. It wasn't the name or the titles that startled him; he knew those of the Marcher Lord well enough. It was the dates: "Born Nov. 6, 1391 died Jan 19, 1425."

Eni backed away, as if the claws of a wraith would pull him in.

How could it know? How could it predict someone's death eleven years before it happened? Unless... unless it was true, that the book was scribed in the devil's blood and burned from the fires of Hell.

18

Ingous was occupied in her nursing duty. She raced down the stairs to retrieve a bowl of water to wet the master's fever. Eni took the opportunity to scan the room. On the far side, buried in the shadows of a nook, an assortment of items drew his eyes. The first to catch his attention was a wooden handle, smooth and polished as if layered in wax that poked out from a round canteen. Eni granted its subtle request for his hand. The handle slid to the right and rotated around the canteen like the moon circling the earth.

It purred as it followed its orbit. Eni could not see the point to this contraption until he gave the handle a final hard twirl and a light radiated brightly for a moment before fading back into the shadows. Eni stood, stunned.

"What devilry?" he said as he spun the handle faster once again. The light again awakened, its blue hue sending the shadows fleeing and bathing the corner in its glow.

As he picked up the canteen, a few coils of the copper rope spilled to the floor. Their weight would have pulled the lantern down with them if Eni hadn't caught them. Seeing the waxed jackets gave him a strange sense of relief.

He turned the handle again. The light's intensity matched his effort. "Eni!" the old woman broke the lantern's hold on him as she entered the room. "That will not help the master! The book… Murdoc says the answers are always in the book."

Eni cast a weary glance to the shelf and staggered over to it like a mule being brought back to the well-worn path around a mill stone. Sighing, he turned the page, saving himself from any further details of the Marcher Lord's death.

He flipped it to near the end, and on the corner of the page, one word out of the thousands caught his eye: 'Medicine'.

Eni failed to see how anything in the article could be of value for Murdoc, as it listed a variety of words with which Eni was unfamiliar. Most he had never heard of, but seeing the words alphabetized on the page, he decided to see if the other volumes would yield their meanings.

He hauled another book from the shelf. Its form was much like its sister's but appeared to have suffered less from the flames that had scared the first one. He tossed back the same thin pages. 'Circulation' provided no cure for his master, but Eni found it of interest all the same.

He continued to rifle through the books. *Each one must be worth a king's ransom*, he thought, as he plopped down each new book on the lectern with quickening abandon.

He held out hope for 'Respiration' but upon reading, he could not see how it would help.

"Maybe we should get some leeches and bleed him out," Ingous suggested with growing impatience. Eni shrugged. Leeches were the standard medical procedure of the day when any illness was involved.

Now she wants to use leeches, Eni thought, looking at the page before him. "Let me see," he answered, feeling like he knew what he was doing. He looked back at the first book that was still sprawled out of the lectern, right above the heading for medicine, and there it was, dark bold print reading 'Medical Leech.'

It was short with little detail but to say 'Once used for the treatment of human diseases.'

"It's in here," he said reading the passage to Ingous.

"Of course it would be," she said clapping her hands as if it were a tale sung with a lute and harp. "Aye, it's been around since Adam and Eve... you go to the pond and gather a few. I'll fetch a bowl from the pantry for the little darlings."

They were easy to catch; Eni only had to walk through the submerged weeds and a handful latched onto his bare ankles. He scraped these into the bowl and hurried back down the hillside.

Eni lit a torch as darkness fell that evening. His eyes ached from spending most of the day deciphering the small black words in the poor light of Murdoc's study. The tomes were scattered between the shelf and lectern, all opened to the last page he had studied as he weaved back and forth from subject to subject consuming the knowledge they contained.

He lifted the lantern from its residence in the corner and perched it on the shelf directly above the lectern. The soft hiss of the crank purred and the blue light glowed from the glass windows of its portal.

It took little effort to generate enough light to read by using one hand to turn the crank and the other to turn the pages of the volume he was studying.

"I see you discovered them…" Eni, startled by the sudden intrusion into his new world, spun around only to see the waking eyes of Murdoc. His voice was weak as he struggled with a shallow cough that convulsed the length of his body.

"Aye," Eni answered, letting go of the crank as the room settled back into the shadows of the flickering torch.

"In the corner…" Murdoc said. He tried to motion with his hand but was too weak do more than wave in the general direction. "Pull the lever," he added breathlessly.

Eni walked to the corner near the window. There a wood box was mounted on a table. It was a simple box of unfinished wood nondescript but for a wooden handle and the now familiar waxed wires running to and fro from either end. One set ran from the box and snaked their way out the window, disappearing into the night.

The other set followed along the bottom of the wall and joined the shadows in the nook. Eni braced the box and slid the lever over; the action was silent but for a small click as the room lit up in a similar blue light that had graced the lantern.

"Now …put that out," Murdoc coughed as he motioned to the torch, its smoke clearly visible as it billowed about the ceiling.

The torched hissed its protest as it sank into the jar of water that stood guard by the door. "That's better," Murdoc sighed as he eased back into the bed.

Eni studied the two blue lights. One was perched on each end of the nook and they bathed the room in light, their waxed wires now clearly visible. Eni glanced back at the lantern and the books that beckoned his attention. He wondered if their allure was true or a curse that destroys men's souls.

"Ahh, you are alert," Ingous announced as she entered, carrying a tray of fresh leeches. "See boy, the darlings did their job," she added, rattling their tray.

It seemed to take Murdoc a moment to understand what she had said. "Leeches," he repeated, as if the word was foreign to him. "You did not put those blood sucking creatures on me, I hope."

Eni shrunk back. "Of course we did," Ingous continued. "Look how they brought you back! They should probably do another milking to bring you back the rest of the way."

"Fools!" Murdoc erupted. "You have the knowledge…and you use…leeches."

"It was in the book," Eni offered, pointing to the still open manuscript. "It said it was once used on human diseases."

"Successfully?"

"Well…"

"Oh, posh," Ingous countered, dropping the tray on the table with a thud. "It was in your unholy books, so leave the boy alone, you grumpy old man."

"Humph," Murdoc grunted, pulling the blanket up tight around him. "Get me some water," he ordered to no one in particular. "… I need to replenish my blood."

19

The walk to the coffee shop was wet but quiet. Wendy was trying to think of small talk but nothing came to mind. She just hurried along, hoping they would get there before the rain came down any harder.

The professor was a good five inches taller than her. He had pulled up his collar against the wind and didn't appear to have any more interest in talking than she did. His stride was longer than hers, but she was sure he was slowing it down so as not to leave her in his wake.

"What will you have?" he asked, pulling out his wallet once they reached the counter.

"Just a coffee."

"Two please," he said to the barista with matching hand signals. Wendy waited with him for the order and then carried her own to the table. They got a seat next to the window with a view of the soggy world rushing by. She set her bag on the floor next her and placed the package directly on the center of the table.

Wendy took a sip as Dr. Brown warmed up his hands on his cup, "So, what is this about?" she said with a smile that she hoped would improve on their poor start.

The professor stared at the package in front of him, "It's about time and money..." He sighed and smiled back at her, "I guess really, it is the search for both, or more accurately, the search for money, with which we could really search for the other."

Wendy looked at the man and wondered why she hadn't left when she had the chance. "I don't have a clue what you're talking about."

The professor nodded, "Yeah, I get that a lot, most don't." He let his words hang there. "You see, I had an idea... Well, it was my doctoral thesis, but I'd thought about it for years, since I was in secondary school. It was a grand experiment. It would change how we thought about time, but funding was… how shall we say… less than stellar."

Wendy felt her phone vibrate in her pocket, so she looked down to see the text. The professor stopped and watched her, holding his tongue until she finished. "Sorry," she quipped with a smile, and slid it back in her pocket.

"Tell me," the professor asked, sliding back in his chair. "Do you have any encyclopedias?"

"Encyclopedias?" Wendy asked, wondering if she had heard him correctly.

"Well, yes," the professor stated in a tone that made her assume that he did not consider this an odd question. He was bridging the tips of his fingers over his coffee. "You know, a multi-volume set of books full of facts and …"

"Yeah, I know what it is. I just didn't see what it has to do with any of this..."

"But do you have one?" he asked, his eyebrows reaching incredible heights behind his glasses.

"Yes… well, not anymore. Everything is online these days, isn't it?"

"Precisely!" the professor said, sliding back to the front of the chair. "That was the key," he added, waving his finger. "Nobody wanted them anymore. They had lots of mass, were detailed, and most importantly, they were plentiful and cheap."

"What on earth are you talking about?" She had met lots of odd professors at University over the years, but this guy was in a category all by himself.

"The experiment, of course," he said, reaching down to the package between them. "It's the whole reason for this," he said tapping on it with his finger as his smile disappeared, "the one thing I thought I got right, but I was oh so terribly wrong."

The book seemed to haunt Eni's dreams that night as he searched in vain for certain words. He was turning the endless pages, looking for the facts and meanings of shifting details that were never fully explained. Foretold deaths mixed with the marvels of cures never imagined. At morning light, it took him a moment to remember what was real and what had been the magic of sleep.

He finished breaking his fast and spent the morning splitting wood and heaving the results of his efforts down the chute. Though Murdoc was in no shape to work and could manage little more than the trip down to the great room, he still required the beast to be made ready for when it was needed.

Finishing his chores, Eni climbed the hill west of the keep. The breeze again was racing over the mountain, cool and damp from its journey across the sea. He lifted his arms, folding his hands above his head as the wind dried the sweat that had gathered from his labors that morning.

It was only then that he remembered the blue lights. He had intended to investigate them, but the thought had abandoned him when he left Murdoc's chamber that strange night. Now the sight of two wires hanging down the walls of the keep brought the thought back.

Eni hurried to the base of the keep to investigate. The dark wires blended in with the green lichens that coated the massive stones and ran downwards until the matched pair funneled into the tall grasses.

Dropping to his knees, he drove his hands into the weeds, parting the green stalks until he could see the pair of wires nestled deep in the sod.

He crawled along, following them as they snaked through the grass toward the mountain, but he only parted the weeds occasionally as he went so as not to lose sight of them. It was slow going; they had been laid long enough ago that last year's grass had fallen on top of them, keeping them hidden but for close scrutiny.

Eni paid little attention to where they led until they climbed out of their trench and shot up an outcropping of rock. The face was too steep for him to follow, so he quickly found an alternative route to the ridge above.

Clearing the obstacle, he was about to seek the twin wire's trail again when he stopped. He knew this place. A higher cliff loomed to the left and a hollowed-out log angled down to the wooden box in the valley before him.

A smile formed slowly on his face; he had no doubt where the wires were going now. He ran down the grassy slope to the box below. A spring of water percolated from where the turning water wheel released it to reform a stream and meandered away, disappearing into the green meadow. Eni dropped again to his knees and inspected the wires that birthed from the enclosed box.

Now it made sense - the spinning wheel mounted on this box. *It's just like the crank*, he thought as he remembered the canteen attached to the lantern in Murdoc's nook. *The water makes the power... but what makes the light?*

That evening, he knew his curiosity was getting the better of him. He could think of little else and spent much of his time plotting an excuse to visit the books. The only problem was that Ingous had other ideas; she was having him grind some wheat through a small mill that Murdoc had made.

The fact that wheat mills could only be chartered by the Marcher Lord himself seemed not to matter to Murdoc. He had built a small one that clamped onto a table and could be turned by either the beast or by hand with a crank.

Because Eni had not fired up the beast since Murdoc's illness took hold and couldn't justify it for such a short and simple activity, he had to spend a couple of hours turning the handle for the month's flour.

He was going to claim a chill in order to justify heading up the winding stairs, but he could feel a bead of sweat gathering on his forehead. Instead, he chose to 'accidently' spill a ladle of water on himself as he tried to quench his thirst.

Ingous mocked his clumsiness, but sent him up to change nonetheless. Taking the opportunity, he headed up past his room to the upper chamber. He had to flatten himself against the jamb in order to sneak past the wood door without opening it any further. Looking in, he saw the old man lying in the shadows. He was facing the wall but Eni could see the blanket rising and falling with each breath.

He strived to move quietly over the wood floor, but his leather boots still seemed to swish noisily with each step. The books were where he had left them, scattered over the lectern, each open to its appointed station.

Moving past them he pulled the lever on the wall. It clicked, bringing the room into the radiance of its blue light. Murdoc held his station, the rhythm of his breathing unchanged.

Eni sighed in relief as he returned to the lectern and tried to figure the best way to satisfy his curiosity. The word "light" proved worthless as it dealt with 'wave lengths.' Eni had no idea what that even meant, since he had never even seen the great sea that lay west of Wales.

The other words were even more obtuse. Photons, optics, and refraction left him more confused than before as he pulled down the balance of the volumes to figure out their meanings. He was looking through the book of 'R', when the pages slipped from his hand and slapped the back of the book with a thud.

"What do you seek?" Murdoc asked in a low voice thick with sleep. Eni turned, hesitant at first, but the old man seemed more interested in his activity than irate at Eni for waking him.

"The copper wire, and the water wheel, how does it work?"

A smile creased the old man's face as he laid there, his face still pale.

"E-lec-tric-ity," he enunciated, sending the boy reaching for the book of 'E'. He watched for a moment, chuckled and rolled back over, leaving the boy to dive into this strange new magic with its magnets and invisible electrons.

It took another week or so for Murdoc to recover enough to go about his daily activities, and with his increasing health, the door to his inner sanctum was once again closed. This came with no statement or reprimand, but simply with the locking of the door which had been open.

The work and routines also returned, and after a morning in the cave and a bath in the mountain pool, Eni wished he had investigated the barrels of stew when he had the chance. He was sure the books would have knowledge of the disgusting concoction and its purpose.

His next task was to stack dried wood in a hole, but it was to be stacked like a pyre so that air could flow between members and produce a fire that was hot and hungry. With the feeding of the beast, he had become quite good at starting fires, but with this one, once the fire was burning good and hot, he was to layer more wood on it and then bury the whole of it.

To Eni this seemed like a waste, but Murdoc was quite determined about it and even made his way out to make sure the lad was doing it correctly.

The day ended with the rolling and wrapping of the wax coated wire. This task, however, took on a new delight. While there was much he could not understand of its power, the concept made sense to him. *Electrons can flow like a river, and the wire is the riverbed,* he told himself. *And the light is like the waterwheel harvesting the power at its end.*

He imagined what other uses there were for the wire and its stream of electrons and imagined Murdoc had other wheels and wires hidden about the keep, but he had not found any yet.

By early November, the weather had turned. An early winter storm had coated both the valley and the keep in a haze of grey and white.

A stone wall that adjoined Eni's bed and formed the corner that he found most suitable for sleeping against also lined the chimney. The fire below radiated up through the wall, and the added heat glued him and his blanket to his bed even after Ingous called him for the morning meal.

Twice the previous week, he had ignored her summons in favor of sleep, and had to go without food until noon by Murdoc's orders, even though there was plenty left.

That Tuesday, Eni was so set on not oversleeping that he had been lying awake for half an hour before Ingous came to rouse him. He was out of bed and would have beat her down the steps had he not had to use the chamber pot before descending.

"Well, aren't we up early? Excited, I would reckon," she said with her typical early morning cheer upon seeing him loiter in the kitchen.

"Aye," Eni said with a shrug, as if it would hide his enthusiasm, but it only brought a laugh from the old lady. Her joyfulness would be considered an asset to most, but her employer took a dim view of such happiness- especially before his fast had been broken.

Murdoc's appearance brought an end to their communion as the old lady dropped her head toward the fire and the sizzle of bacon drew her attention.

"I see the punishment has had its desired effect," he said dryly at the sight of the boy at the table.

"That or the trip to London…" Ingous started, but caught herself with a giggle.

"You know…" Murdoc added coldly to the ever widening smile on the housekeeper. "In many estates, such a cavalier attitude would be considered insubordination."

She turned from her cooking, eyeing the old man from head to toe as if they were equals. "A smile? Really, you English are so dour that you would relieve someone of their duties for smiling? What, is there just too much joy in the world for you lot?"

Their banter was not uncommon and Eni often wondered how Ingous could be so casual about her position, openly challenging her better as she did. Perhaps she didn't think he was capable of really being that harsh, but seeing firsthand how he strong-armed the Baron of Knighton, Eni wondered if she underestimated the old man.

"Anyway," he continued as he opened a steaming biscuit, "there has been a change of plan." He hesitated as he centered a pat of butter inside it. "After a good night's rest, I feel our chances of success, as well as greater income, would be generated with a trip to Wigmore first."

112

"Wigmore… I've never heard of it," Ingous interrupted as the eggs slid onto their plates.

"Oh, the washer-woman has not heard of Wigmore, what a surprise," he gloated, giving the eggs a disconcerting glance. "Overcooked, as usual," he commented as she filled his cup with hot elderflower tea.

"I've heard of Wigmore," Eni interrupted. "It's an estate of the Marcher Lord's, isn't it?"

"Aye," Murdoc nodded, raising his nose with a sudden air of superiority toward the housekeeper, who merely rolled her eyes.

Ingous handed Eni his dress clothes when he had finished eating. Most of them were his own that she had washed and cleaned, but also included was a silk shirt which either no longer fit the wizard, or was too worn for his liking.

Eni felt the smooth fibers on his skin as he put the shirt on. It seemed to flow up his arm like dry water and although he had no mirror he knew he looked good; he could feel it.

He felt his cloak swish behind him as he began to descend the stairs. He was elegant, a councilor to the King and dressed for the part. He sharply turned the corner at the bottom, letting his cloak float as it caught the draft and drifted majestically to the side.

A cold rain met them at the door as they began their long trek, and the swirling winds greeted them as they left the shadow of the keep. Eni wrapped his cloak tightly around him, hoping to preserve his heat.

The clouds hugged the side of the mountain, shrouding it in a grey mist as they made their way down the winding path. The village was quiet as they passed through; even the sheep must have sought shelter from the constant rain. Eni wondered where the green-eyed girl was right then. He hoped she could see him, if only through an open window, but all were shuttered against the elements.

Murdoc said little as they passed into the hills that ringed the valley's eastern edge other than to hand his satchel over to Eni when it

113

got too much for him to carry up a hill. The village disappeared into the grey haze and Eni wished he was back there in front of a warm hearth rather than trudging through the wilds of the March. The cold rain had already soaked through his cloak and the silk shirt clung to his body as they moved into the trees. He began wishing he had packed his silk shirt instead of wearing it for the journey.

The leaves had long since fallen and the bare limbs provided little protection against the deluge. Eni half-expected to see snow mixed in with the falling mist that swam among the hulking trees.

"How far is it?" he asked. His voice seemed to chatter to the steady rhythm of the rain.

"Not far, but we'll camp for the night; one must be presentable to a royal."

"Is it true… that he is the rightful King?"

"Never say that out loud if you fancy keeping your head…" Murdoc advised without looking up from his carefully placed gait. "The desire to lay claim to the crown has ruined many a family and the house of Mortimer has suffered greatly from its position."

"Castles, lands… power and wealth- I could live with such suffering," Eni remarked as a chill swept over him with the passing breeze. "I would be happy with a horse and carriage."

His master cast back a glance of reproach. "You are young and foolish, Eni son of Harold. The life of a royal is typically lonely, painful, and short."

He let his remarks hang in the air as they walked, with only the falling rain and their footsteps breaking up the barren silence.

"Edmund Mortimer's father died when the lad was only six," Murdoc finally said, ending his moratorium. "That makes him both the Earl of the March and the Earl of Ulster, not to mention heir to the throne of England," Murdoc continued as he eased his way to the downward slope.

"Of course, Henry Bolingbroke usurped the crown from his cousin Richard and took the lad and his brother into custody, so two little boys hardly old enough to pee without their nannies were taken prisoners,

114

merely for inheriting the title of 'heir to the throne'."

"But why, if they were only wee lads?"

"Aye, but they were a threat to him. Richard sired no children, so the throne legally would jump back a generation to the next closest line. By the laws of succession, the next in line would be Mortimer through his grandmother…"

Murdoc fell silent, except for his labored breathing as he poled his way up a small wooded hill, leaving a line of impressions from the butt of his staff as it sank into the soft, wet earth.

Eni let him recover once they topped the peak. The view was muted by the streaks of clouds that streamed over the crest in ribbons of grey vapor.

"But he let them go," Eni suggested once he could no longer hear the old man's breathing.

"No… they were stolen away by their uncle and Hotspur about six years later during the Welsh uprising."

"So they were rescued?" Eni interpreted.

"Perhaps…but it's not that simple," he said. "Ask yourself, why?"

Eni knew it was a trick question. Murdoc asked little else, but how the trap was set eluded him. Still, he was thankful for the conversation, even if it would make him feel foolish for falling for the obvious choice, it kept his mind from thinking about how cold and wet he was now feeling, as the rain began to fall in earnest. "I don't know," he finally confessed, loud enough to be heard over the bombardment of the countryside.

The strength of the shower was short-lived and it broke as suddenly as it had started. Murdoc waited it out. "Think…" he finally asked, "Why would their uncle risk so much to free them from Henry's service? By all reports they were safe and treated quite well."

Eni started to say, "They were fam…" but through the stream of water that flowed off the front of the old man's hat, his questioning eyes warned against such a simple answer.

"To be a councilor to the rich and powerful, you must think like the rich and powerful. They will make quick work of you otherwise," the

115

old man added as he turned back to the trail ahead of them.

They trekked silently through the countryside of the eastern March as Eni sifted through this riddle. The land was beginning to flatten. The hills were not so tall or the valleys so deep in this region of the kingdom.

The clouds held back their fury and allowed both the path and his head to clear. He tried to keep track of his thoughts, shifting between the varied points that ran through his mind.

"All right," he announced, once pleased with their order. "The boys were the key to the throne," he said at last. "Since they were the rightful heirs, if Henry had control of them, then no one else could have the right to claim the throne."

The old man kept heading down the path. "So why did their uncle rescue them?" he asked.

"Well, if he could get a hold of the boys, then he could claim by lawful succession that Henry was not the rightful King, the lads were, and since they were so young, he could control them as their nearest kin."

"Quite so," Murdoc answered with only the merest suggestion of a nod. "So why shouldn't Henry kill them?"

"Well they were only little… not to mention family,"

"That would not stop him. He killed his cousin Richard, and he was King. What would him killing two lads mean after that?"

Eni fell silent once again as they continued east. Murdoc struggled up a slope as the boy slowed down behind him, continuing to work at his riddle. The rain was long gone, but as they cleared the crest, a mist had filled the open valley. Murdoc, having spied a downed log several paces off the path, ambled over to it and groaned painfully as he lowered himself to its surface.

Eni lowered himself against a tree. "Why didn't he kill them? There must be a reason," he said low and to himself, hoping that hearing the words from outside his own head would spark an idea.

Looking out upon the open grey sea that lay before them, he wondered what lay buried in the depths. What settlement or village lay

116

covered under this blanket of clouds? It reminded him of a story he heard years ago of when the English attacked a Welsh village during the rebellion.

The English came under a cover of fog, killing, burning, and pillaging as they descended. They tore the village apart as if looking for something... or someone. Then they were gone, disappearing into the mist. Ten people were dead that day, including Clum's uncle.

No one knew what it was that they searched for, and it was only then, looking out over the sea of mist that Eni wondered if maybe it was the young Marcher Lord that drew their frenzied search.

"The uncle..." his voice was soft. "It's the uncle," he said louder turning back toward Murdoc. "The uncle was next in line after the lads; that's why the Usurper kept them alive. That's why he searched for them... killed for them. To keep the uncle from legally claiming the throne, the boys had to live."

"Ah," a sleepy voice answered, as if just aroused. "Now you are thinking like a nobleman. Self-preservation first, followed closely by advancement. The ranks of the nobles will soon be rife with it." The old man yawned and adjusted his cloak. "You'll see... over the next few 'yawn' years if..."

"If what?" Eni asked impatiently, when no answer was short in coming.

"Hmm..." Murdoc mumbled, before yawning, "if you live that long."

Eni was too cold and wet to fall asleep but the old man's head soon fell back against the trunk and he started snoring, as if competing with a noisy rook in a nearby tree. The bird gave a final attempt before fleeing the hilltop in defeat.

The old man's words lingered, though, and Eni wondered if Murdoc knew more than he let on about the future, his future. The next time he had an opportunity, he decided, he would steal a look in the book. Steal a look into his future. He could imagine the great deeds that lay in store for him, the fame and fortune.

As the stories took their path, he too began to drift into dreams, but

Murdoc yawned noisily. "That was what I needed," he said loudly before using his walking stick for support and rising to his full height to stretch.

"Let's be off," he said after a moment, and started his descent into the mist. It took Eni a moment to wake up and realize that the old man had left, but he quickly got to his feet and followed.

The mist was so thick at times that nothing could be seen outside of the trees through which they walked. *If you live that long.* The words seemed haunting, especially in the mist of an unfamiliar forest. Eni wondered what he meant. Truth be told, life was hard for most, with the coming of wars and outbreaks of the plague. But somehow, the old man made it sound more menacing than just a reflection on the shortness of life.

Murdoc was walking quickly as they traveled the downward winding path. The old man showed no more interest in talk, which left Eni alone with his thoughts. There were no sights or sounds in this hazy little world of grey but for the bark of some distant dog.

In time, cottages began to appear in the mist more frequently as the land opened up and flattened out to the east. The path they had followed now turned and joined a road first set in the earth when the Romans were still the lords of Briton.

"The village of Wigmore," Murdoc announced as they came upon a cluster of buildings that seemed to rise out of the mist at his command. "We shall seek accommodations at the inn for the night," he continued, as he made his way to a shabby two story building around the corner in the center of the hamlet.

Eni sped up to follow, but Murdoc turned abruptly and stopped him with the shaft of his stick. "First," he said, his eyes locked onto the boy's, "you must let the Marcher Lord know we are here and seek an audience for the morrow."

Eni felt his neck stiffen. "Of course," he said quickly, although he had no idea how that was to be done. He looked around the shrouded village for some evidence of where to go.

"The castle is to the west, up on the ridge," Murdoc motioned into the blanket of fog. Eni looked but could see nothing.

"Who... How do I refer to you?" Eni stumbled.

The old man raised his massive eyebrows before answering. "You are to say the King's councilor, Murdoc of the March, seeks an audience with his lordship on the morrow." Then the wizard faded into the fog, leaving the boy to his errand while he sought the comforts of the inn.

It was such a grand statement Eni feared he could not do it justice. He repeated it under his breath. "Aye, my lord," Eni called back in acknowledgment, but there was no answer. He turned alone to search for this hidden ridge and its castle, the home of the Marcher Lord.

20

Eni had often heard of fog 'as thick as pea soup'. This fog did not have the greenish tinge that accompanied Abertha's soup- it was light grey and slightly grainier. As for thickness, it wouldn't fill a spoon, but he was reasonably sure he could cut it with knife.

He was within feet of other travelers on the path. He could hear boots kicking up the gravel and the rasp of breathing. The smell of wool or of leather gave him clues to their occupations and yet, as close as they were, none were more than ghosts in the grey mist.

The main road ran north on the west side of the village, its gravel base set more than a thousand years before, when the Romans still ruled Briton. Eni followed it, joining a throng of travelers before veering off to the west- to the gate of Wigmore castle.

He felt the road rise before he saw it, but as it climbed, the world around him slowly grew. First only those around him were visible, but as he ascended, the walls of the Marcher Lord's fortress loomed above him in the mist.

He was following a limping peasant who moved achingly slow, his good leg taking the lead as they climbed higher toward the fortress gate. He was dangling a clutch of stew hens in each hand, his fingers wrapped around their thin legs as they hung upside down, clucking softly with each hobbling stride. Eni wondered if the fowl were a payment of tax, or if the peasant was paid for such a delivery.

The gate was up, with only a relaxed guard on either side to keep the peace. The path narrowed as it climbed the steep hillside. The castle was perched on the top of a ridge that continued climbing to the west, thus making the battlements step ever higher. It was an imposing structure and even the fog seemed to bow to its authority.

A rickety, old cart ambled down the bailey toward him, the oxen doing their best to fight the power of gravity that raced down behind them.

Further up the hill the main gatehouse stood. Its walls were riddled with arrow slots and above, its ramparts were lined with soldiers standing at attention as if they were gargoyles cut from the stone.

This fortified entry was also flanked by twin turrets that rose high into the heavens, overlooking the sea of fog. Eni was so amazed; he almost knocked over the struggling peasant as he took in the size and power of the family seat of the Mortimers.

He briefly caught sight of its helmeted occupants before he passed into the colossal shadow. More soldiers stood guard at its entrance, armed with halberds, but they paid him little heed as he entered the fortified estate.

The mist had thinned so much that the sun was now burning through the haze as he continued up the crisscrossing road that cut across the stone outcropping. Eni realized it had been designed to keep any aggressor in the line of fire from the archers in the inner bailey as long as possible.

The helmeted gargoyles seem to watch his every move from their stations as he cut back again across the hillside. He tried not to make eye contact with them, lest they think him up to no good, but he couldn't take his eyes from these massive walls that protected the Marcher Lord.

As he reached their shadows, he turned, looking back down the path he had traversed; the open hillside was laid bare to the archers above him. He could only imagine the carnage that would rain down on a snake foolish enough to try to raid an egg from this nest.

"What ya want?" Eni spun back around. A soldier with a beard that ran down to the center of his chest stood guard. His halberd stood taller then he, but the man's girth could have snapped it in two if he forced all his weight upon it.

"I…I beg your pardon, my…" he had never addressed an unfamiliar guard before. In Knighton, they all knew who he was and addressed him as the young master. By the look in the guard's eye, that greeting would not be forthcoming on this day.

"My good man," he continued, adjusting the satchel to a more respectable position, and deciding that he still was the soldier's better even here at Wigmore. "I come to beg audience for my master with the Marcher Lord."

"Is that so," the man groaned with a menacing smile as he widened his stance and leaned forward on the halberd's staff as if together they were three legged stool. "And who is your master, boy?"

Eni feared the halberd could snap, but he focused on his task. "I serve the King's councilor, Murdoc of the March," he stated, with as much air as he could muster.

"You heathen scum!"

Eni had little success dodging the stream of spit that was launched in his direction, but he did block most of it with the outer hem of his cloak. He was not so lucky with the butt of the halberd which caught him squarely in the thigh and sent him cascading down the walk to the howls of the gargoyles up above.

"No heathen wizard will step foot in castle Wigmore," the guard yelled after him, as Eni struggled back to his feet.

"Tell that devil's servant to crawl back under the rock he came from," another called from the wall, as Eni felt a warm round of spit roll down to his cheek. He swiped it angrily before hooding his cloak as more rained down about him from the storm of laughter high above.

If he really was a wizard, he would have cast a spell on those bastards! He would have made them pay, but whether they doubted the wizard's power or knew they served a greater power, Eni could do nothing but slink back out the way he had come.

It seemed to take forever to break from the shadow of the wall and out of the range of the archers' spittle. He felt the eyes of everyone he passed fall on him and his spotted cloak as he quickly made his way to the lower gates. "Wish it was still raining," he muttered under his breath, noting the state of his garment.

The fog that had blanketed the land like heavy wool minutes before was now only a thin veil, the change was as abrupt as it was unwelcomed. Finding a grassy knoll, Eni stopped. He unclasped his cloak, laying it out on the wet vegetation. He quietly rubbed his hand over the length of the cloak hoping the blades of grass below would brush off the globs of drying spittle.

He sat on it for only a moment before noticing a larger hill beside the path. It had been out of sight in the heavy fog but now he wondered how he had missed it. With its stone walls quarried from the same rock as the castle, a church stood overlooking the village.

Eni could not deny the sense of guilt and shame that hit him with almost as much force as the cold west wind. He got up and carefully dragged the cloak along the ground to free any remaining fragments before hoisting it back over his shoulders.

He had not stepped inside a church since he had left Knighton with Murdoc at midsummer and feared he would receive similar greeting there as he had from the castle guards. Perhaps it was the voice of his mother ringing in his ear, or the call of God himself, but Eni could not deny it either way. He hurried up the path. He knew Murdoc would not be pleased with this detour and promised to keep it short as he passed though the great oak doors.

The smell of candles welcomed him as he took the first open bench. The massive timber arches framed the altar and the crucifix at the front. There were several other people about but they were praying for their own concerns and no one paid him any heed. He bent his head, said his prayer and left as quickly and quietly as the mice that were rumored to reside there.

The wind caught him as he exited. It surprised him and lightened his mood as he turned and rode it down the hill and into town. The village of Wigmore was far smaller than Knighton and Eni doubted if it would exist if it weren't for the castle that shared its name.

He wondered how Murdoc would deal with his failure. In the two seasons he had been in his employ, the old man had never struck him nor shown any cruelty other than questioning his intelligence and the mix of his blood. But then, he had never failed at a task such as this.

Truth be told, he wasn't looking forward to this meeting and found himself loitering near the hay shed around the corner from the inn. The barn's slotted boards broke the spine of the wind as it drove new clouds in from the west.

After the events of the day, he could have fallen asleep there in the golden curls of hay, but a stable hand armed with pitch fork interrupted his respite and drove him back out into the elements.

Dusk had fallen before the cold and the numbness of his feet drove him into the warmth of the inn. A chorus of laughter greeted him as he walked into the public room. Men of every station had gathered around tables in the fire-lit room telling their tales of the day. No one so much as looked up at Eni as he passed through the throng, hoping to spy his master among the crowd.

Failing to see him, he was about to ask when he noticed a solitary figure seated to the left of the fire with an empty tankard as his only companion. Eni eased to the side, hoping to see the man's profile painted in the orange flicker of the fire.

Murdoc's gaze was frozen on the dancing flames as they practiced their ancient arts. Eni moved closer until he was finally able to draw the old man's eyes away from the fire.

"Oh, there you are… I thought you had gotten yourself lost," he said with a shiver and tightened his cloak about him. "Feared I would have to go out looking for you… Aye, get the lad some supper… " he added, tossing a coin to the innkeeper as she passed by.

She caught it mid-flight, depositing the silver in her bosom and nodding agreeably. "Be back in a moment, darling," she smiled, before disappearing into the crowd. By the time Eni had turned back, the old man was once again mesmerized by the glowing blaze.

He stood there waiting for Murdoc to once again address him, but nothing was forthcoming. The wizard seemed years away from the loud drunken chorus that was being belted out behind them.

"Sir," Eni finally questioned when he could no longer hold it in. "I… "

"Not now," the old man answered sharply, his eyes flashing.

"Here we are…" the innkeeper sang, her voice higher and sweeter than the men crooning behind her. She placed a bowl of stew and half a loaf of bread on the table behind Eni. "Me husband done a fine job cooking if I do say… Can I get ye another, love?" she said, reaching for the tankard that Murdoc was still coveting.

"I must pass," he said, reluctantly handing over his companion. "I'm afraid my voice is not as sweet as the rest of your patrons."

"Come now, ye've only had one- won't start belting it out till ye downed three or four."

Murdoc looked up her innocently, "I'm afraid it is my weakness; one is all I can muster." She giggled before she headed back through the throng as they started on an old sailor shanty that seemed out of place so far inland from the coast.

The stew steamed as Eni dipped his bread into the broth, soaking up the brown soup with flecks of barley and diced vegetables. He had forgotten how hungry he was, having not eaten since that morning at the wizard's keep.

The food warmed his innards, and left him ready to find the comforts of a bed, but Murdoc showed no sign of deserting his watch over the fire. To any but Eni, he could have passed for a silent drunk, but the boy noticed his sudden eye movements break from the flames toward the door whenever someone passed its threshold.

As the night passed along that event came less and less until soon there were few left other than the two of them and the innkeepers, who were tidying up their establishment.

Eni, looking around and seeing no one in earshot, began. "I failed," he started, to which the old man made no response. "The guards wouldn't let me pass…"

The memories rushed back of the events that afternoon, seeing the halberd and the rain of spit all over again. Eni covered his hip as if to protect it this time, but discovered a lump; hard and swollen like a fresh goose egg under his stockings.

He struggled to put aside his injury but his hand kept returning to

125

the scene of the crime. "I'm sorry I failed you," he muttered and sat on his hands to keep them from further investigation. "Shall I try again tomorrow?"

Murdoc gave no response, except to eye another of the patrons as he stumbled out into the night. How much longer they sat there Eni was unsure. Filled with mutton stew he was transfixed by the dying fire, and would have remained that way but for the gust of night air that raced in with a stranger.

"We're closed," the innkeeper called from the bar, where she was polishing the last of the mugs.

The stranger nodded, but made no move for the door. He looked around briefly before answering. "If I may warm by the fire for a moment, I shall be on my way," he said from under his hood, making his way toward the warmth of the hearth.

His cloak was old and simple, but Eni could tell he was not a commoner. His speech was too elegant for one of low station and the leather gloves that hid his hands bulged below the knuckles. His cowl shadowed his features as he wandered toward them.

Eni turned back toward Murdoc, expecting the old man to be watching this charade. But instead of watching the stranger, his eyes were fixed on the flames.

"But how?" Eni mouthed.

"Shh!" the old man hissed, sounding like a pot on the hearth, but a slight smile curled upon his face as he resumed his gaze on the fire.

The stranger rounded the table where Eni had finished his meal, but paid no heed to the boy, who struggled to keep his eyes locked on the dancing flames. The man looked back upon the empty pub and started to pull off his gloves, but thought better of it and stretched out his leathered hands to the fire.

There was an empty silence for a moment before Murdoc remarked quietly as if talking to the fire, "Next time, I would think it wise to leave the rings at home... my lord."

The man said nothing, but his fingers curled back from the warmth before dropping his arms entirely into the folds of his cowl. Eni looked

126

up, but could make out little of the man's face, save for the shadow of his beard, which was short and trim, in the custom of the English lords.

The Marcher Lord must have felt the weight of his peering eyes because he turned and looked down at him. It surprised Eni how old he looked, maybe because of the discussion with Murdoc of his hardships, but for a man of twenty-three, he appeared much older.

Eni stared, and a thought flew through his mind. *In twelve years' time, he will be dead.* Although death by the age of 35 was not uncommon, the fact that he knew the date was unsettling.

"Leave us," the Marcher Lord ordered, his voice as cold as the wind he came in with, and he turned his attention to the wizard.

As Eni got up, Murdoc shook his head, "I beg your pardon, my lord, he should stay. He is my apprentice... and, I would wager, the one you will be dealing with before this business is concluded."

The Marcher Lord cast a disconcerting glance at Eni. "Very well," he muttered.

Eni looked back, stunned, but the men paid him no heed. "There is, of course, the question of the fee for such vital information," Murdoc began in his typical manner. "These are troubled times, my lord, for the entire Kingdom..."

"Your black magic carries little weight with me, old man. I allow you to oversee the valley under your keep, for which you pay me nothing- as was the custom with my father, and what do I get?" he said, his voice beginning to rise with his temper.

He swallowed hard and cast a glance back across the room at the innkeeper, who was sweeping the far side of the inn. Forced to return to a whisper he continued, "Did your rambling arts extend a day to my father's life? No."

"As I have told you many times, my lord, I can only say what will come to pass, not how to change the course," Murdoc offered sympathetically.

"Yes, as you say, yet here you are offering your dark arts at the cost of my purse- to what benefit to me, may I ask? I have both peasants and clergy to deal with on your account. So if this information is of value to me … then we will extend your lease. If not, you may find some other rock to crawl under."

"You are too kind," Murdoc answered, dipping his head only slightly so as not draw attention from the innkeeper. "There will be an attempt made on his majesty's life ten days into the New Year."

The Marcher Lord was silent at this news, and stared into the glowing hearth. Seeing only the back of the cowl shudder, Eni couldn't tell if this was old news to his lordship or a surprise.

The Marcher Lord looked back to make sure the innkeeper was still some distance away, as the sound of her sweeping filled the room. "And…?"

"It fails."

The Marcher Lord nodded his head in acknowledgment. "And who is guilty of this treason?" he asked weakly, his voice suddenly giving way into a cough.

Murdoc waited for his lordship before answering, and when he did, his voice was quiet but solid as he whispered, "the Lollards."

The gasp that followed was loud enough to cause the sweeping innkeeper to stop and look up at them, but all three quickly sought refuge in the glowing embers as they waited for the sweeping to continue.

Eni felt his heart pound erratically as he tried to make sense of what he had just heard. His eyes darted up from the hearth but the cowl of the Marcher Lord remained unchanged. *What is he thinking?* Eni wondered. He took a deep breath as the innkeeper returned to her task and his heart slowed again to the cadence of the broom.

Turning from the fire, the Marcher Lord adjusted his cowl. "I shall make the King aware of this," he said quietly.

"That would be wise, my lord," Murdoc answered as he too rose from his station, preparing to retire.

"The lease shall be extended," he said adjusting his gloves.

"I thank you. You are most gracious, my lord."

As the Marcher Lord turned, he looked down at the lowly apprentice. Eni felt his ears burn, but, as if returning to the character of a commoner, he nodded farewell and thanked the innkeeper for sharing the warmth of her hearth before slipping into the night.

The whisking broom again dominated the inn as Murdoc warmed his hands over the now fading coals. Eni's mind was racing over this news; the Lollards were attacking the King. It made no sense. They were no army, just a bunch of itinerate preachers.

"I have arranged for you to sleep in the stable," Murdoc said as a yawn escaped. He eased up from his perch and held his back as if it might give out under the stress. "I see no reason to rush in the morning... do not disturb me till midday. Then we shall eat and be on our way."

21

Eni was issued a wool blanket by the innkeeper. It was adorned with flecks of hay and smelled of sheep, but he took it with thanks and stumbled out to the stable. Casting the satchel off to the side and wrapping the wool around him, he dropped into the hay, serenaded by the soft breathing of the barn's residents.

He often could hear Murdoc's snoring in the keep, so he was thankful to be as far out of earshot as possible, and he wondered if the other guests would demand a refund for what they were about to endure.

Try as he might though, sleep was not quick to join him in the stable. He adjusted his position several times, adding some hay here, moving a little there, but whenever he closed his eyes, he would relive the conversation that evening, trying to make sense of Murdoc's prediction about the Lollards.

The problem was- it made no sense; why would they do such a thing? He tried to remember as far back as he could, even when he was still small and his older brothers were home. Everything was so exciting. People would gather in the evening after the servants had been dismissed, clutching their small boxes of painted wood.

Under their trinkets and jewelry, a faux bottom would lift up, revealing a hidden compartment where a page or two of the English text was safely tucked away. The assembled would then take turns reading their treasures. Even the illiterate came to hear the Word read in their own tongue for one of the few times in their lives.

They all knew it was dangerous; if caught by the crown or the church, they would be burned at the stake. "It is worth the risk if you believe something enough," his father would say. "God is glorified by our speaking of His word."

That was why it made no sense to go from a simple gathering of reading an English Bible to an uprising against the King. These were mostly simple farmers and craftsmen. A few were minor officials, like his father, with a couple of sympathetic priests; but certainly, none were the type to raise an insurrection against the crown.

As he was lying there listening to the night, a horse shifted in the next stall. In the darkness, he could see little of the animal, but he could sense that it was big, as it snorted and readjusted its stance. Such a horse was rare in the stable of an inn. This was a knight's horse. He wondered why it was here, and not stabled in the castle.

"Oldcastle," he said into the silence of the night as the thoughts flooded his mind.

Oldcastle was a knight. He had fought at Henry's side in the Welsh rebellion. He was at ease in battle and ordering men... It must be ... He must have worked them up... His own little army to seek revenge against the king.

I have to warn them! He tossed the blanket off and jumped to his feet. He caught himself before breaking for the door. Knighton was not far, only a few miles to the southwest, but finding his way in the night gave him pause.

Murdoc's satchel, he thought triumphantly. It was invisible, nestled in the pile of hay, but he hurried over, raking his hand through the strands until he caught the leather strap.

Its clanging contents startled a horse, who snorted his displeasure at the commotion. Securing the bag over his shoulder he slid out the door and entered the arms of the waiting night.

He held the contents securely under his arm to limit their clanging as he stole away. He wanted to move quickly, but seeing a member of the town watch down the road, he held still in the shadows until the sentry finally passed beyond the next row of houses. Eni headed south until he could disappear into the wood that bordered the village green.

The smell of the damp earth filled the air as he felt his way into the thickness of the forest. He wandered about in darkness, as the canopy blocked out what little light the clouded skies allowed.

His heart raced as he blindly felt his way, conscious of the racket that might betray his escape. He would stop and listen occasionally, making sure there were no pursuers, only to find that a swarm of flies had discovered him. Their ability to see their prey clearly surpassed his own sight and they used it to their full advantage.

His arm, which had been occupied securing the contents of the satchel, now joined the combat with the invisible enemy as he clanged his way into the surrounding hills.

He knew full well the tales of the unholy light in the wilds of the March- their appearance was in a good many tall tales and ghost stories of the resident minstrels, and Eni wanted to be sure that he would not be adding to their collection, so he waited as long as possible before delving into Murdoc's pack.

The darkness he could deal with, but the biting flies were another matter and required a change in strategy.

Dropping to one knee, he fished through the bag rummaging by feel for the contraption. The familiar waxed coating, tacky to the touch, gave away the wires which sprang from their coil as he pulled them out, the lantern and crank following close behind. It took only moments to sort out the assemblage and with a whirl of the crank, the wood was aglow with the soft blue light.

He waited for a moment there on the ground, swatting the dark objects that entered this blue world till they briefly subsided. Then, with one hand on the crank, he headed out again.

He felt like he was making good time- not that it was without problems. Turning the crank left him with one hand to both hold out the lantern and negotiate the wilds of the wood.

The light lit only the immediate area around him; its glow faded beyond the first few trees into no more than shadows unless a rodent happened to look in his direction. Its eyes would reflect the blue light.

The first time it happened, Eni almost dropped everything and ran. If the eyes burned a fiery red instead of cold blue, he would have guessed the devil was after him and would have been gone, but seeing

132

the blue gave him pause. It helped that the field mouse, going about its nightly activities, ran into the glow before he could react.

He had gone no further than a mile or two when he wished he had Murdoc's walking stick as well. The wizard had designed the lantern to hang at the end of the pole. The canteen would fit on the stick as well so that the light would hang over his head and free a hand at the same time.

Eni searched for a fallen branch that would fit the notch, but after finding one, he found that it was too thin, and bent so that the lantern ended up hanging too low, and all he could see in front of him was the shadow of his head.

He tried various positions, even walking sideways so that the light could proceed before him, but he found nothing that worked, so he went back to carrying the lantern by resting it on the satchel that slung in front of him.

He wandered for an hour in the forest before coming to a path that brought him to familiar territory. There he was able to pick up speed as he ringed wide around Knighton and the cottages of the neighbors, until he found his way to the outer hedges of the manor house.

He stopped cranking and broke into a run after clearing the last of them, and a smile broke across his face as he heard the dogs' bay at his approach. "It me, lads…" he said, kneeling. Their gruff approach faded into slobbering welcome at the first whiff of his scent.

"Aye, good to see you, too," he added, scratching behind their ears, their heads cocked in enjoyment. The door of the manor flung open, and a sword caught the orange from the burning torch held before it.

"Who's there…?"

Eni rose to his feet and stumbled past the dogs, which were unwilling to let the greeting end so soon. "It is I, father; Eni. I have …"

"What do you want?" his words were terse, and the sword still arched behind him.

"I have come… to warn you," he answered, stepping back from the blade's path. "Mother," he said seeing her face catch the light from

133

behind the door. But she backed away quickly, disappearing into the shadows.

"You come bearing the devil's light, that wizard's black magic, and you desecrate this home of your youth with that…"

"It is not like that," Eni struggled to say. "It is not magic. It's real, like a river, just too small to see… I made the wire with my own two hands."

He could hear his mother shriek behind the door.

"No, you don't understand… It's called electricity. It's like lightning."

"Only God can control the heavens!" his father stormed, the sword waving behind him in his fury.

"Of course, I know that…" Eni answered, over the sound of his mother's weeping, his mind desperately searching for an explanation. "It is like the poke from a woolen sweater on a winter's day…"

"Enough," the Steward answered. "It appears our prayers have gone unanswered," his face was stiff and hard in the fire light. "Go back to your master… this is no longer your home."

Eni couldn't believe what he was hearing. The sword pointed through the night like it was held by the angel at the gate to Eden, sending him into the fall. "No!" his mother wailed, coming from her station behind the door, her arms out-stretched for her youngest son.

"It is too late," the Steward, said catching her in his arms as she staggered out to the boy. "He is one of them now…"

Eni stood there, watching the scene unfold before him. "Be gone!" the Steward ordered over the wailing of his wife, who crumpled in her husband's arms.

"They… they know," Eni said, his voice cracking under the strain. "They know about the attack on the king! It will fail."

The Steward looked up at him, but his eyes were hidden in the shadows. "You are of the devil!" he stormed, lifting the sword that had fallen to his side as if to launch an attack.

Eni stepped back, but his mother held her husband tightly to her bosom. "That's not how I was raised," Eni said, taking a deep breath, unsure of what he was saying. "You taught me to respect authority. You said it was placed there by God. You're being misled by Oldcastle!"

"You know nothing, boy. You are the devil's servant."

Eni swallowed hard. "I know right from wrong," he said, a surge of energy racing through his veins. "I know this is not from God - at least not the God that I was raised with - the God of the Word."

"To hell with you," the Steward spit, tossing his wife to the ground as he rose with the sword aloft. Eni stepped away before breaking into a run. "Run, back to the devil!" his father roared into the night, as if giving chase.

Eni ran until he reached the hedgerow. The Steward had given up the chase and had returned to his wife. Eni watched as he struggled to lift her from where she lay whimpering on the ground.

He couldn't hear any of their words over the heaving of his own breath, but he stayed, fastened to the spot, watching from deep in the shadows of the night. He longed for them to turn back, throwing him a sneer or even a fleeting curse, but there was nothing.

The Steward helped his wife to her feet with the grace and honor he had always seen his parents share. They made their way back into the house arm in arm, closing the door to both the night and the past.

Eni walked back in the darkness. The moon broke through the clouds and it shared enough of its grace for him to navigate. Besides, there was no reason to rush and risk others seeing the wizard's light. It had done enough damage for one night.

To be honest, he preferred it this way. He felt more at home in the shadows, especially after what had happened.

The scene he had witnessed played again in his mind, the sword and his father rising up against him. Was he really the one being deceived? Was he really an agent of the evil one?

Unlike the chirping of the crickets searching for fellowship, he was content in his loneliness. He wandered in the dark wood, silent but for his brushing through the bracken that showered him with its gathering dew. It soon soaked through his clothes. The cool water had saturated his leggings, which he decided to bear as a penance.

Cold and hungry, he walked aimlessly in the wilderness. He wondered if this behavior was evidence of his falling, his taking comfort in the dark rather than the light.

He would have continued in this stupor for an eternity, but for the brightening sky that foretold the coming of dawn. Coming to his senses, the realization that he had no clue where he was caused him to look around. Seeing the lit sky before him and level land of the English countryside, he figured he had wandered mostly to the east and headed north.

He soon found the way; a road set hundreds of years before when Briton was the north edge of the Roman Empire. Its wide stone surface was still intact and was the preferred path for merchants and armies alike. He followed it north with no more thought than a horse being led by the bridle.

By daybreak, the first traveler passed him leading a flock of sheep to the south.

Several more passed, mostly merchants, their carts loaded for the market in some southern town, and a few horsemen over took him heading north when the village of Wigmore came into view.

Eni yawned as he climbed into the hay loft, finding a quiet corner in which to rest until he was beckoned. He questioned if he could sleep with all the thoughts and fears that had powered him that morning. He feared he would see the blade of his father raised against him every time he closed his eyes, but the threat was no match for his exhaustion, and he drifted off quickly, in spite of the comings and goings below him.

22

Midday came much quicker than Eni expected. He could have sworn that he only closed his eyes when the innkeeper sent a boy to let him know his master was ready to depart.

It was a struggle even to stand up due to the low ceiling and the bumps and scratches he had endured from his nocturnal travels. He tossed the bundle over his shoulder and made for the ladder. Maybe it was from not being able to stand straight or the lack of sleep, but he was so unstable that he missed the first rung on the ladder and would have toppled clear down to the stable floor but for the satchel. As he swung onto the ladder, it caught top of the post, leaving him hanging when his foot failed to hit its mark.

More embarrassed than hurt, he recovered to join Murdoc at a table for a meal in the inn. "I cannot remember a better night's rest," the old man crowed as he lapped up the rest of his broth.

Eni had not seen the old man in such spirits since before he was taken by his illness. "It is good to get out from the keep, is it not?" he continued. "The inn boy said it was a struggle to wake you even at midday- I thought it must have been nice not having Ingous wake you at the crack of dawn for a change."

"Aye..." Eni agreed, fighting through a stifled yawn, "but it took a while for sleep to come last night," he answered, smiling ruefully at his truthfulness.

The day was warm and Murdoc was in no rush, having decided that the time spent with the young Marcher Lord extended his lease, though it did not add to his treasury.

For the next fortnight, they made the 'rounds', as Murdoc called it, to the dukes and barons, and even a few wealthy merchants who treated their reception with greater fanfare than the minor royals that they visited.

Eni was quick to note that as they got further from the March, there was a marked improvement in the hospitality of their hosts. Murdoc said nothing of this but would hold his head high and enter through the front gates of these eastern shires.

"The seer of the west" he was called in Birmingham, and there they were treated to a feast in the great hall rather than just being given a basket of food to sustain them on their travels. Most clients offered them a room for the night and were more than happy to pay for the oracle's council when they found a way to put the information to their advantage.

The lords were quick to pick up on Eni's position as the seer's heir and granted him his own room and let him dine with them at the main table. Eni had never eaten so much good food; pheasant, roasts, and pastries. It put to shame anything that Ingous had conjured up.

The time blew by too quickly as far as Eni was concerned. He had no more than settled into the role of councilor than Murdoc informed him it was time to be off again.

"Why do we reside in the March?" he asked as he took up the pack once more for the long trek back to the west. "Here, we are respected; there, we are spit at…"

"Aye, but in the March there is freedom," the old man said, almost longingly. "Mountains to power turbines, hills to deafen the wail of the beast. Here, there is no shortage of lords who demand that you are at their beck and call like a simple peasant."

They walked for some time until the castle was far behind them and the early morning frost dripped away in the low November sun. "But that would never happen, would it? … they treating you like a peasant, I mean," he asked. The idea seemed foreign to him and he wondered if Murdoc was pulling his leg.

"Oh yes, they certainly would… they did, for that matter."

"They did? You mean you used to live here?" Eni asked, his mouth gaping at the mere idea.

138

"No, not me, it was long before my time..."

"You're not the first?" Eni asked, springing up to the side of the wizard, hanging on every step like a young hound on its first hunt.

Murdoc looked at him, surprised by his sudden excitement and lack of protocol. "I am the forth of my kind. I was an apprentice to Alfred the Hermit, who trained under Thomas the Teacher, who was schooled in the art by Harold the Grand Seer. It was Harold who first lived in England but escaped to the March after a local baron demanded fidelity to him alone."

"How long ago?"

"It was five score and five years since he took the books and made for the March," Murdoc answered, still on the move.

"So for one hundred and five years only four men have ever seen the books?"

"Five, with you."

Eni fell silent as he thought about it, wondering what it must have been like to live so long ago.

"It was Thomas who foresaw the coming of the black plague to these shores," Murdoc continued, his labored breathing causing him to slow his pace in order to finish his tale. "It almost cost him his neck, as the Welsh fools figured he caused the calamity rather than was simply warning them about it. Ah, the trials of being a keeper of the book."

"Why not... share it?" Eni said, as much to himself as to Murdoc. "There's so much that could help people. Why keep it to so few for so long?"

The old man said nothing as they walked along, his strides regaining their length as he floated down a small slope.

"Your thought is admirable, but misplaced," he finally said without turning to the lad. "People would not understand it on their own. You yourself thought it was of the devil..." Eni felt his face turn red at the thought of the day up in Murdoc's upper room. "It would be burned the first day by some priest or peasant, thinking they were doing God's will."

"Then there is the practicality of it..." he continued. "How would we get the treasury to do the experiments, to buy the copper, or the iron to build the beast... it all takes coin and plenty of it. No, it must stay in the hands of those knowledgeable enough to use its gifts and wise enough to know when not to."

Though they spoke no more of it, Eni could not peel his mind off the thought of the book. He tried to remember the passages about the cities; of the wonders of the age to come. He wished he had read more when he had the opportunity.

The sun was resting on the ridge south of the mountain when they reached the valley under the wizard's keep. The day had been warm given the time of year, and Eni had packed his cloak away, but on entering the meadow, he felt the first chill since that morning.

Eni knelt to unpack it, knowing his discomfort would only increase with the falling of the sun. Murdoc paid him no heed as he hurried along with renewed energy like a horse smelling the barn when he could see his keep in the distance.

Eni would have caught up to him in a heartbeat but for finding that the fibers of his cloak had been woven into a knot by a burr picked up somewhere on his travels.

He set to work pulling free its tiny hooks, but it broke apart at the first suggestion of freeing its grip on the cloth, leaving scores of the independent burrs embedded in the wool.

He was tossing a pinch of these free loaders to the side when the shrubs behind him suddenly broke apart. It was not that it scared him, per se, but he lost his balance and tumbled into the weeds opposite the path.

He could sense it was large as it broke through the bushes. His mind raced as to what kind of creature it could be as he rolled around to see the unexpected intruder. Wolf, bear ...

Then it laughed, more of a giggle really, and he spun around. The green eyed girl was standing clear of the bushes her hand covering her smile at seeing him sprawled on the ground.

"My pardon, sir," she said with little sincerity. "You won't change me into a frog for my insolence, will you?" Her voice was thick with a

140

Welsh accent.

Eni looked up at her smiling down on him and his wits left him. He struggled to gracefully get to his feet, adding to her merriment. "You're cruel," he said as he straightened up to his full height.

He was taller than her by six inches, but her beauty was more than an equalizer. He figured she must be his age give or take a year or two. She wore a simple wool dress and the smell of sheep soon followed her into the clearing. He looked down at his satin shirt and felt overdressed for the occasion.

"Why is the young Wizard of March alone in the wood?"

"Traveling," he answered. "Stopped to free my cloak from some burrs," he added, picking up the object in question as if merely holding it would provide comfort.

"Ah, that's why it was peaceful for the last fortnight," she said, looking over toward the keep on the far side of the valley. "They said the devil was away..."

"It has nothing to do with the devil. It is a machine, not a creature," Eni said, with immediate regret at his snappishness.

"They mean the wizard," she added with a sudden coldness.

"Oh..." he said with a shudder as if it were a spell, and quickly tossed the cloak on over his head.

"ENI!" Murdoc called from down in the valley, his voice distant but lacking none of his annoyance. Eni blushed.

"I guess you must be off," she said, her smile returning.

"Aye..." he said and turned to go, but hesitated, "What...what name do you go by?"

She looked at him, her green eyes dazzling in the last light of the setting sun. "Dylis," she answered, dropping her eyes to avoid his.

"Hurry up, boy!" The old man called, his voice sounding further away.

"Good day, it was a pleasure to meet you, Dylis," he said hastily before sprinting off in pursuit.

23

The coffee house was getting crowded as more people tried to escape the rain that was taking over the city.

"Of course, I was planning on using a metal frame," the professor continued, talking rapidly about sensors, gauges, pressure indicators, and the rest of the instruments he had planned on including in his experiment. Wendy got lost in the technical jargon but was brought back by his last word.

"Yeah, funding," she repeated.

"Yes, always the funding," the professor agreed, ripping open the wrapping on his biscuit. "Besides, the heat always consumed the Tardis and the costs just multiply when one can't reuse it, so I had to think outside the box, as it were," he said, with a laugh at his little joke.

"I'm sorry, 'Tardis'?"

"You know…" the professor said, losing his smile. "From 'Dr. Who'…? I loved that show. Even though there is no way a small wooden box could have survived the vortex even with shields. I mean come on, it could never produce enough energy for its mass. Still, it's loads of fun."

Wendy was never one to analyze television shows or movies. It took the fun out of them. She was about to say something along that line when the professor interrupted her thoughts.

"So you're a dunker too?"

It took her a moment to catch on and she only did so when he motioned to her biscuit still submerged in her coffee. "Yeah, depends on the type though. Not a fan of chocolate in my coffee."

"Ah, makes the coffee too sweet, doesn't it?"

"Exactly. And I would rather have my chocolate concentrated in the biscuit," she added with a smile. He took a sip and Wendy took the opportunity to get them back on subject. "I still don't see what this has to do with encyclopedias, and/or... more importantly, with my family's heirloom here?"

The professor hesitated, "It will," he said, suddenly serious, "but we have to start at the beginning of all this for it to make any sense to the both of us."

"So what do you propose?"

"Well to start with, how about a name?"

Wendy looked from him to the package, "I...I don't know, that wasn't handed down, only the package."

The professor smiled, "I meant your name. You never told me..."

"Ohh, sorry," she said, with her face slightly pink. "It's Wendy... Wendy Thompson."

"Ah, good. Tell me, Miss Wendy Thompson, when you came here, what suite did you look for?"

"Suite 75, like it said on the bundle."

"And did you find it? Suite 75, I mean."

"No," Wendy answered, but the receptionist greeted me when I walked in so I didn't think about it. I guess it was destroyed in the war or something."

"A plausible answer," the professor nodded. "But this location had a cannery here prior to the war. You see, when we sent out our encyclopedias into the vortex, each was given a different suite number. It was a way of tracking them. We started with suite 1 for our first experiment and ended with suite 250, which was our last."

"So...you are suggesting this package is a result of experiment 75..." Wendy could feel her cynical smile start to erupt and tried to camouflage it with a yawn. "Excuse me," she added with her hand in front of her mouth until she thought she could control it. "So... you are saying that you told my ancestor from who knows how long ago to send this to you now."

"Well, I would have liked it last May, but, yes," the professor answered with little emotion.

Her smile exploded again with no hope of reining it in. "You are off your rocker, you know that, right?"

The professor leaned back in his chair and sighed, but didn't seem to be bothered by the accusation. "So I have been told…more times than I can count. Yesterday…I would have been forced to agree with that assessment, but today," he said, raising his finger in the air as a smile lit up his face, "you came in with this. Today, I'm a bloody genius."

Murdoc put him to work first thing the next morning. He dreaded it and tried to put it off, but since it was a clear morning, the old man made it a priority.

Eni trudged up the hill, winding his way back into the mountain. It had been months since he last visited the concoction and he was not looking forward to the reunion.

Instead of stirring it, this time he had to move the barrels from their tomb. Eni had no idea how he was expected to muscle them through the narrow fissure that formed the mouth to the cave. But once he arrived he found them near empty except for a layer of liquid covering the bottom and a thick sheaf of rotten hay. The stench that had been overpowering before was now little more than an annoyance and the residue sloshed in the bottom as he turned and twisted them toward the opening.

The effort it required still caused him to rest in between trips as the mountain air rushed around him, chilling his mounting sweat.

He was resting from the last of them when Murdoc appeared in the clearing. He was wearing his peasant rags, as he called them, and folded over his shoddily clothed arms lay empty sacks, similar to the ones Abertha had used to store wheat for the winter.

"Aye," Murdoc said, as Eni look from the sacks in the old man's hands to the contents of the barrel.

He groaned, but said nothing more as Murdoc sorted through the bags. He floated one out into the mountain air; it filled and a puff of flour disappeared into the wind. Then, gripping the sack, he held it open next to the closest barrel.

"Agh…" Eni groaned, lifting the rotten mass of grass from the barrel, streams of fluid dripping on his arms. "It has a glaze all over it!"

"Of course," Murdoc answered quietly. "And careful with it…that is the whole purpose of this exercise," he added, adjusting the edge of the sack to fit around the decomposing wad of hay.

Eni looked at his hands; they were green and felt like they were covered in slime with a pinch of sand mixed in. He looked up at Murdoc, "Why?"

"You shall see," he answered, tying the bag tightly and moving it to the side, its bottom already stained by the deep green stew.

Eni was completely covered by the time they moved the fifth sheaf to its new home. The green slime was cold enough as it dripped off his elbows onto the ground, but the thought of having to bathe in the pond in late November sent a shiver, chilling him down to his toes.

"Keep them from dripping on the tile," Murdoc warned as he headed down empty-handed. Eni tied a sack on either end of a wooden yoke. Lifting it onto his shoulders and adjusting it slightly, he headed down the path to the steady cadence of the dripping sacks.

He hung them up in the wooden shed by the wood pile so they could dry and headed back up to bring the rest of them down. He wished he could think of a better way and wondered if the river of electrons could aid him in this work.

Failing to come up with an alternative, he hauled the other three sacks downhill and strung them up to dry before making one last trip up the hill to clean up. Wading into the pond, his breathing almost stopped when he reached his waist. He debated for a moment before diving under the surface scrubbing furiously to remove any remnants of the green stew.

He hurried out, rubbing the water from his skin in an attempt to warm up. *That should do it*, he thought with a satisfied sigh. *Not*

145

another bath until spring.

Over next few weeks Eni returned to the routine chores, with the added work of chopping wood for heat as well as feeding the beast. Murdoc had several villagers deliver logs to the base of the slope. It was the closest any would come to the wizard's fortress with the layer of ice that coated the narrow path.

That left Eni the task of cutting and splitting the logs in the valley and hauling them up the track to the keep.

It took a full day of cutting the logs into workable sizes and the next morning to split the wood so that it would fit either the hearth or the beast's fire box. The impact of the steel ax echoed through the valley that morning as the wood split into pieces. The reverberations even deafened the cajoling of the young urchins from the village who played down the bend, just out of sight.

He took a break to spy on them, but seeing that Dylis was not among them, he was soon back at work. When he decided the pile of wood was large enough or after his hands started to tremor on their own from working the ax, he would take a break and began transporting them up the hill to the shelter behind the keep. It did not take many of these trips for Eni to begin thinking of a better way.

If the beast could run machines in the great hall, he could see no reason it could not be put to work outside as well. Invigorated, Eni set to work gathering ropes that lay scattered in the varied rooms of the keep.

The lengths of rope, once tied together and attached to the turning rod and laced through the pulleys stretched only two thirds of the way down the hill. "Better than carrying it," Eni said to himself as he pulled the empty sleigh up to greet it.

Seeing his plan coming together, he ran back down the hill and began loading the sleigh. Knowing the strength of the beast, he loaded it high till all the cut logs had been stacked and then tied them down lest they fall in their assent to the keep.

He ran so hard up the slope he had to catch his breath before he could think of what to do next. He thought through everything again in his head before he dared to set the beast to this new task.

He shifted the leather strap to the rod. The engagement whined for moment until the strap gripped and held. The rope jumped with a start as the slack disappeared and began wrapping itself up around the rod.

Sweat dripped from his brow in spite of the cold breeze that plucked the taut rope that strung out the open window to the courtyard. From the gear, Eni could see the rope until it twisted around the post on the far end of the courtyard on its course down the narrow path.

The rope wound up the rod forming a thick wad on its midsection as it rotated around. It creaked under the tension. In his mind, he could see it snap and the entire load slide back, falling from edge of the path. He debated stopping it then and there.

It was only then that he realized he had no way of doing so. If he pulled free the leather strap, the weight would pull the rope back off the rod and the load would be free to fall off the mountain. There was no way to lock the rod in one place.

The scene ran through his mind again, the sled falling off the cliff, the logs breaking free of their moorings scattering across the valley floor. Then it hit him, the urchins… that's where they were playing!

He looked around franticly for some device that would wedge the rod. *Murdoc must have something*, he thought. He grabbed the iron poker from the hearth and tried to imagine a way it would serve this task when a movement caused him to glance out the window.

"Praise God," he said under his breath seeing the wood-laden sleigh come into view. He pried the stick under the leather strap, freeing it from is labor. He watched the sled coast to a stop on the level ground in front of the courtyard post.

He thought briefly of rearranging the ropes to have the beast pull the sled the rest of the way, but the scare he'd just had was enough to put the idea to rest. He decided it would be easier to just do it himself, so he untied the bindings that held the load and began stacking logs in his arms for the walk around the keep.

His mind wandered as he followed the same trail cutting through the icy snow. Though he was warm enough to set aside his cloak and carry the freight in his shirt sleeves, the ice somehow overwhelmed the leather of his boots, numbing his toes in spite of the multiple layers of stockings.

He took a break from his labors and aired his frozen feet and damp footwear in the afternoon sun. The melting snow dripped from the shed roof all around him as he reclined back on the rick of wood. It required adjusting a log or two that poked his back uncomfortably, but he was soon drifting off in light sleep.

"Wizard!"

Eni awoke with a start. At first he thought he had imagined it, part of a dream that suddenly felt real.

"Wizard!" It was real, and it came from the courtyard. Eni threw on his stockings and shoes and scampered around his frozen path.

"There!" one of the men called, pointing at him. It was obvious by their weathered wool clothes and Welsh accents that they were from the village.

"Where's your master, lad?" He knew the scowl. He had seen it once before, when he had first laid eyes on Dylis. It was her father. He held a pitch fork in his hand, resting on it like a cane.

He was not alone. Most of the gathered men were armed with scythe, fork or club. Since the Welsh were outlawed from owning a sword or spear due to their last rebellion, it was the peasant equivalent of equipping for battle.

Eni tried to make sense of this gathering. He cleared his throat and tried to claim his right as their better. "What, pray tell, is the reason for your request of my …"

"Tis' not a request lad, it is a demand!"

"Aye!" the rest of the men chorused in a lack of harmony, but with no less enthusiasm.

"I do not understand. Why are you armed such as you are?"

"We have seen the devilry with our own eyes," one answered, nodding at the sleigh still heavily laden.

"Witchcraft, it was!" another yelled, with several grunts of

148

agreement.

"Many of us," one of the men said, motioning among them, "saw the sled climb the hill without a horse or ass. Melkin here even saw the runners slip from the path," he added, pointing to Dylis's father.

"The runners were hanging off the cliff," Melkin agreed. "It was right above the little ones and I saw it sliding off... There's not a beast in God's creation that could have pulled a load like that back up again but there it went up the path like it weighed nothing at all."

"We all heard him cry out and saw it for ourselves," said another.

"Aye, we all saw the devilry... there was no animal pulling the sleigh, yet it ran up the path, pushed by the devil himself."

"No," Eni started to explain and although he knew the seriousness of the situation, he could not keep the smile from breaking across his face. "There was no devil, nor was it a demon or witchcraft. See, the rope..."

"Is this a game to you?" Melkin questioned menacingly, his face red with the fork now leveled waist high.

"He is possessed," another countered as several gathered to seize him.

"No... no, you don't understand," Eni argued backing away. "It is a winching mach..." he tried to say but one of them rushed him and knocked him to the ground.

"Bind his hands," one yelled, as Eni's face plowed into the ice and a knee pinned him in the middle of his back.

A boom like thunder shook the mountain and a gasp rose up from the men. "The wizard!" one of them cried. Eni turned his head to see a black cloud of smoke rise up from a blackened patch of earth several feet away.

"How dare you!" Murdoc raged, his voice deep and menacing as he approached. The men fell back, freeing Eni in their retreat.

Murdoc had candle wick wrapped around his staff, its end glowed faintly in daylight. He pulled a leather ball from the sack that hung from his other shoulder as he spoke. "This is how my generosity is repaid?"

149

He lit the wick that protruded from the leather ball, which sizzled like bacon on the skillet. He looked at it for a moment, and threw it. The ball arced over Eni, who struggled to his feet and landed in front of the villagers who, though retreating, had their weapons bared toward the old man.

The ball hit the ground and bounced unevenly a couple of times before promptly exploding into fire and smoke. Eni fell to the ground as the thunder shook the air around him. When he looked up again, his ears were ringing and a black cloud rose from where the ball had been a moment earlier.

The villagers were no stouter than Eni. A few took refuge behind the crumbled ruins, but most had disappeared down the path. "I took no taxes and gave you freedoms that no other master has given in all the realm, and this is how you repay me?"

"The devilry!" Melkin yelled back, one of the few still standing at the edge of the courtyard.

"You foolish Welsh… You know nothing of the devil but your own ignorance!" Murdoc bellowed as he readied another leather ball. "Be gone, lest I burn your village to the ground for your insolence!"

Eni sat on the frozen earth, looking up as the men slowly withdrew, throwing curses at old Murdoc, who stared after them with his 'fire magic' at the ready lest they countered.

It was only well after the men had departed and he had checked their descent from the cliff that Murdoc looked to his young apprentice. Eni had risen to his feet and stood staring at the blackened earth, watching a wisp of soot that rolled like dust in the wind.

"Creative," Murdoc said, looking at the rope and pulleys that still harnessed the sleigh. "Yes, creative, but it could have been the death of us all the same…"

He plucked the still tight rope. It quivered like a wave down its length with only the knot on the sleigh immune to the motion. Slowly it faded. Murdoc watched it intently until it was perfectly still. Then, as if the sound of his voice alone could cause it to vibrate, he whispered "…and it still may…"

24

With the coming of winter and the shortening of daylight, most of Murdoc's outdoor tasks for Eni came to an end, other than the incessant splitting of wood which remained constant regardless of the season. There were so many logs, each quartered and thrown through the chute and then restacked again along the wall ready to be fed to the beast.

Done for the day, he fished out a splinter that had lodged itself deep in his finger. He was feeling his wound with his other hand, making sure he had got all of it out when an object broke his glazed stupor.

"Treat this with the utmost care..."

Eni looked up to see Murdoc holding out one of the books from his study. The gold-crested 'B' briefly caught the firelight. Eni took hold of it gingerly, opening the volume and brushing its delicate pages with the pads of his fingers.

"Read it and learn. When you have finished, you may move on to another, but if I see this valuable piece of workmanship lying about, I will practice the punishment on page 87. Then you will have learned your lesson."

Needless to say, Murdoc had little more than left the room before Eni shuffled through the pages to find the aforementioned threat.

'Banishment.'

He looked up to see if the old man was watching from the corner, but could see no sign of him. *He is just fooling*, he thought hopefully as he settled in next to the fire.

Eni spent most of the night with this new companion, investigating its words and pictures, but his eyes could not decipher the tiny letters in the flickering firelight for long, so he carried the volume back to the safety of his room.

Given his way, he would have spent every waking hour with it, but the demands of daily living and the requirements Murdoc's chores took precedence.

When the sun fell back to her dark bower and the supper things were put away, he curled up in front of the hearth and partook of a sip of its knowledge. It was mesmerizing, this world that was to come, its cities and countries and even continents that were yet to be discovered. The world seemed so complete the way it was. Sometimes, Eni wondered if the book was really real or if it was only an elaborate minstrel's tale.

"May I ask you something?" he asked one evening as the flame had died away, leaving only red coals to illuminate the room.

Murdoc was snoozing lightly, but he awoke at the sound of Eni's voice. "Of course," he mumbled sleepily.

"It says here that the bubonic plague caused many social changes," he began, flipping back and forth between two pages. "We live in the time of which they speak, yet I don't see these changes."

"Ahh, yes, that is because you are too close to notice them and too young to know the difference," Murdoc answered, sitting up from where he had settled in. "There was a time when peasants were the property of the estate. But since the Black Death, there has been a lack of laborers in all of Europe."

"Even here?"

The old man nodded. "England is no different. A third of the people died, or thereabouts. That means a third of the land can no longer be worked and a third less harvest…"

"And a third less of the profit for the lord…" Eni said answering his own question. "…So then you must make it beneficial to the peasants to stay… or they will leave."

"Aye, they call it economics in the age of the book," Murdoc answered. He always referred to the many volumes as one book. Eni figured it was like the Bible, which also had many books making up one.

Murdoc hesitated and tossed another log onto the coals. "This one is

152

the law of supply and demand. I have found the laws they speak of are quite accurate in this age as they are in their own," he added, watching a flame spring back to life.

"So…" Eni asked, turning to the old man, "that is why you collect no tax on the peasants…only requiring that the villagers fulfill your needs as a landowner?"

"Aye, supply food for our table, wool for our backs. It makes it more desirable to tend their flock on my land than that of my neighbor. Though it would be nice to tax as well, I fear this benefit is needed, given my reputation," Murdoc added. "And that is why we must be more careful. Seeing a horseless sleigh is too much for their feeble minds to comprehend…the foolish Welsh."

Eni dropped his eyes to the book. While he was pleased that it was someone else who was deemed foolish for a change, he felt the blow all the same. It had not yet been three seasons since he had pursued the wizard to resurrect his dead pup. "I probably would have done the same, eh?"

Murdoc looked up and a smile creased his face. "Aye, it's true, but understanding that fact is a true sign of wisdom."

The following days were seasonal, which meant cold to Eni. While it was not uncommon for snow to cover the ground in the early morning, it was not in the habit of staying, and by midday it would melt away even on the higher peaks of the ridge.

Though Eni had been part of the household of the wizard for six months, it was only in the bleakness of winter that he missed his former life. His mother had often entertained relatives. They would come once harvest was complete and share in the season of advent.

Murdoc on the other hand preferred the silence of his chamber more often than not, and other than giving orders or offering direction on a task, Eni saw little of him.

Ingous loved to banter and was quick to offer advice even when he had no need of it, but she spent most of her time working in the kitchen or down in the village. Eni wondered how she managed to live in these two worlds, but it was one of the few areas of conversation she never entered.

He wondered if she had a family there, a husband and children to which she returned each night, breaking bread and passing the cup.

"Breaking bread and passing the cup," he said out loud to the smoldering fire. The volume of "L" had lost its fascination; its words were too cold and passionless, too much like the blowing wind that swirled outside the stone walls.

His mind wandered back to his former life. He wondered how brother Alfonse was getting along. The Brother had been the one person he could always talk with. He wondered what the Brother thought of him now, his being 'in league with the devil' and all.

It was a different life- that could not be doubted- but staring into the fire and looking back over what he had been doing since midsummer's day, he could see little evidence of the devil- only the absence of God.

He wondered how many others in the western world had not partaken of the sacraments for the past six months. Even sailors would make landfall on occasion to attend mass, but here he was in the Welsh March, feeling lost on the sea of logic and reason, with no land in sight.

He longed for the ritual and pomp of the Christmas mass, the spoken Latin and the pageantry of the priests.

He thought of asking Murdoc if he could attend, but he knew the answer. Murdoc had made it clear many times. They were on the outside, and it needed to stay that way.

"Bishops are no different than any other lord," he had said. "If they got hold of the book, they would simply use it for their own gain and glory, because in the end, a bishop is only a prince of Rome, and like all aristocrats, they only care about one thing - their own power."

Eni chuckled to himself as he thought about it. Those words could just as easily have been said by his own father.

25

"The master wishes to see you in his chambers," Ingous announced as she woke Eni from his slumber early one morning. The air was cold and he had no desire to leave the confines of his blankets.

Murdoc's cough had returned the week before and he had not even ventured to the great room for several days. Ingous had brought him his meals, but he failed to eat more than a spoonful.

He looked pale, Eni thought as he slipped through the door. Murdoc was staring out the window into the grey morning and was slow to direct his attention to the lad at the foot of his bed.

"You wished to see me?" Eni finally offered, after standing for some time.

"Oh… yes, what was it again? Um, that's right… the sacks from the cave need to be tended to."

"They are hanging in the …" Eni reminded him.

"Yes, I realize that…" the old man interrupted, his glazed eyes suddenly cold. "But they must be purified, listen clo…" His coughing fit lasted for some time, and when he finally managed to control it, he struggled to finish his thought.

"Break up the stalks," he whispered. "And boil it down with clean water in the hearth until only the crystals remain, but…" he broke off, his voice thickening as if readying for another fit, "…be careful to remove it while it's still damp, because if you let it burn, all will be lost."

Eni didn't say anything given the old man's condition but nodded obediently before heading back down. It did strike him that 'all will be lost' seemed to be Murdoc's favorite saying lately. It flavored everything, from his discussions with dukes and barons, to the lowly green slime that now resided in the dungeon.

After breaking his fast with bread and gravy, he gathered his supplies. First, he fetched water from the stream and brought in wood to strengthen the fire. Then he set to work. The big iron pot was soon boiling and spitting bubbles as Eni freed the dried remains from the sack, crushing and sprinkling the bits and pieces into the simmering broth.

It was not a bad job for early winter, better than spending the day out in the freezing rain that was falling across the March. The warmth of the fire and the light of day made reading easy as he worked his way through the rest of the volume of "L."

The pot simmered away for most of the morning until he fished out the remains of the grass and clumps of green scum that had solidified. As the water steamed away, a layer of white crystals ringed the pot where the water had been.

Ingous had two loaves of bread baking in the corner of the hearth. Their aroma soon overwhelmed his concentration. He spent more time watching her as she shifted them around to keep them from blackening than reading any words.

He quickly set the book aside when she pulled the first one from the hearth. This they ate with a slab of butter, which hardly melted into the pores of the warm bread before he consumed it.

Next to the fire that afternoon, the room felt warm and comfortable, but moisture started to condense on the end wall and on the tools that filled the tables close to it. Fearing they would rust in the humidity, Eni opened the shutters, letting the cold wind swirl in. The swirling air seemed to inspect the goings on in the great room as it weaved, touching, feeling its way like a thief in the dark of night. Its touch was everywhere- Eni had to move closer to the fire to evade its fingers, but in the end, it departed, returning from where it came, taking only the droplets of moisture with it.

The pot hissed as the last of the water percolated through the white residue that layered the bottom. Eni quickly swung the pot from the flames. The iron arm squeaked like an old door hinge as the pot broke free of the hearth and hung out in the room, still hissing away. He tried to go back to his reading, but feared he had waited too long to take the pot from the heat as the water soon bubbled dry. As soon as it had cooled enough for him to tolerate, he set to work scraping the coating from its host.

He gathered enough to fill a small clay jug with the residue. Thinking about the amount of work he put into stirring the barrels, then gathering the slop and cooking it down, it seemed like an awful lot of work for such a frightfully small amount of powder.

Still, maybe that is why he was only the apprentice, he told himself. But still… there had to be a better way. He brought in more water and brought up a sack from the dungeon to start the process over again, first stoking up the fire, then adding the contents of another sack.

The sun was still above the mountain, but Eni wished it would sink faster. The words all blended together on the page, and he found himself turning the page with little knowledge of what he had just finished reading.

"Ye've had enough," Ingous said as she passed by him from one of her many trips up the stairs to Murdoc's chambers. Eni looked up at her with as much interest as he had in the words on the page. "You know what day it is?"

Rising from his stupor, Eni tried to think. "No…" he said. With the activities of the keep and the study of the book, he had lost all contact with days and their role in life outside of the world he lived in. "…Thursday?"

Ingous frowned and shook her head like he was still a wee lad who had misbehaved. "Friday… I just don't know how you can spend so much time looking at those odd dots," she said, pointing to the letters on the page.

"But more importantly, it is Christmas Eve…" she continued as he looked back down at them, "and a brother from the monastery is coming to the village to say Mass this evening. Why don't you come with me? It would do you good."

The vision of last year's Christmas Mass at the Abby filled his mind: hundreds of candles, the choir of monks, the Abbot in his full attire. He could hear the Latin verses even now, like poetry to his ears. Eni sighed. "Aye, it would indeed, but Murdoc…"

"The master is asleep, and in no shape to argue about it… Besides, in his condition he could use a prayer or two, even if he finds no use for them. Not all the world's answers are in that book."

Eni smiled. The open book before him touched on such large array of objects and ideas he wondered if perhaps it really did have them all. "I need to watch the pot," he answered, nodding at the kettle. "He would switch me with a bramble if I let it burn."

She laughed, but watched him carefully. "The whole village will be there…" she added. Eni looked up at her, trying not to show any response, yet he wondered how she knew.

"Most of the men will probably want to draw and quarter me," he said, answering her questioning glance.

"Nah, they are long over that…it just adds another yarn to the wizard's tale. They have many of them from living here in the shadow of the keep."

This was the most he had ever heard Ingous say of the village. "How is it that you can live in both these worlds, being here with Murdoc and yet remaining welcome in the village? I mean, I'm not even welcomed in my own…" his voice trailed off as his emotions got the better of him.

She stared at him, wordless, as if she was ready to join him in having a good cry, but then she smiled. "It's not as bad as all that…"

He turned to stir the pot, sinking the mat of grass that had floated on the top like a lily pad. "We'll see…" he answered, staring into the flames.

"That is fine, my dear, I…I just want you to know that you would be welcomed."

He heard her walk away, but he stared at the fire, wondering if it could be true, wondering if it was possible, wondering if there was a way he could live in both worlds.

26

He lost count how many times he changed his mind as he sat there checking the steaming pot that never seemed to boil down. *The fire will go out before it will have a chance to burn*, he kept telling himself.

He wasn't sure what put him over the edge, the hope of seeing Dylis or the fear that this was all there would be to his life. Maybe he just needed to find out if there was any hope of having a normal life. He looked around at the empty keep: the tools, the equipment, the book, but that was all there was. *There has to be more*, he thought, reaching out to the fire from habit more than the need for warmth. *Something ... more*.

After checking the pot one more time, he raced up the narrow stairs to his room where he put on his cloak, then quietly ascended the stairs to Murdoc's chamber.

The door was ajar so he slipped in. Hearing the familiar breathing of the sleeping old man, he made his way to the nook.

Not wishing to risk waking him with the light, he felt around, opening the cabinets and patting in drawers until he found what he was looking for stacked in a crate under the desk. Grabbing hold of them, he held them out, as if weighing them there in the darkness to make sure he had what he wanted. Satisfied, he slipped two of them into the pocket of his cloak and left as quietly as he came.

The wind bit as he made his way out into the night. The clouds smeared across the moon as they raced by. He considered bringing a torch to light his path but thought better of it.

The track was still free of ice from the heat of the day and the clouds were in too much of hurry to leave such a gift. But he knew the mountain well enough by now to know that even in such conditions it was not uncommon to find a stray patch of ice that had survived the warmth of the day in the shadows or a shallow depression.

He picked his path carefully, making sure of his step before trusting all his weight to it. He wondered how Ingous managed to make the trip so easily. She was up and down the mountain several times a day. If a woman of her age could make it on such a routine, perhaps he was being overly cautious.

Try as he might to be more cavalier in his decent, he would soon find himself back to prodding his foot at the questionable spots that glistened suddenly in the random patterns of moonlight.

The village was dark but for the small church that lay at the center. It was far from the quality of the Abbey or even of the church at Knighton. Its roof was low pitched, and it looked more like a cattle-shed than the house of God.

He could see several people hurrying along toward the building and quickly covered his head with the hood of his cloak as he joined their caravan, hoping to enter unnoticed.

The small church was lit by two sets of candles on either side of the pulpit. The seats, logs split and supported by blocks underneath to form long benches, were filled by both villagers and freemen who resided close by. Eni stayed in back and slid off to one side where he could be hidden in the deeper shadows.

Uneasiness stirred in the pit of his stomach. He watched each individual who entered, measuring those who filled the open seats near him, though most gave him no notice, except a dip of their head in greeting.

This welcome did little to put his mind at ease, though. Most of those who gathered were there with little ones toward the front, down-right excited with anticipation. A high day of celebration was an escape from the drudgery of daily life, none more so than the day of welcoming the new-born King. He remembered the feeling.

Why had he lost it? The idea had no more than entered his mind when a cold chill froze the thought. What if he no longer belonged here? What if God no longer had a use for him? What if he really did

160

belong to the devil now?

The air suddenly felt hot as a few more stragglers jostled into the crowded church. Eni swallowed hard. He would make a scene if he left now so he tried to blend in with the gathering country folk as he lowered his cowl, hiding his features from the light.

"Welcome and Merry Christmas..." the Brother greeted them in English. This alone caught Eni's attention. He had never heard the mass begin in the common tongue. But the voice sounded so familiar that he looked up to see.

He knew him at once, and his reaction must have been obvious since the Brother stared into the corner. "Ahh, my dear friend, come, come! I have missed you so..." Brother Alfonse called out, staring right at him.

Eni was dumbfounded. He stood there looking open-mouthed as the sea of heads opened before him leaving him no choice but to be pushed toward the open arms of the Brother.

"Eni... dear Eni, how I have missed you..." Brother Alfonse whispered as he embraced his former student. "Join these fine folk," he said, offering a place on the front bench.

In the past Eni would have been flattered, not to mention embarrassed, if the Brother had offered to him a place of honor. But the emotions that coursed through him now held none of those traits. It was fear mixed with confusion.

He took his seat, only to feel the strong hand of Ingous pat his knee as she joined him on the bench, and he returned her welcoming smile.

On the other side of him was Dylis with her family. She wore the same simple wool dress, but her eyes were as intoxicating as ever. Her father, who sat beside her, nodded a reluctant greeting, though his eyes held none of the magic of his daughter's.

"Gloria in excelsis Deo... (Glory to God in the highest)," the Brother began. Eni mumbled the words with the rest of the gathering, his mind racing. There were too many questions that confused him as he watched the Brother perform the rituals.

He was so lost in his own thoughts that he almost missed when the

161

Brother veered from the typical Christmas message.

"Extra Ecclesiam Nulla Salus (Outside the Church there is no salvation)," the Brother quoted with emphasis to the gathering, but then slid a glance toward Eni. "Christus ab omni malo plebem suam defedat (Christ defends his people against every evil)!"

The villagers nodded in agreement at each of the Brother's words, though Eni was sure that no one else sitting there understood their context and meaning. He wondered if he should take them as a threat, if he was the evil the Brother spoke of. But if he was, the Brother hid the fact with a smile and the heart-felt joy of one proclaiming the Good News.

There was no fire in the building but for the candles that bathed the front and the few that lined the center aisle, yet Eni felt sweat collect on his brow all the same.

Looking around, he found he was alone in his discomfort. Even Dylis glowed as she watched the Brother pronouncing his Latin with more relish and flair than Eni would have thought possible a year ago.

As the Brother reached the closing "Deus Vobiscum (The Lord be with you)," the community responded, "And with thy spirit." Eni sighed in relief and looked back, hoping to escape as quickly as possible, but the aisle filled and Brother Alfonse was at his side when he turned back, tripping over his feet as he did so.

"How did I do?" he asked, helping Eni to his feet.

"You were wonderful, Brother," Ingous interjected as she joined them.

"Eni?"

"Oh, it was interesting... I never knew some of those were in the Christmas litany," he answered honestly.

"Yes, well..."

"Don't let me keep you from greeting your parishioners," Eni interrupted, seeing Dylis and her father working their way to the rear.

"Normally, yes, of course..." Brother Alfonse started, with a smile for one of the older women who passed him. "...but how often do I get to see my old friend and pupil?"

"Yes, yes of course, Eni," Ingous agreed. "You must spend time with your teacher," she added with a pat on his back.

"Eni, are you not happy to see me?" The Brother asked, as if injured by the boy's reluctance.

"No… it's not that, I just, well… I have responsibilities that require my attention."

"Ahh," the Brother nodded knowingly. "That is something we need to discuss. Come, let us sit for a spell," he said, offering a bench to the two of them.

Eni could not see why Ingous had been included, but she sat next to him, her arm around him like a nun to an orphan as the Brother drew the front bench close.

The Brother hesitated and looked at Eni for a moment before he started. "How long have we been friends?" he said with a smile, but to Eni it seemed forced as the Brother held it for his response.

"Since I was lad of eight."

"Ah, you have been together a long time then," Ingous chimed in. "Seven or eight years, that is a long time to be mentored."

"Aye," the Brother added, "and we had good times, did we not, Eni?"

Eni felt the gnawing in his stomach grow, even as the last few parishioners carried their conversations outside, leaving them alone.

"I do not wish to be rude," he finally said when he could no longer stand it. "But I do need to get back to my duties, so please say what you need to say."

The Brother shot a glance to Ingous who sighed and pulled her hand back from his shoulder.

"Very well," the Brother said, dropping any pretense. "I see you are no longer a child, so I will not treat you like one." His eyes were now cold and distant, harsher than Eni had ever seen them before. "Ingous has informed us that the wizard is not long for this world."

Eni turned to look at the woman he thought of as a friend, "You are an informant?"

She shirked away slightly before fortifying herself. "Aye," she said with sudden courage. "That is how one lives in both worlds."

"We know of the Wizard's books," the Brother continued. "We know they contain the wizard's black magic..."

"There is no such thing as magic!" Eni countered.

"Then you are already deceived..." The Brother's face had turned red, but he quickly recovered. "But for the sake of argument, let us say you are correct and that these books are of some benefit..." he motioned with his hands as if doing a blessing. "Would it not be better if they were in the hands of the lord Bishop of Hereford, Ut In Omnibus Glorificeur Deus (That God may be glorified in all things)?"

"Quite right Brother, the Bishop would be the perfect one to hold on to the books," Ingous agreed.

The often spoken words of Murdoc suddenly made sense to him, "The princes of Rome are the same as the lords of the land. They all want power."

There was silence as Eni pondered what to say. The longer he waited, the more he could feel the smirk grow across their faces. Suddenly he sprang to his feet, "So the Bishop would be in patibus infidelium (among the infidels)?"

"No!" the Brother answered, as if it had been directed at him. "The lord Bishop would see if they are evil, or if perhaps you were right, and they could be used to further the kingdom of God."

"Oh I see," Eni remarked, growing faintly red himself, "and the lord Bishop would never use the books to further his own kingdom! After all, he has enough wine and women already, doesn't he?"

"How dare you! I have come to save thy soul and you mock the lord Bishop who in his goodness allowed me to teach you the knowledge of the written word. And this is how you thank us?"

Eni could not argue this. It was the Brother who had taught him. He could not imagine what his world would be like if he had not received this gift of letters. "I thought you were one of the good ones..." Eni said after a moment. "While the rest of the boys mocked the priesthood as conniving womanizers, I thought you were different – I thought you were a true man of God. I see now, I was wrong," and he turned to go.

"Men!" the Brother called out, and two of the villagers appeared from behind the post and took their positions at the end of the aisle. "Deus Vult (God wills it)," the Brother said, quoting the motto of the Crusades. Eni stopped, seeing that each man was armed with a wooden club. His mind was blank until the pocket of his cloak continued to swing forward with the momentum. "So, you stoop to violence in the house of God?"

"The choice is yours, Eni. Give the Bishop what he wants and you will be welcomed back into the arms of the church."

Taking a step forward, he stared into one of the candles that lined the aisle. Then turning from the men and back to the Brother, he answered, "Deus non Inridetur (God is not mocked)," and pulled a leather ball from his cloak pocket.

In an instant the candle lit the fuse. He watched it burn for a moment than tossed it at the men who dove under the benches as it hit the floor. It rolled for a moment into the darkness before being consumed by a roll of thunder and a flash of light.

By the time they had made their way through the smoke and litter of toppled benches, the boy was gone. They all ran out after him into the night, but the chaos that filled the church was foreign to the village where all was quiet and peaceful on Christmas Eve.

The Brother ran to the base of the mountain path, but he knew the lad was already halfway up to the safety of the wizard's keep. He looked for any sign of the boy, but seeing none, he called out blindly into the night, "If not for God… then for whose glory? Tell me that, Eni!"

There was no answer from the mountain, but the words did not go unheard. High above on the narrow track, a lad was picking his path up the slope. He stopped at the Brother's words, and although he thought about answering, he didn't know what to say. But the Brother's words brought up a question that haunted Eni the rest of the night. *Am I any different than the Bishop?*

27

The rain had let up and after finishing their coffee, they decided to head back to his office. The sky was still in turmoil and gave them doubt as to whether they would make it back unscathed. For her part, Wendy felt a similar turmoil. Sharing a cup with a man she had little regard for just a half-hour earlier had taken effect. But still, there were so many questions.

How did the professor's name get on there, and the address, for that matter? There really was no good explanation for it. It could be part of an elaborate ruse, but he didn't seem the type, and besides, how? She had known this package since she was little. Perhaps, she reasoned, he's not such a nutter after all.

Taking advantage of Wendy's silence, the professor continued his story. "… Since we were lacking funding, we improvised. That's where the encyclopedias come in. We could pick up complete sets for next to nothing at rummage sales. We would package them in the same way each time, keeping the bindings toward the center (less damage, we hoped), and then stacked them using the same method."

He smiled to himself and continued. "Our plan was that by using this process, when they came back, we could study the impact of the vortex by measuring the destruction down to the letter on a given page…"

"But you never got any back?"

The professor shook his head. "Nothing but the occasional burnt embers on the other side. I had such high hopes. We would send them out and expect to get a post that day since we noted the return date to the day we sent it out. But nothing ever came…"

The rain broke and forced them to a run the last one hundred meters, hoping to avoid getting soaked. Their giggles of success were drowned out by the cicada's buzz as they paused inside the door. "Made it," Wendy cheered, as she checked her clothes for damages. She was speckled but they were wide-spread and failed to make it through to her skin, so she considered it a victory given the circumstance.

She followed him back to his office. He took up his chair and Wendy took the one opposite and placed the package down on his desk between them. The professor looked at the address again, "Suite 75..." and turned to his computer that occupied the corner of the desk facing the door.

Wendy looked on in silence as he made his way through the various screens and prompts, "Ah, here it is," he said, after what seemed like minutes. "Number 75 -dialed in to 65.395 x 101.873 at 2.57 gigawatts. Estimated retrieval time 1,325 days. Result was -unusual bright flame total lack of any residual matter including airborne particles- aka smoke."

The professor stared at the screen for a bit before he turned back to Wendy. He flashed a smile but it lacked the sparkle he had at the coffee shop. She thought maybe it was just his office, drab walls, industrial lighting. It would be enough to put her in a bad mood, but then he turned and he stared at the package, cold and unforgiving. "So shall we see what damage has been done?"

The professor picked up the letter opener and the tweezers and hovered over the package.

"I don't get it," Wendy interrupted.

"What?"

"You. I don't get you. If this is the answer to your dreams, your life's work, why do you look like someone just died?"

The professor dropped his hand back to the desk. "We were hoping to go a year or two back in the time vortex. Five years would have been amazing. Ten years, unbelievable."

"So you went several hundred. Even better, right?"

"No...no, no," he said, shaking his head. He thought for moment for the best way to explain it. "You see, I calculated that the most we

167

could get in this experiment was 1,325 days which is like… three years and seven months, more or less."

"Well, we know you beat that since I've known about it since I was ten. So thirteen years at least…."

"Yeah, that's the problem."

"How?"

"We used encyclopedias published in the 1980's because, A, they were cheap and B, all the data was old. No harm in going back ten years with thirty-year-old books."

"Oh," Wendy answered, her expression leaving little doubt that she knew where the professor was going with this.

The professor sighed. "Exactly. No telling the effects of sending a stack of thirty-year-old books of facts hundreds of years back… You studied History. You know the damage people have done with far lesser weapons. Now imagine the results of sending all the knowledge of the future back in time. Who knows? We could be living in a different world because of this. And it's all… it's all my fault."

There was no rousing knock on Eni's door the next morning, nor was there any fire in the hearth once he made his way to the great hall. This didn't surprise him, considering how the night had unfolded.

He decided to start his day with eggs and what remained of the bread that Ingous had baked the day before. But the rope that ran through the ceiling chimed the copper bell that hung high on the wall before he had even set a fire.

Sprinting up the stairs, he could still hear the bell calling out behind him. Walking into Murdoc's chamber, the wizard, white and frail, looked up at him, his hand still wrapped around the rope.

"Where is the woman?" he asked, his voice matching his fragile appearance.

Eni sighed. "She is not here," he answered, wondering how he was to explain this development. The old man stared across the room as if his mind could not accept this information.

"I will take care of you though, sir," he said, hoping to answer the blankness of his stare.

Murdoc looked up at him as if he didn't understand, until he mumbled, "Did she get anything?"

"Um, no... no I do not think so," he answered, unsure how the wizard knew, or how much he should include.

"The nook had been disturbed," he added, too weak to even nod or point in its direction.

Eni looked down at the floor, "That was me..."

"You?"

"Aye, I went to the Christmas Mass last night," he admitted. "But I did not feel right about it, so I took your leather balls, just in case."

Murdoc relaxed, "And..."

"Ingous is a spy for the Bishop of Hereford. She and Brother Alfonse, my teacher in Knighton, were both there. They said you were dying and I should hand over the books to the Bishop."

"And what did you say?"

Eni shrugged, "I used the leather ball to escape."

"They were right, you know. I am dying." Eni looked at him, shocked by the admission, but then nodded. "In the age of the book, they call it cancer of the lungs – not that it matters, but my time is short and you have much to learn."

"So you knew... about Ingous?"

"Aye, that is why I locked the door to my chamber once I recovered last time... and only let you have one book at a time, lest she steal away with them."

"How did you know?"

He gave only the hint of a shrug. "She was too willing to serve, given her people."

Eni shook his head, "I never saw it."

Murdoc's face creased into a smile, "You did. You took one of those, after all," he said, casting his eyes to the nook. "You were just not ready to admit it. You see the best in people."

Murdoc inspected his midsection as it gave an audible groan. "I have not eaten since... I cannot even say when. Go find us something to eat."

The day did not go as planned. With the loss of a housekeeper, Eni was suddenly making meals, caring for Murdoc, and trying to finish his project of cooking down the barrel crystals.

Murdoc was having one of his better days and was more talkative than Eni had seen him for a fortnight. He was not sure if it was that his illness had abated for the day, or that he no longer had to fear Ingous spying on him, but whatever the reason, his trepidations were now gone.

The barrel crystals, Eni's own name for the white powder, were known in the age of the book as Salt Petre. While this information was appreciated, Eni was less than interested in its production, but that failed to stop the old man in telling him about it.

"Urine, lots of urine," Murdoc explained, rather more brightly than Eni thought he should, given the topic. "It took weeks of storing it in that vase there before I had enough," he said, motioning to a large urn in the front corner of the room.

"Matter of fact, I've had that woman empty my chamber pot into it since my illness- you could probably start another batch..."

The urn looked heavy, and Eni could only imagine trying to take it down the winding stairs without having most of it splash all over himself. "Does it have a purpose?" he asked, questioning the worth of such a task.

Murdoc smiled, unfinished food still littering the plate, "Ah the foolishness of youth..."

"...Nay," Eni countered, defending himself half-jokingly. "I just wish to know the value of a task before attempting blindly to repeat it."

"Very well, I will not argue against such logic," the old man responded. "But let this tale unfold naturally, rather than hearing the ending first."

170

Eni had planned to set the latest batch of this salt petre stew on the hearth that morning but seeing his master in such a mood, he quickly decided there was no harm in letting it wait a little longer.

"Once enough urine has been collected and allowed to age, it is poured into the barrels filled with straw. My discovery was to stir the barrels monthly and thus increase the crystal production."

Though he was all too familiar with the stirring of the barrels, Eni did find it interesting to know the reason why. "So where do the crystals come from... the devil?" he added with a smile.

"Aye, the Welsh would think so, but they call it chemistry in the age of the book. One of the ingredients of the urine bonds to the decaying grass and together they form crystals. My understanding is that it works much the same way as baking bread or even cooking an egg."

So I cook it down to get the crystals..." Eni added, trying to move the tale along.

"The crystals will need to dry out the rest of the way in the sun and then be mixed with sulfur and charcoal- which of course you have been making; it seems to have a better pop than the common lot from a merchant."

The wizard talked about this creation like he had taken an elixir for his health, especially compared to the last few days during which he rarely awoke from his stupor.

"The best is to mix the three together: one part sulfur, two parts charcoal, and six parts salt petre. Mix them together with a little water and dry in larger clumps. It's very good," Murdoc said smiling broadly.

"And what is it?"

"They call it gunpowder in the age of the book."

Eni said the word, wondering what it could mean, "gunpowder... you don't eat it, do you?"

Murdoc sighed. It looked as if his illness had abruptly gained ground. "You used it last night..."

Eni thought for a moment, reliving his adventure when suddenly his eyes widened. "The leather balls."

The old man nodded, "They are called grenades in the age of the book, but gunpowder can do more than make a cloud of fire and thunder," he said, then pointed to his walking stick.

"What?"

"Try it," the old man insisted.

Eni walked over and picked it up. "It is heavy," he said, looking at the long pole. It was wrapped from end to end in tight gauze like a bandage but was black as if dipped in pitch. The end had a sheepskin cover tied on tight with a leather cord.

"Aye," Murdoc nodded. "That is because it is not a stick at all. There is no wood, but metal, thin sheets of brass wrapped and bound over and over, layers and layers. Inside at the center is a slender tube, the same diameter all the way through to the bottom, where a small hole is drilled to the center." Eni inspected the walking stick with new respect.

"Then," Murdoc tried to continue, but a cough took hold and he had to take a moment to catch his breath. "You place a small portion of gunpowder at the base," he finally gained the strength to say. "Not more than a couple thimbles full, then stump it down with wool and lead beads.

"What is it for?"

"Defense."

Eni looked at the old man and at the stick still in his hands. He tried to swing it like a sword and then jabbed it like a halberd. "I do not understand…" he finally said, after exhausting his ideas.

"Fire," Murdoc said, plainly too tired to make the lad discover it on his own.

"Oh…" Eni looked again at the stick, trying to see how fire would work with such an instrument.

"Put a wick in the hole at the base to ignite the powder..."

"…And then you throw it?"

Murdoc sighed, he was looking whiter now and his cheeks were hollow. "The powder explodes but there is no escape except through the other end…"

"Oh… but what about the wool and lead beads… Oh, they go with

172

it, right?"

"Aye," the old man answered with an exhausted sigh, but sounded relieved. "It could drop a horse and rider at ten paces, but not much further I expect."

"Fascinating," Eni said, holding the stick aloft like he was expecting a charge at any moment.

"Plant it in the ground if you can. Gives a nasty kick," Murdoc added in not much more than a whisper. "I need to rest... but look under the urn before you go."

Eni went to the large clay vessel and rolled it on the bottom's edge from its spot, its liquid center sloshing back and forth.

There, an iron key, still rough from its casting, was nested in between two floor boards. "It is to the rest of the book, and all my other belongings in that trunk," he nodded to the foot of the bed. "Now that the woman is gone, you might as well have it all. They can do nothing for me."

Eni felt that he should argue with him, tell him to chipper up, or that he would search for a cure, but the old man was already asleep by the time he picked up the key and rolled the urn back to its place. He slipped the key into his pocket and with the walking stick in hand he headed down, more than ready to break his fast.

28

The respite for Murdoc was short lived; his illness set in deeply. Though Eni and the old man would talk, it was less frequent. He would sleep for long stretches and then awake in coughing fits that lasted until blood would come. The whole activity wore him out so that he would soon fall right back to sleep again.

The wooden chest, large and square, had hinges on the inside that squeaked like a mouse as it opened. But instead of finding the books, Eni found a plank of wood guarding the entry like a hatch through a floor.

A row of pegs lined up along the front edge of the wooden plank, each with Arabic numerals above it. The Brother had covered their meanings in his studies, but they were seldom used in regular life and were not highly regarded in the countryside which used only Roman numerals in their counting.

"They will never last," the Brother had said in regard to the ten figures used in the Arabic numbers. "They come from those Muslims, not mother Rome…" Eni had readily agreed, but since he moved here, he realized that Murdoc used only the Arabic numbers and that they were the only ones used in the age of the book.

Over the body of the hatch, he found written in earthy paint with a large English script:

> All will be destroyed,
> lest ye answer rightly
> the year it came among us

The words, black and ominous, caused him to freeze as he

wondered what 'all would be destroyed' meant exactly. He felt the pegs with his fingers. They were firm and solid as they ran through the plank. *The year it came among us?*

He closed the lid, but stopped short of locking it. He could only imagine the effect the message would have on a commoner if they were to burgle the wizard's treasury. It certainly had an effect on him. *The year it came among us.* He had an idea when that was, but the words "… all will be destroyed…" still caused him to hesitate.

It could have been an idle threat, but he knew Murdoc well enough to know the old man would never let the book fall into the hands of any lord of Rome or the realm.

He went back to his chores and hoped the master would rouse enough to verify his answer. He split the day's share of firewood, stacking it under the lean-to in order to limit the dampness.

Coming back in, he warmed himself by the fire until he could no longer stand his curiosity. He raced up the stairs and flipped up the lid, exposing the warning.

He reached for the first peg with the number '1', and tried to twist it, but it held fast. He then pushed it down, till the peg bottomed out level with the board, making a satisfying click.

He hesitated, but nothing else happened, so he pushed the third peg. It was tight, but it slid down and produced the same clicking noise once completed.

He followed the row across and was about to reach for the '0' peg when he stopped. There were eleven pegs in all, and the last peg had '00' painted above it. He had never seen such an inscription before, but the more he thought about it, the more it made sense. "There is only one zero peg…" he said out loud and then gripped the last peg "…And I need two."

The double '0' did not slide smoothly like the other two; he saw movement on the panel and for an instant he panicked. Pulling his hand from the peg, he jumped back, waiting to see what devilry he had set in motion.

The chest was still, so he reached again, only to see his hand quaking in its approach. Placing his palm over the '00' peg, he pushed.

The block of wood that was inset into the panel rose up from its grave as the peg descended. It was only after it clicked that he realized the block had its underside chiseled away to form a handle.

Eni sighed in relief and a smile marked his face as he reached for the handle and pulled up on it. It was heavier than he expected and he gripped it with his other hand, lifting until it showed its treasures.

Dangling from the open lid, several leather balls hung from their fuses. Each fuse ran to the base of the pegs where Murdoc had installed one of his friction matches, a mix of phosphorous and sulfur. "All will be destroyed..." Eni repeated, looking at the impressive amount of forethought and design Murdoc had put into protecting the book.

The chest held not only the volumes of the book, but also piles of notes made on stretched lamb skins and a hefty pouch of gold coins.

The next few days, after bringing Murdoc food- which was mostly uneaten- Eni would spend much of his time with the book. Sitting in the Great hall in the glow of the fire, he would have several of the volumes open before him on the table. He would jump from volume to volume, researching topics that caught his attention, only taking breaks to eat or inspect the final cooking of the salt petre.

He had gained confidence in dealing with the mixture but would still pull it from the heat long before they were soggy crystals, preferring instead to let the kettle dry slowly at the edge of the hearth.

The days moved slowly, but he soon began to exhaust the provisions of the keep. There was still plenty of salted pork, but the more perishable items such as bread had been finished off.

'The woman', as Murdoc now referred to her, had always kept the pantry full, along with her other multitude of duties, most which had slid into oblivion since she left.

His shirt was producing a powerful odor, but he had not yet brought himself to the point of laundering it. There were washerwomen for that; he just was unsure how to obtain one's services when he was in the employ of the wizard.

176

He wondered what type of reception he would receive in the village. He had no doubt it would be bad; after all, he had lit a leather ball and exploded it in their church, not to mention Ingous was there. She may have them worked up to the point that they would bear arms if he tried to pass through.

In the age of the book they had machines that laundered clothes. He thought that it might be a worthwhile project if he could find no one for the task.

Bread, on the other hand, was in the book and although it could hardly be called such when compared to Ingous's, it did rise and bake on the edge of the hearth.

There was little difference, he discovered after consulting the book, between the art of baking and the supposed higher call of chemistry. When one was hungry there was little argument which dog carried the day.

"Tell the woman I want her to make biscuits with butter," Murdoc ordered one day. Eni tried to explain, but the whole episode of her betrayal had been lost to Murdoc. He ate little and could no longer leave his bed or sit up without exhausting himself.

"I will tell her to do better," Eni would oblige, but he had no idea how she had created her delicacies, and their store of butter had been empty for some time now.

He did share Murdoc's desire for butter though, and, truth be told, he was tired of being in the keep. He had not been out since Christmas Eve and their stores needed to be replenished. Taking a small purse of coins, he locked up the chest and scribbled a note for Murdoc on the slate in the event that he should wake.

Dressed in his work clothes, he bolted the front door and slipped out through the wood chute, padlocking the gate with the same key from the chest upstairs. Armed with both Murdoc's walking stick and several leather balls, he headed down the path to the village below. He looked back, hoping he was not forgetting anything.

Once in the valley, he headed southeast and away from Knighton. A path curved around the mountain, winding over rock outcrops that had weathered for a millennium in the March.

He felt odd walking with the wizard's staff, planting it with every stride. In one way he felt powerful, knowing what lay seeded in the belly of the shaft. But it also made him feel like an interloper, holding authority he had little right to possess.

The rolling hills of the March gave way to the level farmlands, and the exposed rock into the rich earth of eastern England. The wind raced past him, in a far greater hurry than he that morning. Soon the path meandered across a road. It was little more than a two track, rutted from carts cutting through the frosty shell of mud. Staying off to the shoulder, Eni fell in line with the other travelers making the journey east.

The walk was uneventful. The town was large enough that he melted into the crowd that migrated around the square. He ate at the public house and purchased a crock of butter in the market from an old woman who thanked him with a toothless smile.

He enjoyed sitting where he wished, unnoticed and unheralded by both villagers and merchants alike. He paid for his goods and was off by noon for the walk home.

Grey clouds racing north in the overcast sky added little cheer to the already drab winter landscape, and the wind that had passed him on his walk over, now bit his hands and face on his trip home.

He tied the crock of butter to the staff much like he had seen Murdoc do with his cooper pots that day in the spring. But the crock just dangled behind him near the center of his back, as he did not dare risk damaging its contents on the ground.

It was not until he passed the open arms of the mountain that he escaped the wind's assault. Seeking the warmth of the fire, he gave little attention to the village until he heard someone call his name.

He turned with a start to see that Dylis was running toward him. She was alone but he dropped the crock with a thud as he readied the staff in the manner Murdoc had instructed.

Her eyes had lost none of their magic, he realized, and she smiled upon reaching him, "my lord..." she said, trying to catch her breath, "there is someone to see you."

"Me?" he said, gesturing with his hand, "Don't you mean Murdoc?"

"No, my lord," she said again, playfully. "He asked for Eni of Knighton. That *is* you, is it not?"

"It used to be…" his voice carried none of her merriment.

"He is a Welsh lad…" she said, "…with red hair." Eni stood there looking at her, not knowing what to do. "He said you were friends," she added, as if that would explain everything.

Her eyes made him want to smile, to take her hand and follow her that instant and greet the one friend he had on this earth. But he stood there, looking at the most beautiful face in the March, stone-faced.

After all, stories of sirens and temptresses reach back to the Greeks and the Proverbs… He wanted to believe her, he wanted to have faith that Clum was still his friend. But after Ingous and Brother Alfonse… He could not shake the thought, *this has the makings of a perfect trap.*

29

Eni was not quick to join Dylis. He first delivered his purchase to the keep and checked on Murdoc who was once again asleep. The slate lay face down at the head of the bed, so he knew that Murdoc had been awake and had read his note.

It was only after latching a knife to his belt and lighting a long smoldering match that he made his way back down the path to the waiting girl.

Dylis sat upon a bolder that had long ago fallen from a much loftier position on the mountain. She eyed him in his descent. The magical smile was no longer there but had been replaced by a cold hard stare. "What is this?"

"What?" he asked, stopping short on the path.

"You look like him, dressed for battle rather than meeting a friend."

Eni looked down at his clothes. He did not think he looked much different than when he went up. "I fail to see how."

"You are armed and you carry the wizard's fire. I thought this was your friend we are about to see."

Eni followed her gaze to the curling smoke that rose from the burning wick lashed around the top of his staff. It reminded him of looking down at village from the courtyard, but rather than offering heat and warmth, its tiny chimney was seen as threat of the wizard's power.

"I don't know who my friends are anymore," he said blankly, and continued down the path to the valley floor.

"Follow me," she said, jumping from the rock and taking the lead. She led him around the village. Given the open meadow, they were easily visible from the huts, but they could also see that no one gave chase as they turned towards the north. Her pace was quick. She kept one step ahead of him with not so much as a word or glance in his direction.

They passed over the knoll from where he first set sight on the village that mid-summer's day. Dylis slowed from her frantic gait as they entered a swatch of trees, but even so, her lead increased as Eni looked about the forest, wondering what might lie hidden behind the trunks and boughs of the forest.

He was so intent on this search that he failed to see the most apparent attack until it was too late. Dylis had turned back and stormed toward him, her eyes bearing more fire than even the belly of the beast could handle.

He stumbled back and reached for his knife, but her attack landed before he could mount a defense. Her crossed arms hit him square as her protruding elbows struck his shoulders like a ram, sending him toppling to the ground before her.

"You don't trust me?" she demanded. Her hands were on her hips as if he were a wayward child. This was no lady of an English court who politely greeted him with a curtsy and a giggle. This was a Welsh lass of the March, he was painfully reminded, as she gave a quick kick to his shin when he tried to right himself before she had finished with him, "Do you?"

Eni looked up at her, stunned, confused, and slightly scared. It seemed like forever before he could finally speak, and when he did, his voice was weak, making him feel more like a lost lamb than a wizard, "I don't know… should I?"

In an instant, her magic returned. "Eni of Knighton, I will never deceive you. This I swear," she said, and held out her hand.

Maybe it was her touch or a spell, but somehow, he knew. He knew he could trust her. He would have liked to hold on to her hand, but she pulled free, leading him onward through the thickening wood.

Following her through the branches of the underbrush, a voice whispered from the corner of his mind, *She is a siren of the woods leading you to your doom. Run, fool, before is all is lost.* He fought the

181

doubt, but even so, how could he know for sure?

"This friend of yours, is he a bit timid?" Dylis asked after traveling in silence for a distance.

"Aye, it must have taken an awful lot to get him to come," he said as they came to a clearing dominated by a large rock outcropping. The ragged stone angled skyward as if a giant had stepped on it awkwardly, leaving it unsettled.

"This where I left him," she said, looking about the clearing.

"Clum…" Eni called out.

There was no answer, but for the call of a rook somewhere in the woods beyond. "He was sitting right here," Dylis said, pointing in answer to his sideways glance. She led him all around the ancient stone, but it showed no evidence of a recent guest.

Looking over her shoulder, he began to wonder if the voice was right and she was loitering there until the Brother and his men arrived. The Brother would know about Clum; he could have concocted the whole story to lead him far away from the safety of the keep.

"He was here," Dylis said at the sight of his unsettled face.

"Clum... are you here?" Eni yelled again, trying not to look at her.

There was a crunch of litter behind them and a red head poked up from behind a rotted log. "Eni?"

"Aye… Clum, it is good to see you."

Clum did not answer as he pulled himself up from his resting spot. He rubbed his eyes, recovering from his impromptu nap and then stumbled to his feet.

They waited by the rock as Clum climbed over the fallen log and reached back for a woolen pouch. Slipping it over his neck, he inched forward. His face was white and he looked down at his feet as if forcing them forward against their will.

"Your Mum told me to give you this," he said, slipping the pack from around his neck and setting it on the ground in front of him. He stepped back, watching Eni carefully as if he feared an attack from the young wizard.

Eni stooped down to the sack and picked it up. It was not as light as he expected, but before he could put it on his shoulder Clum blurted out, "He is dead! Your Father, I mean. He... he left with some others from the village... I don't know why. He made it back, but was bleeding something awful."

Eni staggered back, feeling as if the wind had been knocked out of him. "St. Giles field and the Lollards," he muttered. How could he have forgotten?

"This is for you too," Clum said, handing over a piece of parchment. "Your mum said not to let another living soul look at it..."

Eni unfolded the cloth. He knew it was his father's handwriting. He had seen it many times, but his letters looked unstable and weak.

> *Eni, my son*
>
> *Forgive me, although I do not understand,*
>
> *I do have faith in you.*
>
> *Go forth with the word and with God.*

"He died the next Lord's day," Clum continued as Eni stared at the words before him. "The whole south of the March is ablaze, like when we were little and the rebellion started. They sent men to track down the survivors. They got the bishop's blessing and all. The guards are looking for scraps with words on 'em and calling 'em heretics if they were caught with 'em. But the Steward... he was a good man, Eni. We Welsh knew that."

"Did they bury him in the cemetery?"

Clum dropped his face to the ground.

Eni followed his gaze and held it there. "...It matters not," he said finally and then folded the parchment and placed it under his shirt. He let out a long sigh and shook his head as if it would help clear it.

"I'm sorry," Dylis said, putting a hand on his shoulder.

Eni looked at her, her expression a mix of concern and pity. He tried to cast a reassuring smile but was sure it failed.

He pulled out the rest of the purse of coins he had taken with him that morning. "For your efforts, Clum," he said, taking out two coins, "and give this," he added, tossing over the balance of the coin purse, "to my mum."

"I will," Clum answered, pocketing both in his belt.

"Thank you, my friend," Eni said, raising his arms to embrace his oldest friend.

Clum looked at his feet with extra enthusiasm, but glancing up and seeing Eni still holding his arms aloft, he consented and stepped into the embrace.

Eni patted his back and whispered, "Fly back a different path, and tell no one of your task today, lest the lash this time be in a dungeon."

Clum nodded and left the clearing. They watched him disappear into the wood like the mist in the coming sun. "You look worried," Dylis said, glancing up at his face.

"Aye…" he answered, patting the satchel that hung at his side. "Time to go."

30

Murdoc was still asleep when he returned that evening. Brushing off the snow that had begun to fall on the trip back, he built a roaring fire in the hearth, trying to rid the damp and cold that clung to his clothes and infiltrated the keep.

He set the satchel and its contents on the table along the wall. It looked odd among the leather punches, setters, and mallets that resided there.

He milled some wheat with one of Murdoc's contraptions. It looked similar to the lantern's crank, but was a larger box with metal teeth that shredded the grain into a powder.

Mixed with an egg, salt, water, and a bit of lard, the cake was soon turning golden in the corner of the hearth, being made ready for fresh butter. He turned it every few minutes until he could no longer resist its aroma.

The steam continued to rise after the cake joined his pile of books on the table next to him, but before he could begin, the bell rang, sounding more like the harness of a rampaging bull than the beckoning of an old man.

Taking the stairs two steps at a time, he quickly reached Murdoc's chamber. Out of breath, he stumbled into the darkness.

"Light!" the old man groaned, his voice weak and hoarse. Eni fumbled along the wall, kicking the wires with his foot, until he found the box and flipped the latch.

The room filled with light, but pulsed, one of the lanterns flickering as its bulb began to fail. Eni stared at it for a moment before turning to the groaning old man. Murdoc's face was splattered red as drops of blood cascaded to the bedding.

"Oh dear," Eni stammered, gathering a stack of rags that had been piled in the nook. He tried to wipe Murdoc's face clean as even more blood trickled from his mouth with each gaggled breath.

Eni lurched forward as the old man grabbed his collar, "Power corrupts… They must never…" he mouthed voicelessly, unable to produce so much as a whisper "…get it, promise me…"

"I… I promise, but we'll get you through this."

Murdoc shook his head, his pupils moving wildly about his eyes. "South Hampton…" he said, closing his eyes with a cough sending more bloody spit trickling down his cheek.

Eni cleaned him up the best he could as Murdoc faded back into an unsettled sleep. Eni stood vigil for some time before his groaning stomach brought the cakes back to mind. He ignored it for while, but seeing Murdoc sleeping comfortably, he could no longer resist.

His meal was cold by the time he made it downstairs and the fire was near embers but was revived with a few oak logs. Taking a kettle from the hearth, he crushed some dried elderflowers, steeping them in the still hot liquid before finishing off half the skillet, saving the balance for the morning and started paging through the volumes of the book that he had with him.

Try as he might, he could not find any reference to the strife that Clum had spoken of in the south of the March. The Lollards were nothing more in the book than a few paragraphs, a mere blade of grass in a meadow of facts and events.

Slamming it shut, he shoved it across the table and took refuge in the dancing flame of the hearth that now crackled and popped with delight. He wondered how events that meant life and death to those around him could warrant not even a mention in the age of the book.

He added a touch of honey to his elderflower tea and nestled in the chair with the steaming cup and the warm fire before him. He straightened his legs, which had grown stiff from his journey that day and relaxed.

The day's events seemed distant. The trip for supplies… its memory was so vague he could almost question if he had gone at all. Only the butter in the larder was his proof, but even with that, he questioned what was real.

The flickering blue flame reminded him of a mouse in search of crumbs as it dodged back and forth under the blackening oaks.

He felt that at any moment Ingous would come waddling in, her arms laden with clean sheets. Her hearty laugh would wake him up to find it had all been a dream. She was never a spy and Murdoc was healthy, full of ideas and planning a trip to London to see the young King Henry himself.

It could be, he thought, letting his mind wander through the fantasy, *if not for the satchel.*

He turned to the table, hoping it too was part of the dream, but it was there, catching the orange firelight that filled the room behind it with shadows. It was real, and with it, the cold truth. Father was dead.

Eni wondered how it had happened, if they marched in formation, fought with sword and shield, only to fall in the glories of battle, or if, as was more likely, there was sudden shower of arrows, blackening the sky, each marking out a Lollard as they scattered in a panic, trying to escape.

"All for a book…" he said out loud, his voice echoing in the empty room. It scared him, not so much the sound itself, but the sarcasm behind it – he sounded like Murdoc.

What would Murdoc do if he knew Wyclif's book was here? he thought, but he knew the answer. He would toss it in the fire, Eni had no doubt. It would be an 'unacceptable risk,' another arrow in the quiver of his enemies.

It served no purpose but to antagonize the princes of Rome. Its presence alone would provoke an attack that not even the Marcher Lord would dare protest. How could he, when it had caused an insurrection against the king?

No, the logic was undeniable; the book should be destroyed for the good of all involved. There in the darkness he would have done it. He would have thrown the whole satchel and its contents into the fire - gone in an instant.

Eni turned again. Perched on the table, the wool strap dangling over the edge, but it was out of reach. Two steps were all it would take, two steps and it would be gone, one less adversary to the lords of the land, one less conflict that would have to be dealt with.

It was only two steps, but his legs had walked enough for one day and the warmth of the fire bade him to stay. *Maybe later,* he thought and he snuggled into the chair as if it were a wool blanket, listening to the crackling tongues of the fire that soon whispered him to sleep.

He woke with a start, freezing. The chair was hard and the hearth was white with ash. The only redeeming grace was that the eastern sky glowed with the promise of a clear day.

His neck had a disagreeable crook to it. He wondered how he had made through the night. He ambled out to gather more wood. *At least Murdoc slept through the night,* he thought, as the night's snow peeled off the logs onto the kitchen floor. He passed the silent bell.

A roaring fire came quickly and with it a boiling kettle soon joined the morning chorus. Eni finished the cakes, warmed enough to melt the butter, but left one for Murdoc along with a cup of tea.

The light streamed through the window as he rounded the stairs into the room. "Time to eat," he said in a cheery voice, hoping to lighten Murdoc's typical morning mood as he set the plate and cup on the table.

There was no answer.

"You all right?" he asked, turning toward the bed. He should not have been surprised... even the old man knew it was coming, but to see his lifeless form still startled him. He had no doubt the breath of life was gone, but still he touched the cold flesh with the back of his hand, more to judge the time of his passing than anything else.

He figured it must have happened soon after he left, peacefully in his sleep. Eni walked back down the winding stair, leaving the plate and cup on the table and took his place once again in front of the fire, staring at the flame as if it were a crystal ball, hoping it would grant some sense of direction.

No church cemetery would take him, that Eni knew for sure. Murdoc was evasive to faith and so apathetic about the church that Eni did not know where he truly stood with God, but still...

After watching the fire fade once again, he gathered tools and set out to the mountainside. It took a while to find a spot. It had to face east, just in case God's mercy would extend down to Murdoc's lot.

Eni finally found a spot up a small hill from the turbine and the stream that trickled from it. The spot would catch the sunrise and on a clear day, one could see the lowlands of England. Satisfied, he began squaring up a hole and set to work.

Though on the surface it appeared more earth than stone, he soon found out the opposite was true. The sun brought sweat to his brow as he worked a pick ax, breaking up the rock in order to make it deep enough to be a proper crypt.

The work was slow and he had not burrowed more than a couple of feet before hitting a slab of rock. The pickaxe seemed to only bounce off its hardened shell, leaving little more than a chip in its wake.

He worked until the sun had receded past the peak that loomed above him. His progress had slowed to the point that the flakes that sprang from the pickaxe were not much larger than the grains of sand that kept caving in from around the perimeter of the hole.

Using a sudden breeze that sent a chill across his frame as an excuse, he donned his cloak to inspect his work. Finding no better way to gauge the size, he jumped into the hole and lay down.

The grade of the land floated above his chest by six inches or so, enough to cover the body but not deep enough to keep the wild animals from finding it... *Just like the pup*, he thought, laying there in a dead man's crypt.

Staring up, a smear of clouds was the only blemish to the pure blue sky. Watching them float through the earth-framed window, his mind raced. There were no more wizards to solve his problems ...or fathers. He was alone now, alone in a stone keep, inheriting the titles of both heretic and outcast.

The ridges left by the pick ax stabbed into his shoulder so that he soon stood up and took his place again with the living. *This will have to do*, he thought, after giving them a few cursory whacks, trusting it to knock down the tallest of the annoying peaks.

With his appetite clearly getting the better of him, he made his way back down the slope. The keep, draped in shadows, appeared to be morning the loss of its lord as he lay in its upper chamber.

Funerals were church affairs. First a wake, then a funeral mass, and if the passing was a wealthy person, the guests would be treated to a meal where they would remember the person's life.

There was no doubting Murdoc's wealth. His purse was proof of this, but being Wizard of the March was a lonely position and although there would be few to refuse a free meal, even from him, Eni was having doubts. It was not the cost that concerned him, it was the attention.

If I have learned one thing being here, he thought, staring at the fire that night, *it'd be that seeking attention for oneself would likely bring one's downfall.* The lords of both Rome and the state did not take kindly to competition, especially from a sixteen-year-old lad.

'Cost/Benefit analysis' they called it in the age of the book. It was a strange name for a simple process of adding up the good and the ill and seeing which had the greater account. It took no scholar to see which won in this regard.

He was not quick to rise the next morning. The cold kept him under his covers until he had to relieve himself or burst, but once up, he saw no reason to wait with his task for the day and set to work. He started wrapping Murdoc's body in his blanket, binding both ends with a leather cord. He first readied himself, and then hoisted this package over his shoulder. The load was not as great as he had imagined. It was only now he could feel how the illness had whittled the old man away.

Eni tried, although unsuccessfully at times, to treat the parcel with the reverence it deserved. With the winding stairs and a lopsided load, either the head or the feet always seemed to be in contact with the wall. When he tried to adjust, the other end would smack unceremoniously on the stone as he descended the circular stairway.

190

Each time, he groaned, almost as a way of paying penance. He tried to slow down and perform this task with more dignity, even if he were the only witness.

The day had been warmer than those past and the ground was soft and free of snow and frost. He had to step carefully lest he slide and stumble as he climbed the muddy hill.

Reaching the grave site, he set the body down in order to catch his breath. The sun was high in the sky by this point with large fluffy clouds racing in the wind. Of all the varied weather on the mountain, this was Eni's favorite. He loved to see the billowing shadows as they crossed the open valley to the hills beyond.

"You'll have quite the view," he said quietly. It was strange to hear his voice, or to hear any voice, for that matter. Dropping to his knees, he set the body in the hole, laying it as neatly and straight as the ragged rock walls would allow. It seemed wrong to be doing this alone, an outlaw burial, done without the blessing of the church.

He wondered if his father's burial in Knighton was similar, if he too was buried as an outcast, or if by some act of grace, he was allowed into the churchyard. To be sure, there was no man who loved God as much as his father, and for him to be laid to rest outside the fold... He shook his head, casting the thought as far as it would fly.

Eni grasped the tailings that he had mined the day before. They were cold and the sharp edges dug into his skin as he dropped them, chip by chip and grain by grain into the pit. "Ashes to ashes," he said out loud, but his voice sounded weak and useless so he gave up on the second part and only grunted as he pushed a load of the dirt into the hole.

Goodbye, father, he thought, as the last of the blanket disappeared from view. He snorted, disgusted by his sudden foolishness, and set to work in earnest, leveling the ground.

Sweat gathered as he moved the last of the shavings and then started to mound the grave with larger stones that were strewn about the area. Even though the work was strenuous, he was surprised that he felt so warm, given the biting wind and darkening shadow in the west.

He had done all that needed to be done, but as day passed into evening, he didn't want to leave. He kept gathering stones until the darkness had thrown enough tendrils across the great bowl of the sky that he had to quit. His throat ached and eyes stung as he sat down next to the mound that entombed his master. Cursing his weakness, he finally let the tears fall and he mourned with the stars bearing witness.

31

They sat in silence for a moment both watching the package as if it would provide them with some sort of sign of how to proceed.

"How would we know?"

The professor looked up either shocked or confused so Wendy asked again, "How would we know if history has been changed?"

He thought about it briefly. "We wouldn't. Well, unless …"

"Unless what?" Wendy interrupted.

The Professor shrugged, "I guess unless we find the encyclopedias. We could see the differences from what was written in them compared to what we see in this new reality… It's just conjecture really, though, I mean this was protected and cared for. Who knows how many volumes made it through the vortex much less survived the rigors of decay traveling through time the normal way."

"Well then, you really shouldn't have much to worry about," Wendy suggested. "How much knowledge could they have even gotten from it? Probably nothing more than your name and address."

He thought about it for a moment and smiled, "Yeah, maybe you're right. So Wendy Thompson, shall we see what's in this artifact your family has been saving for me?"

'Lead on, Professor Brown."

"Please, call me Angus," he added with a reluctant smile as he fished out a pair of plastic gloves from his drawer.

"It's probably safer to keep you a professor."

He wasn't sure what she meant, though with the twinkle in her eyes he doubted he should take it too seriously. He added, "Maybe, but the way this is going, I don't think I'll be in the professor gig too much longer."

Sliding the package from its plastic sheath, he stopped to take a picture of it with his phone before pulling at the leather cord that bound the package in its leather skin and then took another. "Hard core science technology here," he said, waving his smart phone. Then setting it down, he picked up a tweezer and pulled the leather cord that held the bundle closed. "I doubt this is original," he said, as the cord pulled free from its knot.

"Are you going to carbon-date it?" Wendy asked. She could have sworn she felt the pulling of the old leather cord. It tugged on her like it was somehow attached to her insides.

"I would love to…," the professor started, as he checked the quality of the photos he had taken and then added, "…if there was funding."

"Yeah, I get that. Not so fun, huh?" she asked, but the professor continued to click photos from every angle he could think of.

"Not so much..." he finally answered. "But that's life in academia these days."

"I guess all you can do is buy a bridge and get over it, huh?"

The professor stopped and looked at her, slightly stunned, before a smile finally made a claim. "I guess… or I could just crawl down in a hole somewhere, which would probably be less stressful."

Delicately, he lifted the package and let the cord fall free and set it to the side. He again inspected the bundle and sent it through another round of picture-taking before deciding on the best way to proceed in unwrapping it.

"It's crazy," the words caught him off guard. And he came up from his inspection eyeing the girl across his desk.

"Come again?"

"It's just… Well, I didn't want to come here," Wendy continued. "I was embarrassed for being late and all that, but now, thinking about all this, I'm wondering if maybe you wish I never came. It's just crazy how our perspectives changed."

The professor slid back in his chair again, thinking about it, "Yeah, I'm not sure what I feel right now. It's a good question. I've been on a roller coaster today; that's for sure." He looked over the package and found the edge of where the leather had been folded. "Hopefully," he added, as he placed the tweezers on the flap, "this will tell us, one way or the other."

The days slipped by and Eni did little other than read and tend the hearth. The beast had not groaned to life since before Murdoc had taken ill. The work tables sat unattended but for the gathering of cobwebs. Eni had little desire to work on any of it, so instead he planted himself in the fireside chair to read and eat.

Of course, the latter required firewood, so he made frequent trips to the shed in order to supply the hearth, but like the rest of the provisions, even the stores of wood were falling low.

It was the 28th of March when, in the midst of the book of "S", a pounding echoed through the great hall. For a moment, he was dumbfounded as to what it could be.

"Aye, wizard! Eni, are you in there?" The voice was weak and muffled by the thick wood door but was followed by several heavy thuds that resonated through the chamber.

Eni slammed the book shut and looked about for the staff. He had planned to have a few leather balls with him, but they were still in the upper chamber.

Half the volumes of the book were strewn about on the table next to the fire. "Foolish… never should have this many out," he said to himself, using his voice for the first time since Murdoc's death. As he started to pile them up, the door sounded once more. Boom… boom…boom, "Hello, is anyone there?"

"Agh…" he groaned, slapping a volume down on the table and picking up the staff, striding to the end of room. "A moment!" he yelled out, taking one last look at the pile of manuscripts just asking to be pilfered.

Reaching the door, he called out, "Who's there?" The gruff,

annoyed tone of his voice surprised him. He knew he sounded unmistakably like the previous master of the keep.

"Eni, is that you?"

He knew that voice. "Um… aye, Dylis, are you alone?"

"Aye."

Eni slid the bolt and pushed the door open, his staff at his side with a smoldering wick at the ready. The bright morning sun blinded him for a moment, but when he could see, he noted the way that she stared at him.

"What?"

"You all right?"

"Aye…" he said with a shrug, "why?"

"You look…" she shifted uncomfortably.

"What?"

"Well, more like a ruffian than a wizard. Old Murdoc is such a dandy. How does he let you get away looking like a drunkard?"

"Ah, he is still under the weather," he answered, thinking wryly about the morbid truth in his words.

"I hope he is healthy enough to come down the mountain; that's why I'm here. There is a knight in the village. He comes from the Marcher Lord. He needs to parley with the wizard.

"Oh! No, I don't think he could…Why did they send you, anyway? You're just a girl."

Her eyes widened, her inner fire burning through her green eyes, causing him to step back in alarm. "I am Welsh," she said in open defiance. "I go where even the English knights dare not tread… or wizards, for that matter."

"Aye, I see that. A thousand pardons, mum," he said with a mock bow.

"It's true, you English swine," she added indignantly, with enough pomp to transform her peasant's dress into the finest silks.

"Aye, my lady," he said, bowing again, "but I am only half the swine you think me to be. My mum was Welsh and proud of it."

"Ah," she smiled. "I thought there was something redeeming about

196

you; that must be it."

"It must be indeed, my lady," he agreed. "Let me bolt the door, and I will accompany you to the village, if you would permit me."

"In all seriousness, my dear young wizard, you must clean up. You're in no state to see a knight of the Marcher Lord."

Eni looked down at his attire. It did not seem that bad to him, but still, he had not changed clothes since Ingous had broken from their fellowship. Perhaps a change was warranted. "As you wish, my lady," he agreed.

"May I?" she asked, following him to the door. "Ingous had told us stories, but I have always wanted to see inside the wizard's keep." Eni stood back and let her pass, but a horn of warning sounded in his ear.

Dylis was wide-eyed as she entered the great room, looking up and down the mighty stone walls and massive timbers that spanned across the room to form the ceiling high above.

"I've never seen a room so large," she said, turning in a circle to take it all in. While her attention was drawn to the architecture, his was called to the volumes of the book that were still stacked on the table by the fire.

He quickly moved to them, using his body to shield them from her. He added their fallen comrade to the stack and proceeded to hoist them in his arms.

"Are those the ones…" she asked, drawn to the urgency of his task.

He looked at her; the magic of her gaze was far more potent than what any wizard could devise. "Aye," he said. Then turning with his load stacked to his chin and threatening to topple at any moment, he started toward the stairs.

"Could I help you?"

"…No" he answered, before the words were out of her mouth. "Murdoc would not allow it," he added, hoping to cover his rashness.

Dylis turned to the hearth, inspecting its massive stone work and the plates and blanket that were strewn about the front of it. Eni was passing the last of the tables when she turned back to him, "He is dead…the wizard."

Eni stopped mid-step, sending the first few books to the ground. He slid the stack on the table, pushing over the tin snips to make room in the process.

A tremor raced across him as he sought a suitable answer, but looking up, he saw her face, frozen with determination. Who was this girl who had such power over him? Was she really a friend or was she a conniving spy for the Brother? He tried to think up a lie, an excuse, anything... but he couldn't. This was a battle he could not win. "Aye," he finally said, his shoulders drooping.

She shook her head, and he saw her eyes melt at the recognition of his deception she then turned her attention again to the upper timber.

"I am sorry..." he started, but stopped when no other words came to his rescue.

"You are a fool, wizard," she finally said, casting her eyes back down toward him. "I do not know those books of yours, nor do I have any desire to steal them- no matter what you may think."

Her body shook as she spoke, and in that instant Eni thought she was like the Beast when it was burning bright with a full head of steam. "I thought I was your friend, but apparently you have no need of one. So farewell, wizard, be with your books until you rot, as that is all you care for," she spat, making for the door.

"Dylis..." he called out, but she ran out the door before he could think of the right words, so he stood there, alone with the book in his keep of stone.

32

His heart pounded as Eni descended along the winding path, his staff testing the ground with each stride. He had taken Dylis' advice and cleaned up, even going so far as to dip into the ice cold pond in order to scrub off the layers of soot that had accumulated across his brow.

He was still chilled as he made his way down the slope. The linen shirt, though clean, did nothing to keep in the warmth against the wind. He wondered where he was to find the knight, but a commotion in the village erupted as he came into sight, and a man dressed in a level of finery not often seen in the village appeared before the gathering crowd.

He was a large man, big and powerful like a bull in a coat of deep purple velvet. A long sword hung from his waist, his gloved hand tapping against its hilt to some unknown melody.

"Where's your master, boy?" he asked, his voice deep and Norman. The peasants gathered behind him as if he were one of their own.

Eni looked about the crowd, but there was no sign of Dylis, and he wondered if she had told.

"My lord," he started, with extra emphasis on *lord*, "I fear Murdoc, the Councilor, has taken ill and is unable to greet you, so he sent me in his stead."

He thought he had done quite well, but the knight merely spit on the ground in front of him. He had a typical short beard which he quickly wiped with the back of one hand, the other still wrapped about the sword hilt. The crowd surged forward around them, and to Eni it felt as if they were egging him on in hopes that he would free them from the wizard's rule.

"Tell your master that he shall meet the Earl of March at second bell on Wednesday next at the keep in Knighton... lest the devil take him before then."

"I shall inform him, sir knight, of your good wishes," Eni answered with a small bow. "If that is all, I must attend to my master and I bid you safe travels, my lord."

It was short and to the point, Eni thought, hardly worth cleaning up for. The crowd, too, was obviously disappointed, grumbling among themselves that no blood was spilled in the encounter. They only dispersed after the knight had made his way back to the stable.

Eni hurried up the path until he was high enough that he could look down from behind a rock unnoticed.

The villagers paid little heed to the knight as he readied his horse and rode off to the east. From behind the rock, Eni watched the man till he passed the far side of the meadow. As the knight's figure faded, he turned his attention to finding Dylis.

At his elevation, it was difficult to make out individuals; most wore similar grays and browns, and the distance blended them into one another. He was even unsure of the gender of some of them, as cloaks and dresses took on similarities.

With numbed fingers and a steady wind to chill him, he soon gave up and retreated back to the keep, reestablishing his position by the fire. It took some time for the flames to lick the warmth back into his body.

"You are a fool, wizard," he said aloud, staring at the tongues of yellow and orange, in their careless frolic, dipping and bowing as if dancing. A flame was never alone; there were always two or more. If one happened to fade, another would jump in to take its place. He figured it had to do with the chemistry of gases or some such thing, but he really didn't care.

Why must I be alone? he thought. "I do not wish this for my life." His voice cracked as he spoke, but with no one to hear him, it didn't matter.

"I cannot live being the most hated man in the March, always fearing, never trusting... this is no way to live," he told the fire. It

200

crackled, sending sparks flying as some trapped moisture hissed its way to freedom. Odd, he thought, that fire could set water free.

Eni debated what to do; he thought about leaving the day next and spending the evening with his mother at the manor, but he worried what kind of company he would make. He could not figure out the reason the Marcher Lord wished to meet, or what he would do once he found out that Murdoc was dead.

Why at Knighton and not Wigmore? Why so early in the day, rather than at night; the hour of their last parley? So many questions, and as he had come to expect, so little help from the book.

For the next few days he had spent most of his waking hours pouring over them, except for a brief exploration around the mountain in order to settle a nagging doubt. It had done him good. The pages of the book were like a prison that day. It felt good to run once again and be free.

Trouble was, he had to come back to his cell and toil in the chair, trying to solve a hapless riddle. Why would the Marcher Lord want to meet now?

He was having no luck when a piece of paper fell to the floor. It had been planted in between the last two sheets of book of "E".

Happy for the excuse, he picked up the folded document. It was perfectly square as if cut by a blade, but the fibers were not as fine as the pages that embraced it, though it was thinner than the vellum sheets of the Wyclif.

Opening it, he saw that the writing was of a mechanical type, similar again to the book, but larger, and lacking its crispness of text:

```
To whom it may concern:

If you are reading this note, it is
hoped that you have also discovered the
accompanying encyclopedias. While we
understand that due to their age they are
```

virtually worthless, they are of great help to our research.

Due to the nature of our experiment, we ask that you keep the books safe and in the condition in which they were discovered.

Please return this letter, along with the date and location found, and what remains of the encyclopedias to us on or after May 18, 2017.

A generous reward will be offered as a thank you gift for your time and dedication to this research.

Thank you,
   Dr. Angus Brown
   TVR, Suite 75
   1001 Bowlsy Rd
   London, England

Eni read it several times. An experiment, he thought, dropping the letter onto the open book. Not from the devil at all, only an experiment of some sort. He stared at the three volumes he had taken out for the night. These treasured volumes carried no more weight to the person who sent them than Murdoc's urine had to him, and yet…urine produced salt petre, which had set him free on more than one occasion.

"It makes no sense," he said out loud. He had lost Dylis over this 'virtually worthless' book, used merely for someone's experiment.

Now, men die over the right to read a book in their own tongue, but in the age of the book, these treasures have no value. He read the paper again and could only shake his head in dismay.

He accomplished little else that evening. Instead, he spent time in front of the fire, trying to wrap his head around the idea. "I will see Mum afterward," he decided, after a yawn brought him back to the problem at hand. After all, night was already falling, and he had the meeting on the morrow.

He had no luck in deciphering the Marcher Lord's plan; there was the South Hampton conspiracy, of course, but that was still more than a year away, and he doubted the Marcher Lord would want to bring it to anyone's attention. Eni decided he would save the information for later use, but could use it as a blind dagger -if one were needed.

He secured the keep for the night, storing the books in their chest, which was fully armed and ready to blow up anyone foolish enough to pilfer it. Try though he might, he still slept poorly; he woke almost hourly but only rose for good once the sun's halo touched the eastern sky.

He was soon off with only the bare necessities: the staff, a couple of leather balls and a smoldering wick at the ready, and also a decently sized dagger. He took it with some trepidation, but convinced himself he did not know what lay ahead, and it was better to be prepared. He turned towards the valley and the rising sun, leaving the key under the splitting stump, sunk a few inches into the damp earth.

It was a beautiful morning as the sun came into its full circumference. The rowans were budding and the woods rang with a chorus of birds. Some were new arrivals from the continent, calling for their loves among the branches as they flitted about from limb to limb.

Eni welcomed spring after being held hostage to the keep all winter. He liked nothing more than wandering through the wilds of the March, investigating the hills, vales, and secret places. The seasonal waterfall and the rocky crag each held an allure.

The kiss of a warm spring breeze met him as he crossed a ridge and followed the path into a wooded vale. The leaf buds were further along here, nestled on a south slope as it soaked up the April sun.

Under the trees, the aroma of soft damp earth, growing things, and fresh shoots that poked their heads through the trampled litter was rich and calming. He looked about, reveling in this miracle of nature, when he saw a blur from his right and then....

He tried to breathe as he slammed face first into the litter. He tried to move, but couldn't, something was on top of him- or someone.

There were leaves; leaves in his mouth, leaves in his eyes. He was suffocating in leaves. Air... he needed air... just a breath, a gasp, but there was none before everything faded into black.

When he came to, Eni was propped up against a tree like a shovel. He blinked, but the canopy above him was hazy. The dream of what had happened was lost in a fog.

"Ah, good to see the light in your eye. It wouldn't do for you to die," said a voice that sounded as cheerful as the song birds above him. "Gave me quite a scare, yes indeed. Your master might turn me into a frog for such an indiscretion."

Eni turned his head to its source. He expected the action to hurt, but strangely it didn't. The man, leaning against a rock, looked vaguely familiar. His clothes were worn and he had a hard bread roll that he held like an apple, biting a piece free. A large dog sat next to him, wagging its tail as the man spoke. The wizard's staff and the leather balls were displayed in front of him, like the trophies of a hunt.

"Got the wind knocked outta you was all," he continued, chewing the pastry like cow's cud. "You'll be fine in time, no harm done. Just needed a bit of coin was all," he added, patting the pouch on his side.

"Are you in the habit of ambushing travelers, my lord?" Eni said flatly. His emotions were still mired in the fog.

Edmund de Mortimer stopped chewing and looked down at his ringless fingers.

"I assume you are after the key?" Eni asked, still devoid of emotion.

The Marcher Lord did not answer, but the cheerful disposition was gone as he swallowed the morsel. "How did you know?" he asked, his speech now fitting for one of his noble birth.

Eni adjusted his position against the tree. "Your dog, my lord," he said, motioning to the animal. "... He still has his tail. No commoner would be allowed such a creature un-bobbed."

The Marcher Lord shook his head at this lapse of detail in his ruse. "You are quick on your feet, that I'll give you. So charades aside, let us get down to business shall we? Did you warn the Lollards?" he asked, as stone-faced as the hill behind him.

Eni looked at him, wondering how he knew.

"The night we met in Wigmore," the Marcher Lord said, answering his questioning glare. "The guards on the walls later saw the wizard's light heading towards Knighton." He was watching for Eni's reaction, watching for some sign.

"I sent my Steward to check, and he confirmed the wizard never left the public house that night, but you..." he eyed Eni like a butcher considering a hog at the market. "It never crossed my mind to check on you. So I ask again, did you warn the Lollards?"

33

The leather flap pulled free from its station where it had been posted for centuries, but it flipped back the moment the tweezers let go of its edge. The professor freed the remaining two flaps, but the memory of embracing its treasure lingered and it was only the added weight of an ink pen on one of the side flaps that kept it open.

"Let see what we have here…" he said, delicately pulling first the top document from the open end of the package and then carefully one by one pulling the contents out onto the desk. They both looked at the small pile of papers. They were yellow and discolored, but otherwise they appeared no worse for wear from their trip through time to the modern era.

The top paper, neatly folded, had the name 'Dr. Brown' written on it in the flowing pen stroke of a quill. The professor stared at his name and sighed deeply as he looked up at Wendy.

"At least it doesn't say Angus…" she said with a giggle.

He looked up at her with a questioning glance.

"Sorry," she continued. "I just never liked the name Angus… reminds me of cows."

"You can call me Brian then," he said, still rotating the camera around the desk.

"Angus Brian Brown… Your parents were cruel…"

I never said my parents named me Brian, just that you could call me that."

"Oww, aren't you the clever one,"

"Takes one to know one, so I'm told," he said proudly and took a picture of her for good measure.

"Are you going to open it?" she said with a nod to the still folded parchment in front of him. "Or are you just going to flirt with me?"

"I consider it harmless banter, unless you want to…."

"Open it already," she said, ready to do it herself if he took much longer.

"Right." He took a deep breath and held it in as if to steady his nerves. Then, using the tweezers, he carefully pulled the letter open.

Dear Dr Brown,

For sixty years I have lived with a secret: a secret known only to my wife and I, but since her passing this April last, I know my end is near and I am now alone and cannot share it with anyone, even our children. For if they were told, they would think me not right in the head.

So it is with great joy that I write you, so that I may finally share the history of my life, even if it is only by ink and paper. It is fitting I suppose, since that is the course of how this came to be, words on paper traveling to and fro across the millennia. For even now, it is hard to imagine that it was truly real. I would think it a dream but for the evidence.

Sir, I believe you are the only other person that will truly understand how it came to be...

The Professor stopped and sniffed, wiping his nose with his sleeve as he looked up.

"A kindred spirit?" Wendy offered.

The professed looked back down at the handwritten letter. The characters did seem a touch wobbly, showing the author's advancing age. "Wonder what it was like?" he said, working his way back down to where he left off.

Go help you fully understand, I have included several other documents. Most notable to you, I gather, a page from the book, one that means the world to me. It is all that I have left of the wizard's book.

They burn Lollards, was all his mind could offer. Being caught with merely a passage from Wyclif's book was a death sentence and he had left a full copy next to the hearth. Key or no key, an oak door could only take so much.

"Did you warn the Lollards?" the Marcher Lord was growing impatient. The rightful heir to the throne of England, in spite of his young age and smaller stature could inspire a dreadful fear. In the March, his word was law, equaled only by the king himself.

"Aye," the word fell so quick from his lips that both of them appeared surprised to hear it. "I warned him, my father, but he did not listen…"

Edmund de Mortimer watched him. He offered little reaction, given such a confirmation. "You know you will be burned at the stake for such a heresy," his words so soft they could have been lost among the bird calls.

Eni sat for a moment, "We will all die, my lord, some later, some sooner… even you."

His lordship smiled darkly, but only for a moment and then it was gone. His face was blank, but he seemed so much older than his twenty-two years. "Does seeing your name in the Wizard's book make you feel protected?" he asked mockingly.

Eni smiled. "I am not worthy to be mentioned in that book, my lord.

208

It is only the powerful that mark its interest."

"You are lucky," the Marcher Lord said without emotion.

"How about me?" a voice rang out behind Eni, who turned to see a knight three paces off, sitting on a fallen log. "Am I in your devil's book?"

Eni knew him at once, and seeing the outlaw John Oldcastle side by side with the Marcher Lord answered the painful question of who had hit him. "Aye, you are in there."

"Hear that, my lord? I too am considered one of the powerful and mighty," the old knight said with a halting laugh.

"More for the basis of a playwright's fool," Eni answered, forgetting briefly who bore a sword.

But Oldcastle merely smirked at this. Banter and battle went hand in hand for men like him. It may have even raised the old man's opinion of him.

"So when do I meet my maker?"

"You do not wish to know, Sir John," the Marcher Lord interrupted.

"Ah, but I do…"

"No my friend, you do not. I asked the Wizard for that once. It cost me plenty from my purse, I might add. There has not been a night I do not dread its knowledge, especially on the 18th of January, knowing it is but one step closer to my destiny." The Marcher Lord shook his head. "No, there are some things meant only for heaven to know."

"All right then, lad," Oldcastle said, folding his arms. "Answer me this, do we win? In the end, are all the blood and tears worth it?"

Never give without payment. That was what old Murdoc said, and he had all intentions of obeying, but his head nodded of its own accord.

"Ah, I knew it! God be praised," the old Knight said, slapping his thigh, "We get those moral beggars in the end."

"No… it's not like that," Eni said, throwing out Murdoc's number one rule. "The Lollards never win a battle, never overthrow the king. They are all losses, all of them," he added, looking back at the Marcher Lord.

Oldcastle's forehead wrinkled like a rotten melon. "But you say we win…"

"Aye, but it will be… the years are more than seven score," he said, adding up the dates in his head. "It has nothing to do with the uprising, it has to do with the king's problem with women."

"Preposterous," the old knight snapped. "I don't believe it! Women!"

There was a commotion in the woods and a young page came running toward them. Sir John promptly turned to work on his pouch thus hiding his face from the new-comer.

"My lord," the lad stammered as he tried to catch his breath. His attire was far better than his master's, who quickly donned his velvet coat that had been hidden behind his rocky perch. "Riders from Knighton approach."

"Very good, Harold, we are finished here. Hail the Baron at the forest's edge. I shall join him shortly."

"As you wish, my lord," the boy bowed and dashed back through the wood. The Marcher Lord did nothing more till the lad had gone. Then he jumped to his feet pulling off his coat and shirt.

"We have little time," he said, tossing the worn shirt into the bushes and pulling out a satin one from his bag. "…The lord Bishop is gathering a horde to storm the keep at Wizardsvale. He is after the book…" He pulled his velvet coat back over his satin shirt, dusting off specks of earth that had violated it. "Let the wizard know that I should be here in Knighton for a fortnight and if he cannot protect book, I shall, in Wigmore."

The Marcher Lord turned and followed the path his page had run moments before, leaving the wizard's stick where it lay. Eni watched him till he passed into the grey of the wood.

"So…" he turned back, but Oldcastle, the outlaw ghost, had disappeared. He wondered where he could go- who would take in a wanted man. *Only in the March*, he thought, *a villain from the Welsh war could become a hero for challenging a king over a book which most of them couldn't even read anyway.*

210

Taking up his tools again, Eni started the long walk back, which felt longer on account of his bruised gut. From all he could figure, he landed on one of the leather balls which knocked the wind out of him.

He also was reasonably sure that it was Oldcastle that tackled him. It was the second time the old knight had gotten the better of him, he thought, remembering back to the summer before.

The wind had shifted from the morning. *Probably a storm front*, he thought. It was a term from the age of the book, a meaningless term to anyone but him. He wondered what it would be like to live in a world of storm fronts, knowing when it would rain days in advance, and having the river of electrons cook his food and heat his home.

Life would be so easy. They must all be like the Marcher Lord, sitting around all day, ordering their electron servants to do the work rather than flesh and blood.

There were some peasants in the fields, but he saw no sign of Dylis among them. The sheep had been lambing and there were a good many of the little ones trailing their mothers as they moved on to greener grass.

Up on the elbow of the mountain, the keep looked desolate. The dark clouds cast it into shadows that gathered around the edges of the higher slopes, like suds in a washer woman's pail.

At least the Bishop has not yet come, he thought, drawing up the path. The door was solid, and there was no evidence that any had passed that way after the telltale marks of the wizard's staff from his morning's exodus. Though he was sure it was safe inside, he lingered, looking instead about the courtyard, trying to devise ways of holding back an army from his doorstep, alone.

He knew of castle defenses from Knighton; being on the March meant it had to deal with Owain's rebellion. The castle had porticos with murder holes where pots of boiling water could be poured on invaders from above and platforms where piles of logs could be staged so that by merely pulling a pin they would roll into the lower passage, taking out the first few raiders and slowing progress of the company.

The key, of course, was having archers lined up on the high wall, raining down arrows so that by the time any actually made their way to the inner passageways, they could be easily dealt with by sword. This took men, men to set up, men to pour the oil and free the logs, and men to fight.

There may have been a day when the wizard's keep could have done such things- back when it had walls- but they had fallen many years before and now lay only as rubble on the slopes.

Eni looked out over the valley, empty except for the sheep and the villagers, but for how long? He was alone on this mountain, waiting in a fallen fortress with no manner of defense.

Still, he must do something. He could not just hand over the wizard's book to the Bishop. He knew what he had to do- or at least he thought he did.

"I have to sleep on it," he said to himself, looking out over the valley. The mist boxed in his view as the grey reached down, making the courtyard feel as if it were early winter instead of spring.

He started a fire in the hearth that evening and made a meal of a couple of eggs mixed with flour in the skillet. He was out of lard, and it burned to the pan, but given how hungry he was, it went down fine.

He did have one asset that the failed defenders of the past lacked- he had the book. Having learned from his mistakes, he took only one volume back down with him: 'C' for castle.

He had read enough to know that there were no castles still in use in the age of the book, that they had been relegated to tours and museums or made so pompous and grand that they could no longer defend a hen and her egg, much less a village and a vale.

The more he read, the less hope he had. While castles improved over the years, the improvements were structural in nature. Bow loops were larger and walls were thicker, with higher towers and deeper foundations, none of which were any aid to a force of one.

The pages ran through his fingers as the words flowed through his mind. The cascading letters meant nothing until five of them froze suddenly in midstream.

His heart stopped as he flung the volume open flat and pulled back

212

several of the pages, racing over each in search of the word. "…Couldn't be," he murmured, thinking his mind had got the better of him as each page came up empty.

Turning another page, he was beginning to think he had imagined it. After all, how could it be? But there it was - tucked in at the end of a paragraph, as real as the page itself.

Hand trembling, he read it slowly, word by word as if it were an illusion playing tricks on his eyes. "No… there must be another," his voice cracked.

Eni stared at the text for a moment before ripping the page from its binding. He slammed the book shut and pushed it away where it ground to a halt on the far side of the table.

He could only imagine how Murdoc would have erupted at such an action; it was so emotional, so Welsh. The page fluttered in the air before he crushed it between his hands, ready to pitch it into the fire and see its prediction burn.

It was not that he thought it changed anything. Perhaps a year ago he would have. Then there was magic and the power of the devil, now there was only science, but its tail stretched further than any demon's could ever reach. Seven hundred years into the future and back again, and yet, after all that- there it was, still long enough to crush his dreams, his dreams of girl with green eyes, his dreams of Dylis.

34

It had been warmer lately and the light lingered later in the evening, so he could have easily gone without it, but he needed warm food. After the initial hot roar, the glow of the embers faded under layer of ash. A small flame rose, after its brethren had already fed. Alone it nourished itself on the blackened wood, the last of its kind.

It turned from blue to orange and back again, showing its colors like a furling banner riding the breeze. Eni watched it from his bench, small and insignificant until it vaporized into a whiff of smoke.

The room darkened with its loss, the curl of black smoke matched Eni's mood. He would have left it that way, brooding and alone, only to see the tongue pop back into reality a moment latter.

Weak and blue, it struggled for survival, fighting for a breath in the darkening world. Eni picked up a stick with the intent of knocking apart the tongue's fragile hold, dooming it once and for all.

But as he reached, the tongue turned a brilliant orange as if it had found a hidden fuel deep within the blackened wood. The hearth glowed, and Eni could feel the heat radiate across his face once more.

The stick, its end blackened from previous work, waited above for the command to attack, but in the fiery glow, Eni was centuries away. "10 and 700," he said, under his breath, unsure if the two had any bearing.

The tongue continued to flicker, holding more yellow than blue. It stretched up to nibble the end of the stick like a deer straining to reach a high apple in a tree.

"It would be off by... a lot," he concluded, not feeling up to the figuring. The flaming tongue touched the outstretched stick, bearing offspring that leapt to life.

Eni tossed the stick into the hearth, multiplying the tongues that glowed in exuberance. He turned from them, hoping to make sense of these sudden thoughts, but finding little inspiration in the darkness, he soon returned, trading in the remaining logs for their radiant wisdom.

I wonder... he thought as the glow of the fire washed over him anew. *Why should it not work?*

He sat for a moment, adding it up once again, and with a feeling in his heart something like determination, he went out through the dungeon and into the night with nothing more than the shirt on his back and the key in his pocket.

At first glance he questioned the wisdom of leaving the crank lantern behind, but his eyes adjusted quickly. Clouds, long and narrow, snaked past the moon which, though less than full, provided ample light for travel.

He ran down the path, breaking to his left so as to pass clear of the village, which lay dark but for a few glowing hearths.

The night air was cool and damp, with a low mist blanketing the countryside as it readied itself for bed. He cut through it as he ran, leaving an eddy that slowly swirled behind him before falling back asleep.

He soon was through the valley and into the wood. The darkened trees cast an eerie shadow over the path, the budding branches denying the moon the right to follow. There were spots here and there that he questioned if the trail veered to the left or right, but they were short lived and easily rectified.

He was a stag alone in the forest, running powerful and free, the woodland prince, at home in his domain. Each stride barely touched the earth, a mere whisper on the fallen leaves.

It was only when the castle in Knighton came into view with its scattering of glowing windows reaching up the tower that he began to tire.

Stopping on the small knoll, his breath charged ahead, shaking his frame like it was the beast at work.

Though it was still prior to Compline, the courtyard was quiet as he retraced the path he and Murdoc had last taken from the keep. The river gurgled its familiar song as he opened the servant's gate that had yet to be locked.

He failed to see anyone until he reached the kitchen, whose citizens were busy cleaning up from the feast that indicated the presence of the Marcher Lord. They bantered as they worked, free from the oversight of their betters. He knew most from his youth and a few stared as he passed through, but none said a word or impeded his way.

The sounds of the dinner echoed from the hall, for the Baron and his guests were clearly enjoying themselves. Eni stood there in the servant's passage outside of the laughter, second guessing his decision to come.

"Can I help you?" A man appeared. Well dressed and middle aged, he spoke in clear crisp English, unbridled by any Welsh influence.

"Who are you?" Eni returned, regretting his tone upon hearing it.

"I was about to ask you the same," the man said with a voice as courteous as it was pompous. Eni knew he was under inspection. Becoming aware of a bead of sweat trickling down his cheek, he wiped it with his coarse shirt sleeve, realizing he looked more like a peasant than councilor to the king.

"I am Thomas, Steward to the Baron," the man continued, sensing he was not getting anywhere. "How did you get in here, lad?"

"I am no lad!" Eni snapped, developing a quick dislike for his father's replacement. "I am here to see the Marcher Lord."

The Steward looked away, "I do not see that as being possible," he said, returning his gaze, clearly displeased with this aspect of his job. "His lordship does not meet with commoners."

"I hurried to bring him news... I can assure you he would welcome my information."

"Indeed," the Steward answered. "And who should I say you are?"

Eni thought he had done well with his last line, but now he hesitated. If he claimed to be the wizard, then all would know that Murdoc was dead– the only detail that kept the Bishop from mounting his assault. "I am in the service of Murdoc, councilor to the king."

216

"It is your master who should seek audience with his lordship, not someone of your standing," the Steward answered. "I suggest you be on your way, lest we have a guard escort you."

What Eni did next caught him unprepared, and it made for all the more ruckus as the good Steward crashed into the maid servant who was passing by. Her load of plates and silver echoed as they toppled in the passage way.

Eni staggered for a moment, realizing what he had done, but then he sprang for the great room as the Steward lunged for his leg. His "Stop, you!" was lost among the laughing and conversation of the assembled.

Eni quickly made his way toward the front table where the Baron and his guest of honor were still enjoying their cobbler. He was unsure if they were alerted by the Steward or used to such attempts, but he only made it around the corner before confronted by two guards with ready swords.

"My lord, a word!" Eni called out, as silence quickly filled the room.

"Ah... Eni," the Baron said, as if ready to ask him to join them. A guest behind him murmured, "That's Harold's lad."

The Steward raced in, grabbing Eni by the arm. "My apologies, my lord! I ordered him to be gone, but he pushed by me."

"It is alright, Thomas. This is..." the Baron started.

"How dare he," the Marcher Lord interrupted, his blank expression suddenly full of fury. "I will not put up with such insolence. Toss him in the dungeon!"

"But my lord Edmund..." The Baron started, only to be silenced by the younger man's glare.

"Very good, my lord," the Steward quickly agreed with a nod, seeing the Baron's retreat on the subject.

Eni stood there, struck dumb by the turn of events as the two guards latched on to his arms, dragging him backwards toward the door. The guests, both Welsh and English alike, counted his father as a friend and groaned in their disapproval at this treatment.

"Bring out more wine," the Baron ordered, fearing the change in mood. He knew from his years of experience that keeping the peace in the March required keeping people happy. He could only hope that the young Marcher Lord would figure that out before starting another war between the Welsh and their English masters. He smiled at the young lord, who merely nodded his emotionless face in return.

Eni quickly learned what it was like for the mouse when the cat got hold of it. 'To the dungeon' apparently carried few restrictions for the Marcher Lord's men, since they took every opportunity to fling him into each wall, bench and door that appeared along the way.

The Steward shadowed behind. "That will teach you for messing with Thomas, it will..." he repeated gleefully upon each impact. Once they reached the stairs they dragged him down the first few, allowing his feet to dangle well behind, and then let go.

He could hear them laugh as he toppled down head first. He curled into a ball hoping to protect his head from the cut stone steps. This worked, but kept him tumbling down like a mountain boulder until he smashed into the heavy wood door that sealed the bottom.

He started to unfold but the guards were on him before he could gain his bearings. They hoisted him as one, unbarred the door, and tossed him headlong into the darkness.

35

It stank as he lay in the blackness. It was moist and rotten, making Eni think for a moment he was back in the high cave, having fallen into one of Murdoc's barrels. Coming to, he wondered what his chances were of refining the salt petre and blowing his way out, forgetting completely the need for the other ingredients.

He unfolded his arm, feeling up and down the length of it to see if anything was broken. Satisfied, he continued through the rest of his limbs, giving each as thorough an inspection as possible in the darkness.

Soon the sound of a constant drip hitting standing water seemed to ricochet around the room, bouncing off the stone which magnified it. The steady *whamp* gave the impression of something deeper than a puddle, more like a cistern or a well.

He lay there, not wishing to engage any of his limbs in any activity where he would have to listen to their painful protests. Instead, he rested, listening to the steady beat of the water, waiting for his heart to slow.

Though he would deny he slept because of the knot that swelled in middle of his back from either the fall or the uncomfortable floor, he somehow was aroused by the clanging of the lock hours later.

A torch led the way through the door and drove the darkness to its hidden corners. A helmeted guard followed it into the dungeon. "Up, you!" he ordered with a hand on the sword hilt, lest there be any protest.

Eni struggled to his feet, but staggered as his bruises failed to follow the command. He started to wobble and quickly steadied himself along the wall when another entered behind the guard. He wore a hooded cloak, under which even the torch cast no light. "That will do."

"Sire?" the guard questioned with eyes firmly attached to the prisoner.

"I don't see him as a hardened criminal. I think I shall be safe enough," the cloaked man answered wryly.

"As you wish, my lord," the guard answered, handing off the torch and withdrawing up the stairs. The man stood for a moment, listening to the retreating footsteps.

Eni had no doubt to the identity of his visitor, and was not mistaken when the Marcher Lord pulled the hood from his face. "Well done," he said with a forced smile that Eni could not remember seeing before. "I doubt any will suggest we are in league together after that performance."

"Aye, I even question it myself," Eni agreed, putting more of his weight against the wall.

"Come now, you left me little choice, with the Bishop of Hereford at the other end of the table!"

Eni paused. He had not seen the lord Bishop. Of course, he was not looking either. He was so intent on his discovery that he failed to look at the situation as logically as he should have. Murdoc would not have been pleased.

"So, what have you come to tell me?" he asked, as a drip of burning pitch oozed from the torch and splattered to the floor.

A flood of thoughts and ideas coursed through Eni's head like a dam giving way. He tried to add them up, performing a cost/benefit analysis in the matter of an instant. He knew he could not catch every drop; something was bound to fall through. Still, he gambled, "Murdoc is dead... He died soon after the turn of the year."

The Marcher Lord's face lost all emotion as he stomped out the fallen flame with his shoe. "Who else knows of this?" he whispered.

"No one," Eni answered, gaining confidence that he had chosen correctly. "That is the reason I have been safe this long from the lord Bishop... and from you."

A sharp glare from the Marcher Lord told him he was right. "But you are in a dungeon," he said, trying to sound as unthreatening as possible under the circumstance. "If what you say is true, why tell me now... here?"

Eni smiled. "Because, my lord, I know the future..."

"So will I ...when I get the wizard's book."

"No, you will never get it. I am sure of that, at least." Eni was vaguely aware of how aloof he sounded. But he was calm, separate.

"And the lord Bishop?"

"No, my lord; neither will he. It was a mistake for the book to be here, just as it is a mistake to let it rule your destiny."

The Marcher Lord's eyes caught the gleam of the fire for a second before they again fell under his control. When he finally spoke, his voice was low and rough, "But God does not make mistakes..."

"No," Eni agreed, "but man does."

Eni doubted there was any real intent on keeping him locked up except for the reason the Marcher Lord had originally shouted about. All the same, he found it difficult to read the Marcher Lord and his true intentions.

The first few steps were the hardest, made none the easier by the steepness of the stairs. He was sure he could say quite honestly that every part of his body hurt, but he waited until he was a ways from the castle to inspect his damages.

The day had just broken when he passed back through the servant's gate. The sky was overshadowed by dark clouds that had no intent on passing quickly to the east. Whether it was the grey and unsavory color palette of the morning or the revelry the night before, none were about but for a few boys at play.

It was hard to imagine that it had only been last night that he felt as swift as a deer running through this forest; now he was sore and hobbling. There could scarcely be a more pitiful sight.

So close to the village and its demand for firewood, there was not so much as a fallen branch in all the forest that he could use as a crutch till he was a good mile away and had already climbed the steeper of the

221

slopes.

He rested at the top of one of these as a light rain started to fall. He knew he should hurry back; after all, if the Bishop should get ahold of the wizard's book, he knew the consequences well enough.

"They would probably fight over who got to kill me, either drawn and quartered for treason or burned at the stake as a Lollard." He began to laugh, but stopped, feeling like the grouchy Oldcastle.

He knew he should be worried; logic told him that. But yet, he rested on the same old rock that had supported his master that first trip to Wizardsvale. There he sat, in spite of the pouring rain that enclosed the hilltop in a sheen of gray mist.

He felt like the old wizard as he got up and hobbled his way down the slope. He was thankful for the rocks and stone edges that made for better footing than the mud-filled pools dominating the center of the path.

One of these caught his attention- not the mud or the blades of grass that bowed down around it. It was the face he saw staring back at him.

He lifted his hand to his forehead and touched the lump that felt more like an apple than his own skin. He rubbed his cheek smearing the blood that had poured from his nose, kept damp by mist and rain. "Hideous," he said to the rippling picture before continuing on.

It was down this back slope that he found a stick, not far off the path, yet still taking some effort to reach in his condition. It was adequate to support him yet light enough to move with his hindered gate, though it was shorter than he would have liked it and probably made him look like a hunchback at a distance.

With not so much as an outline of the sun able to chisel through the mountainous clouds, he had little idea of the time, but the churning of his stomach told him it was past noon when the village came into view.

The keep itself was insulated by the gray sky. The sheep and their villagers were scattered along the field in the valley, the sheep moving here and there, appearing the happier of the two parties. Eni continued shambling forward, eyes down, making sure he would not add to the spectacle by slipping and crashing in front of them.

He could already imagine the women running up to pull their children away from this hideous creature that came stalking out of the wood. He would be a new woodland fable to join the sprites and goblins of legend.

With renewed effort and a sense of pride, he increased his pace. He could feel their stares and was thankful Murdoc had instituted such a gulf between them. They would let him pass unhindered and unspoken to- and then laugh into their ale at night.

He heard it coming up behind him, an urchin to be sure, coming to mock him. He hoped the parent was close at hand to drag their brood back to the nest.

"Eni?"

The folds of a wool dress came into his peripheral vision and he wondered if it was a curse or grace.

"What happened? You look…"

He did not want to look at her. He wanted to ignore her and continue on his way, but he didn't. If her gasp was not enough to tell him how bad he looked, the look in her eyes certainly did. "Hideous," he answered for her.

"Aye," she said, and in an instant her magic was back. "Let me help you."

Eni looked back down at his bruised legs and their wooden assistant.

"I do not deserve your help," he said, biting his lip. "You were right – you were my one friend and I failed to trust you." Then looking up at her, he added, "I am sorry."

The deepness of her eyes held him and though her smile was gone, her face was not unpleasant. "Does it take a whipping for you to realize that?"

He shook his head. "I knew the moment you walked out the door, and I was just too…" he hesitated, hoping to find a better word, "too scared."

"I guess you had a reason to be," she said, acknowledging his injuries.

223

"Aye, and this is from one of the good ones."

"Dylis!" Melkin called out. He had been working nearby and now came with several of the other villagers. "Leave him alone and come back to work now."

"Father, he is injured and needs my help," she answered, without leaving Eni's side.

"He made it this far on his own. He can make it the rest of the way- or get the devil to help him."

"Father!"

"He and that wizard are in league with the devil, girl. Get away from him, lest the devil get you too!"

Eni could feel her trembling next to him. "I am no wizard, sir," Eni answered. "I am Eni, son of Harold, the last Steward of Knighton." The crowd had gathered as he spoke, so he raised his voice, making sure they could all hear.

"I was ordered by the Baron to serve Murdoc, the wizard, which I have done, but no more. The wizard is dead." At this the crowd began to murmur among themselves.

"In a fortnight the Marcher Lord will claim what is rightfully his by law and birthright." The crowd erupted in a mix of rejoicing and rebukes of their English masters.

Eni hobbled over to Melkin in order to speak quietly with him. "Sir, in my current state I am unable to perform the tasks needed to ready the keep for his lordship's arrival. I promise on my honor to keep her safe and pure if you grant me your daughter's assistance in this matter."

"She is needed on the farm," Melkin countered. Dylis rolled her eyes as they began to barter for her.

"She will be, of course, well compensated for her time."

Melkin eyed him. "But you're English..."

"My mother is Welsh."

"Aye, I don't trust 'em either."

"Father…" Dylis reprimanded.

"Oh, all right," Melkin agreed, "but you best keep her safe, lad, 'cause no Marcher Lord will save ya if anything happens to her."

"I will protect her with my life, sir…" Eni added, and as they shook hands Eni whispered, "Sir, do you know of any by the name of Cotterhouse?"

Melkin drew up his nose, "Cotterhouse? No, never heard of 'em. Why you ask?

"Heard he was from around these parts. Just a rumor, I suppose."

Dylis took the place of his crutch as they headed up the path toward the keep, checking on his condition every few feet. Although he had read about anesthetics in the age of the book, it had made little sense to him how anything could dull the pain like they had described. But walking there with Dylis under his arm and feeling her supporting his every step, he knew what it must be like, and it was better than he could have ever imagined.

36

Dylis cleaned up his wounds and brought down clothes from his upper chamber. She had started a fire and fixed a meal from the meager stock of the pantry by the time he was done changing. The blood soaked rags of a Welshman were gone and he was once more a part of the dignified English race.

"Now," she said, after waiting until he had finished eating his first and only meal of the day, "what is this all about?"

Eni was unsure how to begin, but also unsure of what he had just unleashed.

"I think I just told the lord Bishop it was time to attack," he said, staring at the fire. It had been his only companion for so long that it felt odd to share his thoughts with another person.

"The Bishop?" she asked, sitting on the bench next to him, "but how?"

"Surely there are more than a few villagers that will tell him what I said."

"More than a few, I reckon," Dylis agreed, "but why?"

"Both he and the Marcher Lord want the wizard's book."

"But the lord Bishop is a man of the church."

"Aye, but is he a man of God? That is the question."

Dylis shook her head. "Even so, why would he want a book from the devil? It is against everything he holds dear."

"Ah, it is not from the devil, but from a man, much like any other, prone to mistakes like the rest of us. And if the bishop got control of it, well he would quickly claim it as a gift from God... which perhaps it is, at least to me."

He stopped talking and stared at the fire, wondering if his ranting made any sense to her. "You see," he started again, "the princes of Rome would use it like they use the other book to give themselves power and control." He motioned to the table behind him with the satchel, "And that won't happen this time."

She retrieved the bag from its station and returned to her seat next to him by the fire. "This is from your red-headed friend, is it not...?" she asked, feeling the outer shape of the bag before reaching in and pulling out the bound vellums. "What is it?"

Eni hesitated to answer. He could have lied; he knew a Welsh farm girl would not know her letters, but he had promised her his trust. "The other devil's book," he said simply.

She gave him an odd look, but then she realized what he meant. "A Lollard!" she gasped, dropping the book as if it would burn her. "But it is death..."

"Aye," he interrupted, hoping not to hear the fact he knew well enough and turning his attention back to the dancing flames. "It is my inheritance."

She joined him in staring at the fire, hoping to see what it was telling him. And while it seemed he could understand the fizzles and pops as the fire ebbed and flowed, she could not. She waited for a moment before seeking an interpretation.

"What are we going to do?"

He did not answer right away, and she wondered if he had heard her, but then, rising from his trance he turned and looked her in the eyes, as if the fire had been trapped there. "Destroy it – by fire and water."

She doubled back, "Magic?"

His swollen face cracked, and for the first time that he could remember, he smiled. "No," he laughed. "Not magic, only the beast ...and gunpowder."

He would have loved to sleep the rest of the afternoon, for after sitting by the fire he had tightened up and now ached like an old man. But it was only a matter of time. The Bishop would know of Murdoc's death by now and would certainly act before the time the Marcher Lord was to come.

Dylis had left for the day, volunteering to gather whatever hay was left in the village from the winter past. First cutting was due in a month's time, and it would be little missed. "Drier the better," he had warned her, lest she got talked into the damper fare.

He had since been spending his time gathering the candles and miscellaneous butts and ends that Murdoc had accumulated for his waxed wire. After dumping the lot into a kettle just off from the fire, he raided an upper storage room that Ingous had commandeered to do her sewing prior to her departure.

Stuffing a bolt of gray tweed under his arm, he headed back down, hopping from step to step on his better leg. Clearing off the nearest table, he spread out the fabric, cutting its length at the table's edge.

The liquid wax was like honey, and using a horse hair brush from the cobbler's table, he scrubbed it into the fibers while brushing it from the edges to keep the cloth from sticking to the table.

He cleared off another table and repeated the process of coating and sealing the fabric in a white wash of wax. By the time he had finished the second, the first had cooled and hardened to a point where he could remove it from the table.

Eni found it worked best to stand them on edge as he leaned them against a bench and started another, using the last of the cloth. It only stretched half way across the table, which was fine, since he was almost out of wax as well. Once cooled, he layered them and brought them down the steps.

Try as he might, he could not forget his rolling down a similar staircase the night before. This descent was a slow, laborious affair.

The door to the ramp was still padlocked and with the beast having not been fired since late fall, he staggered into the total blackness of the dungeon. *Odd*, he thought, since he was carrying what had been, a short time ago, hundreds of candles. *I should have kept one to light my way,* he thought wryly.

He worked his way back to the northeast corner, hoping it would be

228

drier there than right under the bulwark of the hillside. After using his shoulder as his guide along the wall, he stopped when he could go no further and set them down in the blackness, trusting his ears that they remained leaning in place.

Night had fallen by the time he was back up and now with the hearth casting the only light, he started searching the tables for other materials that would ease his mind. The leather table had a few hides, but he knew they lacked durability. As for the rest, he could find little that seemed useful until he came to the pile of copper wafers that had yet to be processed into the long thin wire.

He had doubts, but he had all night if needed, so using tongs, he warmed several up in the fire and hammered them together on the anvil to form flat copper plates the size of his open hand. It was far from pretty and would garner mockery from all but the greenest of apprentices, but it worked- or at least he thought it would.

It was well past Compline when he had finished, but it was still quicker than he expected. He had pounded the plates so thin that it was easy to use a punch pierce two holes on their outer edge.

Using the largest of the cured skins and the leather thread Ingous had used to mend everything from jerkins to boots, he settled down next to the fire. He had never mended clothes before, but finding a needle, he began lacing the copper plates to the hide with the leather thread.

Finishing the first, he held it up for inspection. He had staggered each row of the copper plates similar to a thatched roof. It was off kilter, but just a little, and feeling the pinch of time, he decided it would have to do. He fought the call of sleep for the most part, and when he did doze, he shuddered awake, as if dreaming the attack was already under way.

His fingers soon burned as much as his eyes as they fumbled along, his cadence only broken by his ever present yawning. Lifting the hide with its now flashing scales, it looked more like a fish or a dragon than the native woodland creature who once wore it. It was smaller than he had hoped, but he was out of copper and he could no longer focus on

229

such tedious work.

Exhausted, he took it below and tried to assemble it, but working in the blackness of the dungeon he had little idea of the result. Taking the last of his strength, he followed the winding stairs up to Murdoc's room. He fumbled around until he found the crank and lantern.

With the blue light as his companion, he made his way back down to inspect his work. It required a few modifications once the light had marked his errors. Some straightening here and a little more support there, and then he stepped back. "It should work," he said out loud, as if the spoken word would add a measure of completeness to the project. "But," he sighed, "only time will tell."

37

Boom…Boom…Boom!

Eni awoke with a start. He had been wrapped in a blanket by the fire before the sun could cast its glow on the eastern sky. It seemed only minutes ago, but the high windows were alight with the glory of the morning.

He laid there a moment before the sharpness of reality truly woke him.

Boom… Boom…Boom!

He tried to spring from his place of slumber, but the bruises that had resembled an apple the day before were now more closely related to the eggplant family, showcasing dark purples and greens that Eni didn't think were entirely natural. The muscles that had borne such fruit were not pleased, given their lack of rest, and screamed loudly in reproach.

He crawled the first few feet until he reached a table. He hoisted himself up, then, using it as a crowbar, he pried his body open, stretching his back and each limb as they protested. It was only when his body knew that it had lost that his muscles submitted and began to cooperate.

Boom… Boom…Boom!

He hurried to the door, but hesitated. "Who's there?"

"They're coming!"

Eni pulled out the iron bar from its grapples and the massive door swung open as Dylis hurried in, bearing a sack of hay. "They had to have seen me! What took so long?"

"I was sleeping, and…"

"Never mind," she said, dropping her bundle to the floor. "I was climbing the path when I saw them on the far side of the valley. We have little time."

"All right," his heart was pounding through his chest. "Take the hay to the uppermost chamber," he said. "I need to start a fire."

She was about to question the wisdom of his orders but thought better of it and took up her sack. Eni's muscles, as if aware of his fears, were in sudden agreement as he hurried toward the hearth.

It would take too long to start a fire from scratch, so feeling through the cinders, he found some coals buried deep in the ash that glowed in thanks as he freed them. Scooping them up in the shovel, he carried them down to the dungeon, leaving a plume of white smoke in his wake.

Cobwebs draped the opening to the firebox and withered to the corners as the hot coals were shoveled through. He gathered the scraps of bark and litter off the floor and fed them to the coals, which smoldered as they dined.

A tongue lit up in the darkness, allowing Eni to sigh in relief, however short-lived. He had used his store of wood to warm the hearth, leaving nothing but a stick or two where a cord had been stored. "Agh!" he bellowed, racing back up.

There were only two more logs by the hearth, and seeing no other option, he heaved a bench against the stone wall. It merely fell with a thud spilling its contents on the floor.

"What are you doing?" Dylis asked, seeing the bench lying on its side.

"Wood, I need firewood!" he was out of breath from running up the stairs. "Lots of it. We need to break this up!"

"I can do it," She said spotting a sledgehammer among the blacksmith's arsenal. "I left the hay up there. Why, I don't know."

"Aye, I'll take care of it," he said, running his fingers through his hair but wincing when one caught the lump. "Get as much as you can, two or three at least."

He was half-way up when he heard the crush of the hammer collapse upon the bench. *Should have thought of that...* he thought, but as he reached Murdoc's room his mind was consumed by what lay in

232

front of him.

Seeing the hay piled on the floor, he kicked it over to the chest and then sprinkled handfuls on top till it was blanketed in the golden threads. He searched the nook for any other of Murdoc's inventions that would be suitable. There was a flask of an evil smelling liquid with the word 'Turpentine' labeled in Murdoc's typical scrawl.

Eni remember reading about it but the only fact he could recall was that it was flammable so he poured half the bottle over the chest and pocketed the rest.

Checking out the window, he could see no sign of the attackers, so he ran back down the stairs. Dylis was on her second bench. "Good," he said, answering her glance.

He picked up an armful of the broken wood and started down toward the dungeon but stopped. There on floor amongst the rubble of the destruction was the wool satchel, its contents still lying where it had been unceremoniously dropped next to the hearth the night before.

He looked up at her and nodded. He expected her to refuse or at least protest but she only smiled before scooping up the book, she placed it deep in the satchel and pulled the straps over her shoulders. "Are we ready my lord?"

Eni sighed as he gathered his load and headed down the winding stairs to the dungeon.

"Where are we going? We have to get out of here!" Dylis called from behind him.

"I know, but this has to be done," he called back as they reached the glowing fire box. He started shoving the wood in, overwhelming the small flame that had taken residence there.

"What is this?" she asked, her eyes wide as she took in the iron arms connected to the massive flywheel.

"It is the beast," Eni said calmly. "Come, let's get you out of here."

He climbed up the ramp and undid the bar that kept the gate locked shut, and helped Dylis up the ramp. He spied around the building and seeing the courtyard still empty, they hurried up the hill behind the Keep.

They dropped into the swill where the pond was lined with chirping birds who complained at the interruption of their courtship. Tracing Murdoc's waterwheel from the water's edge, Eni fell to the ground and began searching through the dead stalks that were bowing in submission to their greener offspring.

Dylis had continued down the slope, but stopped. "What are you doing now?" she said, her voice hushed but hurried as she looked about at the ridge above them.

"Looking for... ah, here!" he pulled out the wax wire from its burrow. The length of it pulled up a tent of dry grass with its ends still planted in the earth. "This," he said, stripping the grass free, "is important," and he started to bend the wire back and forth in between his hands until the wire suddenly snapped.

He stripped back the wool as flakes of wax fell off. "All right, see this?" he said, motioning down as Dylis stepped closer. "If they get in, put these two pieces of copper together like this." And he touched the wires together like they had never been broken.

"Where will you be?"

"I have to go back. All is not ready yet," he answered.

"Then I'll go with you. I can help."

"No, it's too..." he started.

She clutched his arm fiercely, "Then don't you either. It's only a book, for heaven's sake!"

"I have to." he said, standing up and taking her hands in his. "I promised."

"They will kill you," she exclaimed, her eyes piercing his being as she spoke. "Armies like that don't gather unless it is for blood."

He looked at her there in her simple wool dress, a Welsh peasant, and he marveled, "You are wiser than any of the lords of England, my lady. Don't worry, I will get out. I promise you. This will be only the first of our adventures together."

She tried to smile, tried to let her magic bend his will once more. "How do you know?"

He placed her hands together and smiled as he stepped away.

234

"Because I am the last of the wizards, and I know the future."

He backed away and then turned up the hill toward the keep that was breaking the horizon of the morning sky.

"What will happen when I touch the copper?" she called after him.

He turned at the top of the hill and said with a smile, "Magic," before the rise swallowed him and he disappeared.

38

Eni bolted the gate once in the dungeon and fed the last of the broken benches to the beast. It took a lot of heat to get the water boiling, and he only hoped he had enough time.

While the courtyard was still empty, he could hear the clatter of armor as knights forced to dismount in the valley clanged their way up the path. The time was at hand and he still had preparations to complete.

He headed back up the stairs, first smashing the rest of the benches and a table for good measure. He carried them down, stuffing the fire box with all that would fit. The flames roared, their glow piercing the depths, and the mirrored glow of the copper plates radiated back through the darkness.

The massive wheel creaked to life as the arms groaned from their disuse. Eni picked up a table leg. Square and plain, it was solid oak, and he weighed it in his arms as he timed the wheel.

As the iron spokes passed, he placed the table leg against the frame, and held it there until the next spinning spoke caught it, wedging it deep into the iron with a grunt as the wheel suddenly ground to a halt.

The arms groaned and Eni sighed in a mix of both fear and relief. He watched for a moment and then sprinted up the stairs.

The gathering army made no secret of their approach as the men formed up outside the door, filling their battle lines as they trickled up the path.

Eni watched from Murdoc's room, staying out of sight below the sill. Only one more thing to do, he thought, as he circled around the pile of hay filled with the smell of turpentine.

He dropped to his knees and pulled hard on the wires that coursed through the room, snapping them free from the lantern. Stripping off the wax and wool for several inches, he then crawled out over to the hay. It took longer than he wished, but he finally found the finest and driest blades of grass. They were so dry they would crumble to his touch. He then laid out the wires parallel to one another but with a hairs breadth between them. Then, he nested the fine blades between them, layering more grass over them with some of the heavy smelling pine oil.

He scooted back, careful not to disturb the wires, and stood up to inspect his handiwork, only to be interrupted by the gathering forces below.

The first words were in French. Peering over the edge, he could see the French knights in full armor as they took their place in front of their columns.

"My brothers," one man said. Eni did not recognize him but figured it must be the Bishop to lead foreign knights in such a foray. "You know why we are here! This black wizard has been a blight on our land for many years, an abomination to God."

"Aye!" the men's voices rose in agreement, almost shaking the tower in their exuberance.

"Now is the day we take it back! Now is the day we send him back to hell!"

"Burn it!" one of them yelled, and the others cheered. They were ready to break ranks when the Bishop struggled for control. "No, no my brothers. No… that is what he wants; fire will allow him to escape."

"Ohhh," the masses groaned.

"No, we must kill him and then take the wizard's power- the black devil's book," he commanded. "Only then could he not haunt us and our children. We must take the book, for only then can such evil be subdued."

Eni was caught up in the Bishop's rapturous speech as much as his men. It was only when he heard a loud ping deep below him that he was brought back to reality. He knew the sound. It was a screw bursting loose from the beast.

Eni hoisted the leather satchel he had prepared the night before. He was now ready. He had laid out his plan, taking all into account but this, his escape. Whether it was an idea from the book or the voice of God, he always thought the way would just appear to him when the time came, but standing there hearing the beast echoing its destruction, he began to panic.

"Oh, God," he groaned as he thought about how foolish he had been to neglect this part, but then he saw it in the nook and it made perfect sense. He had seen it before, hundreds of times. Leaning in the corner was the odd iron poker with its curved black scythe, and instead of a handle, the iron formed a loop that was knotted with a heavy rope. He smiled, not knowing if he should thank God or old Murdoc.

"We must take the keep!" the Bishop continued to roar below as Eni raced with the poker and its coils of rope down one flight of stairs to a room that overlooked the back slope.

He hooked the curved blade on the sill and dropped the rope to the grass below. His quick descent was more of a drop than a climb as the men's war cry, "Death to the deceiver!" echoed across the mountain. He tugged on the rope, freeing the poker from the sill, and it thudded to the ground beside him.

He was over the ridge before the invaders could round the keep. They were like flies on a carcass as they darted about, all striving to be the first to gain entry to the stronghold and seek the reward for bringing back the wizard's book.

Even from a distance he could see Dylis's shoulders relax as he came into view. "Now," he mouthed, and nodded as he ran to join her. She drew the two wires together and closed her eyes –but nothing happened.

She did it again and a flicker of blue appeared at their joining. "Is that it?" she asked, looking up at him.

"Aye, that is it."

"Good thing you are leaving, Eni of Knighton. You are not much of a wizard."

"Touch them, then," he dared, as he dropped to the grass next to her.

238

She looked down and rubbed her finger across the shiny metal, only to be bit by the tiny blue spark. "Ow!" she exclaimed, tossing it the ground.

"See? Magic," he said, bending down and fastening the two wires together once more. He bent the wires over and folded them together so that the connection would hold unassisted. Then offering his hand to her, as the men's voices gathered in excitement, he whispered, "We must fly."

They quickly crossed the glen and climbed up the next hill, checking to make sure that they had gotten away unnoticed. They quickly dropped over the crest on the far side, staying out of sight of the keep.

They passed on the leeward side of Murdoc's grave, though it bore no mark, but for the piled stones. Eni paused, wondering what the old man would have thought of his decisions, how he would have reacted to seeing the fall of the keep.

It was a fine spring day, he thought looking back to the east, too fine of a day for the likes of this. Somehow, he had always imagined that castles would only fall at night in the midst of thunder and blinding lightning. Or perhaps a winter storm racing over the mountain, full of cold and fury would be fitting for its demise. But a day like this, a sweet spring day, with the birds in song and the flowers in bloom—somehow it did not seem right for this to be the last day of such an ancient keep.

"Come..." Dylis beckoned. They were on the far side of the elbow where it joined into the mountain. It was steeper there, but they were hidden as they climbed to the vale where the singing pond held court, protected by the halberds of tall grasses.

Smoke, black from the burning turpentine, rose high from the keep's upper windows, and they could hear the invaders cursing the sight. Dylis watched and started to move toward the edge to see the source. "Come," Eni called her, "they will be very unpleasant in a moment."

She smiled and took his arm to go, but then a boom echoed across

239

the valley, and she spun around to see a black, skirt-like plume rising from where the keep once stood. Its dark billows glowed by the fire of its undergarments.

"We have to get out of here," he said, grabbing her hand and pulling her along the cliff. He pushed a coppice of branches from the crack in the wall. Stepping inside, he pulled the wicket gate shut, closing them into the darkness.

They waited but a minute and a low rumble shook the ground. Dylis gasped and steadied herself, looking on in horror as Eni sighed in relief. "Thank God."

The distant voices groaned in failure. The Bishop's voice rose far above the chaos. "Search for them! This is the devil's work, my brothers. Put all to the sword for this deception. They shall know the wrath of God!"

Eni turned back to her, smiling, but she only stood there. "We won't be safe here. We have to keep going," he said, nodding into the cave. Then, stepping past her, he walked in several feet and bent over. She could hear the clanging of metal and rustling of clothing, but her eyes couldn't penetrate the darkness.

"Ready?" he said, and with a whirl their world was cast into an unearthly blue tint.

"The wizard's light!" she cried, stepping back, her silhouette trembling in the opening.

"Dylis, no, it's all right."

He could see the horror in her eyes, as he let the light fade back into the darkness. Her haunted glare, the reflection of stories told at night of the evil wizard prowling the wilds. Stealing children away, stealing them to the very depths of hell, and here she stood, next to wizard's heir, already underneath the earth.

"Do you trust me?" he asked, staying where he was.

She blinked, and steadied herself against the rock, ready to bolt into the clearing at the slightest movement. "Did you make the earth shake?"

240

"We both did… the fire we built in the dungeon," he said slowly. "It had water above it in what was like huge copper kettle. What happens when you boil water?"

"Steam comes out the spout," she answered, her silhouette still tense against the filtered light from the wicket.

"Aye, but if you stopped the steam, if you plugged up the spout so that the steam would be trapped, what would happen?"

"I…I don't know…"

The steam would build in pressure and then the kettle would explode, ripped apart by the steam when it could no longer hold it, and that is what you heard and felt, the huge kettle exploding in the dungeon. It was no magic. It was only steam."

"And the wizards light?"

Those sparks you felt on the hill; that is what makes the wizard's light. I can make the spark by turning this crank. It is like a little water wheel in a box but instead of water it makes sparks. Let me show you…"

She hesitated, thinking it over.

"Over here, I found tracks!" a voice called out to the others from the edge of the pond.

Dylis sprang from the entry into his arms. "Let's go!" she whispered, and they eased themselves into the darkness. They stumbled in the blackness, waiting till they were far enough away from the cave mouth lest it be discovered.

But after negotiating several turns and catching a bruise or two on the outcroppings, they stopped.

"Here, I will give you the power," he said, feeling for her and then placing the strap over her head. Reaching for her hand, he placed it on the crank, "turn… there you go."

The blue light slowly came to life, only to die back again. "Was that me?" Dylis asked.

Eni smiled. "Yes, but you didn't do any magic at all, see?" She smiled back at him shyly and turned the crank again as the passageway lit up. Eni led with the lantern in one hand and steadied his satchel with the other.

There was a place or two that required them to crawl through on their hands and knees before opening up to a larger passage where they could again walk.

"How did you find this?" Dylis asked, brushing her dress free of the mud.

"Murdoc stored things in the cave, but as for where it leads… Well, I had figured that for the keep to fall all those years ago, there must have been another way, so I went exploring."

They had gone for a while, and whatever fear the light had spawned in Dylis dissolved once she began to use it. First spinning it faster so that the light was so brilliant it hurt to look at, and then stopping, letting the cave fall into darkness and forcing Eni to stop mid-step.

"Are you quite done?"

To which she would only laugh and grant a trickling glow. "So, wizard," she asked, after tiring of this game. "Are you going to tell me now what few trinkets were worth saving from the keep?"

"I have no secrets, my lady," he answered without turning or slowing down. "But the time is not yet right to share all. Ah, but look there."

It was dim, but every step brought it closer. The glow of day soon appeared. It was softened under the canopy of trees, and was accented by the rush of water that fell in front of the entrance to the cave.

They swung around behind a waterfall and scampered over some rocks that were wet from the ever present mist which kept the cave secret from any viewers below.

"Does it look like Hell, my lady?" he asked, watching the water cascading down the rock face and splashing into the pool beside them.

Dylis licked her lip and thought about swatting him as if he were one of her younger brothers, but decided against it. "No, it's quite lovely. Thank you," she said, keeping her manners.

"And you were worried," he teased.

"Aye, so I was…" she said, and smiled with the full force of her powers. "So what now, my homeless wizard?"

242

Eni leaned back against the stone. "I'm not quite sure," he said, patting the satchel, "but I have a few ideas in here."

"You could come... I mean, I'm sure my father could find a place for you to stay."

Eni smiled, "That would be nice, but for the good of all- I was killed up there today," he said nodding toward the Keep. "I have to get away from here. If they caught me in the village they would kill you for hiding me."

Dylis nodded. "Will I..." she started, but then biting her lip, she turned to the waterfall. "Will I ever see you again?"

Eni rummaged through the satchel, pulling out the coin purse Murdoc had left him. "I promised your father I would pay you."

"No, you don't need to..."

"Aye, I must live up to my word. Here," he said, placing a silver farthing in her hand.

She looked down. "That is very kind of you, but I'm not sure I was all that much help," she said, wiping away a tear.

"I would like your father to hold on to these for me as well," Eni said and he pulled her around to face him, depositing three gold coins in her hand, each one a year's wages for a sheepherder.

Her eyes opened wide with wonder. He smiled, looking into their mesmerizing depths. "It may be a year or two, but then I'll want them back, you understand, or he'll have to give me something of greater value–like his daughter's hand in marriage... If, of course, you are accepting of that?"

39

The professor scanned over some of the other papers. All were yellowed from age but the writing, though faded, was still legible.

"Don't you think you should get more experts involved now?" Wendy interrupted. "I mean, this proves you were right. It proves the science. Doesn't it?"

The professor sat back in his chair with its familiar squeak and rubbed his beard until he found a hair that was longer than the rest and began to play with it with his fingers. He looked over the smattering of papers before him.

"He called them the wizard's book…" He stopped and shook his head as if trying to understand it all. "Seven hundred years… No, this was a mistake, this…" he started, but stopped as a different folded bundle caught his attention. His voice changed from worry to surprise in an instant, "Hey look at this… I think this is for you."

He pulled it free from the rest. The word "Heir" was written in ink. It was smaller than the rest with the edges of the parchment folded in on itself. "It's heavy," he said, as he handed it over to Wendy.

She weighed it in her hand. It did seem heavy but not overly so. "Open it," the professor prompted.

"You think I should? I mean…"

"Hey, do what you want, but I would."

It went against her better judgment. History should be treated better than this, but how could she refuse? The curiosity was killing her. The parchment unfolded and released its treasure and treasure it was, two coins fell into her hand.

On the back side of the parchment was a note. The handwriting was in the same wobbled script as the others. She cleared her throat and read out loud.

My dear child,

I thank you for delivering this to Dr. Brown. I do not know how our family has fared over the years, but I wanted to at least reward someone for the diligence of performing this errand that required the participation of so many generations of our house. I know this is not much of a reward in the age that you find yourself, but please receive it as a token of my thankfulness.

Grandfather

"Very nice," the Professor said, nodding his head. What are the coins?"

"Not sure, but I think they are gold," she said as she studied them. They are in very good condition for being so old.

"Probably worth a couple of hundred pounds I would wager."

"It all helps," she said with a smile.

They went through the papers until they came to one that was different from the rest. "Ah, this... this is one of ours. See? It still has a scorched edge from its trip through the vortex," the professor exclaimed, his voice unable to hide his excitement. The folded paper stuck together and the professor had to use his instruments to separate the thin sheet from itself. It took a while, but he was able to pry the page open enough to read the page number on the corner. "Let's see..." the professor muttered as he enhanced the page with the magnifying glass, "The letter C and page 350." He let go and the paper jumped back to the position it had held for centuries. "Reach over into that pile of boxes, if you would..." he said, pointing to the corner of the room on Wendy's side of the desk. "Yeah, that one."

Wendy pulled off the lid and started heaving out the heavy books until the gold letter C caught the light.

"Good, good. Put it here," the professor said, clearing a space on his desk. "Let's see what was so important to our mystery man, shall we?" Maybe it was the anticipation, but it seemed to take them a while to find the page, and then they both chased down the lettered columns.

"Here! This must be it," Wendy pointed triumphantly.

Ely Cotterhouse, Sir (1397??- 1488) English Inventor, adviser. Little is known of his early life, but he is thought to be originally from Wales or the west March. He was knighted by the Earl of March in 1415 and granted land in Herefordshire. He was considered a father of the English renaissance although he never visited the continent. He brought scientific thought to the forefront and is also known for the introduction of paper into England. Though known to be a Lollard, he was so well connected in court that charges were never brought. He was credited with continuing Lollard thought until its acceptance in the English reformation well after his death. With his wife, Dylis, (??- 1485) he is believed to have had four children.

June 1415, Wigmore Castle

The Steward knocked. "I am sorry, my lord, but there is a young gentleman to see you," he reported.

Dropping his quill to the desk, the Marcher Lord rubbed his eyes, "Not another one?"

"I'm afraid so, sire. Shall I send him away?"

"Who is the lad? I hope not one of the Dorests, those scheming..."

"I have never seen this one before, sire, but he is well dressed and well spoken."

"No, I have had enough for one day," the Marcher Lord sighed.

246

"Very good, my lord," the Steward answered, retreating to the door. "Oh, I did promise the lad that I would tell you that it had to do with your... what was term he used? Your destiny. So I have told you. Good day, sire."

"Wait..." he called out, leaning back in his chair. "Utter foolishness, to be sure," he added under his breath.

"Sire..."

"Send him in. Just send him in." He waited a moment and then again picked up the quill, but it seemed to twitch in his hand. He held it there, watching it vibrate against his will.

"Sire, Mr. Ely Cotterhouse," the Steward announced, and the young man entered with a formal bow to his lordship. "Do you wish me to take notes, sire?"

"No, that won't be needed," he said, looking up at the visitor with not so much as a crack in his expression. "You may attend to your duties, Thomas," the Marcher Lord said, setting the quill back in its well. They waited in silence until the Steward had left, closing the door behind him.

"I thought you were dead."

"That was the idea, my lord. It has a way of freeing one to start new life."

"Yes, I suppose it would... and the wizard's book?"

"Destroyed."

"What about the other one?"

"It is safe, and fulfilling its destiny with a number of scribes."

"Ah, yes, destiny... I have thought often of the morsel you gave me that night. I admit that its knowledge had given me hope, but your death had, well, let's just say I am thankful you are alive and well. Mr. Cotterhouse is it?"

"You are most gracious," Eni answered with a bow. "Yes, the name was a gift from the book, but to business, my lord. I had promised Murdoc on his death bed that I would deliver one last piece of council to you and to your King."

He waited for a response, but the Marcher Lord said nothing, so he

247

continued. "In two month's time, an attempt will be made on the King's life and it will fail. All those accused will be executed."

"And you tell me this because…?" he said, opening his hand as if picking an apple from a tree. "Have you forgotten that my death has already been foretold?"

"He is your king. I would naturally assume his wellbeing is of your concern?"

"Naturally," the Marcher Lord agreed in a casual almost jovial manner.

"Also, my lord, I am afraid this plot is to place you on the throne of England and those accused are of close kinship to you. And as for your foretold death, well my lord, let us just say the facts of the book are not always what they seem, often rather, they are merely reported that way."

"I see," he said, picking up the quill again. He twirled the feather in his fingers for a moment, watching it spin as he gathered his thoughts. "So what was the cost of this information?"

"It is free, my lord. A gift, if you will."

"That is kind of you, Wizard."

Eni smiled. "Oh, I am no wizard, sire, only a merchant and adviser if you so wish."

"My apologies, good merchant. So you have imparted your wisdom. How do you advise I use this information?"

"For this, I fear there is a price…"

"Name it," his lordship snapped, leaning back in his chair. His eyes were piercing and he still clutched the quill, holding it off to the side out of habit lest it drip on his finery.

Eni hesitated and took a deep breath, "I wish to be knighted and given a small estate in Hereford," he said as elegantly as his pounding heart would allow.

He had spent the past two years rereading the torn page and thinking about this very moment. He had played out the scenario many times in his head and was well aware that the ramifications would be disastrous if the Marcher Lord was hasty in his response.

248

"Knighted? You are a schemer!" his lordship bellowed. "What have you done to deserve such an honor?"

"I believe that is the appropriate wage to save your life, my lord," Eni answered as confidently as he could muster.

"You never..." he started, but stopped, clearly puzzled for a moment, and then continued in a more reserved tone. "Can you save me from my destiny?" A thin smile crossed his face. "Can it be done?"

"It will cost you everything, my lord," the younger man said, watching closely for a reaction.

"No more riddles, wiz... merchant. Tell me all you know."

"Very well, sire. You know the Biblical story of the rich young ruler who went to the Christ Lord, asking the price to be saved? You are he, sir."

Again Eni waited, but the Marcher Lord sat there at his desk, staring at the feathered quill. "You see, the wizard's book said that Edmund de Mortimer was thought to have died in Ireland in 1425, but what if it was someone else?"

"You are playing a game with me!" he snapped.

"No, my lord, the wizard's book... It was a book of man, not a book of God. It was prone to errors, just like the act of any mortal man."

"The wizard's book was never wrong! Why... how could it be now? It foretold of my father's death, of King Richard's. It knew all of this."

"Yes, it did," Eni sighed, wondering if he would even leave the room with his head intact for what he was about to say. "My lord, let me be the last to ever accuse you of treason, for the book claimed that you had no knowledge of these attempts on the king over the past few years, and yet I met you in the forest with none other than the outlaw knight John Oldcastle. Now in two months' time your own kin will be accused and die at the hand of the King, and yet you again are not accused even though you are the one they wish to place on the throne."

The Marcher Lord scoffed, "I was foolish enough to have told my dear brother-in-law of my destiny after a night of drinking. No, no it is not for me that he would go to such lengths for the throne, but for his heirs who will have inherited it when I am gone."

Eni could feel his mouth go dry. How could he not have considered this? He was well aware that the lord's young nephew Henry would indeed one day sit on the throne, but it was years away. Old Murdoc was right; it was indeed a different world for the royals and the curse of the throne was not yet done with this family.

"I can only advise, my lord," Eni interrupted their silence, "just as only God can look in the hearts of men. In the end, only you can judge if the book was truly correct in assigning guilt, and even then, I cannot promise that it will work, only that there is hope."

The Marcher Lord did not say a word. He only stared, stared straight ahead until he could no longer keep his eyes open. Whether he prayed or simply thought, Eni could not be sure, but when he opened them again his voice was soft and quiet. "What must I do?"

"When the time approaches, send only troops to Ireland who do not know you in the flesh. Keep on the lookout for someone of similar stock and build as yourself and whom you can trust. Teach and train him to be you and send him in your stead. Then you must disappear forever into the countryside giving up all claims and titles you now own. For on January 18, 1425, it will be reported that the Marcher Lord is dead, whether it will be you or someone else only God knows."

He thought for moment, "What would I do? Who would I be?"

"You would be free, my lord. Free to be anything or anybody. You could give yourself an estate in some far flung district under an assumed name, where no one has ever met you, and you can live the rest of your life free from the book and free from its destiny."

"Ah, free…" he said, sinking back into his chair. He stared into the ceiling, his face blank but for the wonder in his eyes. Then slowly, as if churning the idea like cream into butter, a smile formed, a real smile, perhaps the first in years. "Yes, free from everything," he said at last. "Now that has possibilities."

"So, that must be our man… and your forefather," the Professor said proudly, after reading the excerpt.

"That's amazing," Wendy agreed, "and a lord, no less! I wonder what he did to earn that? Having all the answers probably greased a few wheels, huh?"

The professor didn't answer, his attention drawn back to the pile of documents, moving the pieces of paper off one another until they were neatly arranged on his desk. The next one to catch his attention had the word Experiment written on the front.

In opening it, he was less careful than before and the paper tore at the fold. "Oh no," Wendy jumped, her face cringing at the sound, but the professor merely placed it back together in a readable fashion.

Dr. Brown,

The volumes you used in your experiment made it back through the passage of time with little damage but for the singeing of the outer pages and the blackening of the covers that I believe formed the outer layer. I was not, however, there to witness the event. From my understanding it arrived in the year of our Lord 1300. I came into its possession in the year 1413 after becoming an apprentice to Murdoc, Wizard of the March, who was the fourth keeper of the book.

Due to the politics of this age, I fear that I could not keep the book in the manner you had requested. Using the knowledge I had gained, I attempted to store it, both to keep it safe from those who sought its knowledge, and in the hope that you could one day find it. They were left protected under a shield of copper and wax and buried in the northeast corner of the dungeon

251

in the ruins of the keep, located two leagues west of the dyke on what was known as wizardsvale, though I have no knowledge of what it is called in your age. These names seem to change over the passage of years.

   To this day, June 18, 1485, it has not been discovered or disturbed. I cannot assure you that it even survived the explosion and the destruction of the keep when I was forced to abandon it. Given the miraculous gifts that you have in your age, I hope that you will still be able to fulfill your quest from this experiment.

   I beg of you, sir, to end this experiment now before more damage is done, for my experience has shown me that such knowledge can intoxicate even the most worthy soul. I have given it much thought over my long life, wondering if I had acted correctly in destroying the wizard's keep and burying the book and work of those who held it before me. It was such a waste, and yet, here at the end of my days, I am at peace, for there is too much evil in this world for this knowledge to be known only by a few, even with the best intentions.

"He buried it." Wendy said, looking up after reading the letter. "We could go right now and find it!"

The professor said nothing as he read it again, feeling each word with his lips.

"Well?"

The professor sighed, and slid back on his chair with an uneasy smile. "There's not really any need. It's like the guy said, this was a mistake, over and done with."

"But you're a scientist. It's what you do."

"You don't understand," he said, his lips almost turning white. "This was not science. Science has to be systematic, observable and repeatable. It… it went back seven hundred years, virtually unscathed- we had no models for that! This wasn't science… this was a freak of nature." He took a breath and shook his head.

"I mean," he continued, "there was no way that it should have happened, and with what we know, mathematically, it could never happen again."

"We know," he pointed to the both of them, "that it did happen, so on some level, 'Hooray, I was right.'" He waved his hands aloft in mock celebration. "And no one can take that away from me- cool. But at what cost? How many lives were lost on account of me?" His voice cracked and he cleared his throat. "Please… I beg of you, Wendy Thompson, let this end, here and now."

Wendy dropped her head and looked at the old pieces of paper on the desk – her family's treasure passed down from generation to generation. "What about the reward that you promised?" she asked with just a hint of a smile.

The professor looked up, startled for a second. "Well, it's too late...funding, remember."

Wendy took a deep breath and tried to look as menacing as possible, "It said there was a reward. We kept this for seven hundred years," she said, pounding the desk for added effect, which was lost along with her widening grin. "I think we earned something, don't you?"

The professor shook his head in mock sympathy, "Sorry, but I might be able to find enough resources to take you out for dinner tonight."

"Dinner?" Wendy gave a deep and long sigh for added effect. "Well, it's not like gold coins, but I guess it will have to do."

The End

Author's Note

This story is considered historical science fiction, though you may wonder what that means. Well, the story was written to be as accurate as possible to the known historical facts. This means the people, the dates, and places of the major events were used as they were recorded in history.

The Lollards and the laws imposed against them and against the Welsh people were also real. That said, some creative license was used to further the story.

One of these was the castle in Knighton. In reality, the castle was destroyed thirteen years before our story took place during the Welsh rebellion. The author also created the location of the wizard's keep, as no such place was known to exist.

Science moves forward at an alarming rate, but to the best of my knowledge, time travel of any manner (other than forward, and at the usual rate) is still in the realm of fiction, and therefore the term science fiction is used to describe this tale.

About the Author

S. Van Haitsma was born in Holland, Michigan, the third child of exceptional parents. He now lives in Hudsonville, Michigan and plays on a working farm with his wife. He has one son, two daughters and a dog, Pippin.

Discussion Questions

Time plays a major role in the story, how does the book portray the passing of time? If the technology to go back in time really existed, how do you think it would work?

Eni struggles with a perceived conflict between faith and science. How does he come to view this relationship?

In the book, science and magic are one and the same. We live with scientific breakthroughs on a regular basis. Have we lost our awe for the unexplained?

The two books in the story both have power, and are both controlled by a few and desired or hated by others. Talk about how this has often resulted in censorship, and how Eni handles his situation. What would you have done if you were in his place?

In the 1400s, the Welsh were second-class citizens with limited rights and opportunities. Discuss how this is similar and /or different than the American experience with African-Americans after the Civil War.

The Marcher Lord wanted to know his future. If given the chance, how much of your future would you want to know? Do you think you might try to change it? If so, under what circumstances?

Eni proposes a way for the Marcher Lord to escape his destiny which is based on the idea that recorded history is not necessarily true and accurate. Do you agree? And if so how big of an impact do you think this has on our lives and history as we know it?

How does opening the package change how Wendy and Professor Brown view themselves?